SECOND NATURE

His Chance Series Book Two

ALEXA LAND

Dedication

To Aerielle
Thank you for the inspiration

Acknowledgments

Thank you so much to
Anita, Kim, Melisha, and Jera
I truly appreciate your help and support!

Thank you as always to the members of Alexa's Land, my Facebook
readers group, for your enthusiasm, encouragement, and friendship!
Emily and MJ, Harper thanks you for his pet chicken.

Cover Design by Angsty G

Contents

Chapter 1

I'd imagined the moment when we found each other again a thousand times.

It was supposed to be like something out of a movie, and I had it all planned out—the things I'd say to him, the way I'd sweep him off his feet. I wanted to be so suave. But because I was totally blindsided by our reunion, all I could do was stand there with my mouth hanging open.

Four years had passed since he put me on a bus to Reno, where an aunt and uncle I'd never met before were waiting to get me into rehab. I'd begged him to come with me, but he'd refused. He said I didn't need a junkie like him dragging me down.

He'd saved my life. I knew that for a fact. In a matter of days or weeks, my addiction would have killed me.

I never should have let him stay behind, because it was impossible to find him after that. When I returned to San Francisco, I tried like hell to track him down but he'd disappeared without a trace.

Until this very moment.

My friend Will introduced us, totally oblivious to the fact that he was about to throw my entire universe off its axis with three little words: "Gabriel, meet Riley."

When I turned to face the person who'd just joined us, my heart stopped and I whispered, "Angel." I'd only known him by his nickname. That was part of the reason it had been impossible to track him down.

It took a couple of seconds for recognition to dawn in his big, brown eyes. No wonder. I'd come a long way from the scrawny, strung out nineteen-year-old he'd put on that bus. Then his breath caught, and he grabbed me in a hug and exclaimed, "Oh my God, Riley! I never thought I'd see you again!"

He'd always had a habit of looking by touching. When he let go of me, his fingertip grazed the thin, silver ring that pierced my left nostril, and he brushed back my dark hair before running his hands down my biceps. I'd put on forty pounds of muscle since the last time he saw me, and it felt good to hear him say, "You look great."

"So do you." That was a total understatement, because Gabriel was perfection. With his glossy, dark hair that hung just past his shoulders, artful touches of makeup, and androgynous clothing, he had a style all his own that accentuated his natural beauty. He was dressed in slim-fitting pants and a black off-the-shoulder sweater, which made him look polished and sophisticated. Unlike me.

Even though I'd tried to dress decently for my weekend getaway to Catalina Island, all that meant was going with a less worn-out pair of jeans and a T-shirt that didn't have any holes in it, along with the vintage black leather jacket I'd picked up at a thrift shop for ten bucks. If I'd had any idea I was going to run into Gabriel, I would have—well, okay, I'd probably still look exactly like this. My wardrobe was pretty lackluster.

"We have so much catching up to do," he said, as he squeezed my hand. "How long will you be here?"

"Two days." Not nearly long enough. "Do you work here?"

"Yeah. I mostly cover the front desk, but we all help out wherever we're needed. I live on-site, too."

"It's really nice." We were in the tropical courtyard of someplace called Seahorse Ranch, which belonged to one of Will's friends. I'd been expecting something rustic, not a luxurious resort.

A party was gearing up around us, since Will and his boyfriend Lorenzo had gotten engaged just minutes earlier. The couple was actually nowhere to be seen at the moment, so I could only assume they'd snuck off to celebrate in private. Gabriel gestured toward the huge, white, Spanish-style building behind him and said, "I was making dinner with a couple of the guys before you arrived, and I need to get back to it because my dessert's probably about to go up in flames. You're coming to tonight's dinner party, right?" When I nodded, he said, "If you don't have plans, can we get together afterwards?"

As if I wouldn't have dropped everything to spend time with him. "I'd love that."

"Okay, good." He gave me another hug and said, "I'll see you soon."

I watched him as he cut through the crowd. He turned back and looked at me when he reached the doorway, and the sweetest smile lit up his face. That made my heart feel like it was going to explode. Then he disappeared into the building, and I whispered, "Holy shit."

It was pretty chaotic all around me as about a dozen people worked on pulling together an impromptu engagement party, so I retreated to the empty lobby. Then I bent over with my hands on my knees and took a few deep breaths. The enormity of what had happened was just beginning to sink in, and I could barely process it.

Someone entered the lobby a minute or two later, and I straightened up and tried to act normal as my friend Phoenix exclaimed, "That was so great! I had no idea Lorenzo was planning to propose this evening."

"No one did. It seemed pretty spontaneous."

"Let's take our stuff upstairs. I want to freshen up before dinner," he said, as he handed me my backpack and grabbed his duffle bag and guitar case. Our things had been abandoned at the reception desk when the commotion of the engagement took us by surprise.

"Good idea."

As we headed for the stairs, he said, "This place is great, isn't it? I love the fact that it's closed to regular visitors right now. It should be nice and quiet this weekend."

I glanced at him and asked, "So, you're planning to relax?" It was a trick question. Phoenix didn't actually know the meaning of the word.

"Not exactly. I have a stack of trade publications I've been meaning to review, a bookkeeping program I'm trying to learn, and I've been slacking off on my songwriting, so I hope to make some real progress over the next two days. Oh, and I really need to put out some feelers for my next job, since my contract with Will is running out in three weeks."

Phoenix's dream was to make it big as a singer-songwriter, a goal already achieved by his identical twin brother Dallas, which was awkward. In the meantime, he worked as an incredibly skilled personal assistant. Part of the reason he was so good at his job was because he was a total workaholic, so it was no wonder he'd filled every minute of what was supposed to be a weekend off.

When we got upstairs, we found our rooms and opened the connecting door between them. After I tossed my backpack and jacket on the bed, I leaned against the doorframe and asked, "Remember when I told you about someone I used to know named Angel?"

Phoenix paused in front of a mirror, took off his blue baseball cap, and tried to finger-comb his shaggy brown hair as he said, "The long-lost guy you're totally in love with? How could I forget?"

"Well, about ten minutes ago, I found him."

He turned to me with a startled expression and blurted, "Are you serious?" When I nodded, he asked, "Why didn't you say something sooner?"

"Because I didn't want one of his friends to overhear this conversation, especially the part about being in love with him."

"Tell me everything."

"Will introduced us when everyone was gathering in the court-yard," I said. "All of a sudden, there he was. I didn't know what to say or how to act. I'd dreamt of that moment for years, even though I knew finding him again would take a miracle. Well, one just happened, but I was so dazed that I might have instantly blown it."

"I doubt that. How did you leave it?"

"We're going to get together after dinner to catch up."

"Okay, that's good."

"But how do I handle this? What do I say?"

"The most important thing is to take it slowly," Phoenix said. "It's been four years. The last time you saw him, you were a nine-teen-year-old kid battling alcoholism and a heroin addiction. You're not the same person you were back then, and I'm willing to bet he isn't either. You need to get reacquainted. Also, maybe don't lead off by telling him you're in love with him. He doesn't even know who you are anymore, so I doubt he'll be able to respond to that."

He was right. I sighed and muttered, "I thought it was going to be different when we saw each other again. I expected it to be—"

"Romantic? Like in the movies?"

"Exactly."

"It was," Phoenix said. "You just found this man against all odds. But that's not the end of your story, it's the beginning. Just enjoy yourself, and don't try to force it to meet your preconceived ideas of how this was supposed to go. Take the time to get to know the person he is now, and let him get to know the man you've become."

"You know, you give good advice."

That made him smile. "I try. So, was he the gorgeous guy with dark hair you were talking to downstairs?"

"Yeah. Turns out his real name is Gabriel. I only knew him by his nickname, which seems odd to me now, since we were so close. Or I thought we were."

"See what I mean about taking the time to get to know each other?"

"I do, and you're totally right." I chewed my lower lip for a few moments, and then I muttered, "I just hope we aren't doomed from the start."

"Why would you be doomed?"

"Because submissive bottoms don't usually end up together."

Phoenix leaned against the dresser and scratched his short beard. Then he said, "Admittedly, it's pretty unusual. But that doesn't mean it's impossible. If you both want to be together, you'll figure it out."

"I hope so." He went over to the bed and unzipped his duffle bag, and after a pause I asked, "You're not planning to get dressed up for dinner, are you? I didn't expect this place to be so fancy, since it has the word 'ranch' in its name."

Phoenix was wearing what he always wore—jeans, cowboy boots, and a flannel shirt over a T-shirt. A few pieces of silver jewelry took his look from farm boy to indie rocker. "I didn't bring anything dressy," he said, "but I don't think we need to worry about it. Everybody I've met since we got here has been dressed casually."

"That's true." I pushed off the doorframe and said, "I'm going to take a few minutes to get cleaned up. Come get me when you're ready to go downstairs, okay?"

"Definitely."

I shut the connecting door and found the toiletry bag in my backpack, then went into the bathroom and tried to fix myself up a bit. After brushing my teeth and combing my hair, I debated shaving but decided the five o'clock shadow really should stay. I looked like a kid without it, and there was no point in reminding Gabriel I was six years younger than him.

At that point, I ran out of ideas on how to make myself look more presentable, so I gave up and went out onto the balcony. It felt like I was about a million miles from my tiny studio apartment in L.A. I wondered how Gabriel had ended up here, of all places. It was probably a great place to live and work, since everyone I'd met had been really friendly. But it was also in the middle of nowhere, not just because it was on an island. The hotel was located way outside the town of Avalon and the developed part of Catalina, so it felt like some kind of lush, tropical oasis, totally apart from the rest of the world.

Well, maybe not the tropical part. It was actually pretty cold since it was late February, so I went back inside and dumped the contents of my backpack onto the bed. Fortunately, I'd thought to pack a black, V-neck sweater, and I pulled it on over my T-shirt before frowning at my reflection in the mirror. I usually didn't give a fuck about how I looked—until today. Now all of a sudden there was someone I wanted to impress, but I didn't have the first clue how to go about that.

Phoenix knocked on the door a few minutes later, and we went downstairs to the dining room, which was just off the lobby. It was open and airy with high ceilings and lots of windows, and like the rest of the hotel, it looked like a huge pile of cash had been spent on it.

There were two groups of people drinking cocktails and chatting, but I didn't see Gabriel. I turned to Phoenix and whispered, "I'm so nervous."

"I know, but you'll be fine. Just breathe."

"Do I look okay? This sweater was a mistake, wasn't it? Do I look like a nerd? Or a dad? Or a nerdy dad? I was cold, but it didn't seem right to wear my leather jacket to dinner."

Phoenix grinned at me and reached up to fix my hair. "The sweater's fine. Seriously, you have nothing to worry about."

Gabriel appeared a moment later, and Phoenix quickly pulled his hand away. I stammered, "Hey. Um, meet Phoenix Jaymes. Phoenix, this is Gabriel—"

I actually had no idea what his last name was, but Gabriel filled it in for me. "Moriarty."

They shook hands as Phoenix said, "It's great to meet you, Gabriel. Please excuse me, because I need to go and…do something. I'll talk to you later." Good lord, he was as smooth as I was. My friend grinned at me and hurried away, so we could have some privacy.

"He seems nice," Gabriel said. "Is he your boyfriend?"

"No! I mean, Phoenix is just a friend. He acts like my dad sometimes, but in a good way. We met last year on the set of my first movie, and I think he took pity on me because I was so lost and clueless. He's a personal assistant, which means his whole life is spent taking care of people. I guess he just sort of started taking care of me by default." Okay, why did I say that? It made me sound like I was five years old.

"Are you an actor?"

"God no. I can't imagine a scarier way to make a living than standing in front of a camera and like, trying not to suck while a bunch of people stare at me."

He grinned and asked, "Then what were you doing on a movie set?"

"I'm a makeup artist. Normally I just get to assist, but I met Will on the set of his current film and he actually asked me to do his screen makeup. That's huge. This is only my third movie, and normally it would take forever to get a break like that."

Gabriel seemed surprised. "I never would have guessed you'd go into that field. What made you choose it?"

"It was because of you," I admitted.

"Seriously?" When I nodded, he asked, "How did I inspire you to choose your career?"

"It's a long story."

He touched my cheek and searched my eyes as he said, "I still can't believe you're here. I missed you so much."

"I missed you too, Angel. I mean, Gabriel. Why didn't I know your real name? We used to talk about everything, and that's a pretty big thing to miss."

A little smile curved the corner of his full lips. "I told you my name was Gabriel the day we met, and you immediately started calling me Angel."

"I thought everyone called you that."

"Nope, only you. It was sweet. You told me it was fitting that my name was Gabriel because I looked like an angel, and from that point on you always used that nickname for me."

"I can't believe I forgot that. All this time, I was so upset about not knowing your real name, because it was impossible to track you down without it."

"Hey, don't beat yourself up," he said, when he saw me getting upset. "We were both dealing with addiction at the time, and there are a lot of holes in my memory, too."

"I hate to think what else I've forgotten."

"Let's start fresh." He stuck his hand out. "Hi, my name's Gabriel Moriarty."

I shook his hand. "Riley Palma. I was right when I said you look like an angel." He grinned at that, and I added, "I always thought you were Latino, but with that last name I'm doubting myself."

"I am. My mom and her family emigrated from Mexico, and their last name is Morales. But she decided to give me the name of the rich white guy who knocked her up, because she hoped his stuck-up family would welcome me into the fold. Big surprise, they never wanted a thing to do with me."

"So, you should just tell people you're named for Sherlock Holmes' arch enemy."

He grinned and said, "That's a much better story." Then he asked, "Your last name's Spanish, isn't it?"

"I looked it up once and Palma can be Spanish, Greek, Portuguese, or a bunch of other stuff. In my case, it's probably Italian, according to my aunt and uncle. They weren't totally sure, though. I don't come from the type of family that takes pride in its heritage."

"You're talking about your relatives in Reno, right?" When I nodded, he asked, "What are they like?"

"They seemed nice. They didn't really know what to make of me when you sent me to them, but they cared enough to make sure I got into rehab and checked on me a couple of times. Afterwards, they gave me some money and suggested the best place for me would probably be back in California. I got the message, and I didn't blame them. Why would they want to open their home to a stranger with what was then a very recent drug problem?"

Gabriel frowned and said, "Because you're family."

"I was more of a stranger. They were estranged from my mom,

and they'd never even met me before I showed up on their doorstep four years ago."

"Did you ever reconcile with your parents?"

"That's not an option," I said. "My dad took off before I was born, and my mom didn't bother to let me know where she was moving after I left home at sixteen."

"That breaks my heart."

"It is what it is. What about your mom, are you two close?"

"We've had our ups and downs, and I don't know if I'd call us close, but we get along pretty well." I'd almost forgotten we were in the dining room with a lot of other people until Gabriel leaned in and whispered, "What do you think about blowing off this dinner party? I just really want to keep talking to you, instead of sitting around making polite small talk with everyone."

I looked around and saw Phoenix chatting with Will and Lorenzo, so I told him, "I'm all for it. My friends are amusing themselves, so they probably won't miss me."

He grabbed my hand and led me into the adjoining commercial kitchen, where a couple of guys were getting ready to serve a mountain of food. Gabriel said, "Colt and Ren, this is my friend Riley. We have a lot of catching up to do, so we're going to be antisocial and skip out on dinner. Hope you don't mind."

The older of the two was a handsome guy with dark hair and a short beard, and he smiled at us and said, "We don't mind at all. Have fun."

Gabriel found some silverware and used a dishcloth to pick up one of the desserts on the counter as he said, "I baked six pies for a total of fourteen people, so I'm going to steal one of them. I think there's still plenty to go around." Then he asked me, "Do you want some of the main course, too?"

"Actually, I'm good with just the pie."

"Me too." We said good night to his friends, and as we left the kitchen he asked, "Where to, my room or yours?"

"Yours. I'd like to see where you live."

We left the main building, but we didn't go to the second, nearly identical building like I'd expected. Instead, we took a path through some thick landscaping and eventually came to a tall fence. On the other side of it was a palatial mansion, and I blurted, "Holy shit, is this employee housing?" It was sleek and modern, and it jutted out over the edge of a cliff and tapered down a couple of stories, like a sculpture of wood and glass.

"Yeah. So, a few years ago, Ren built Seahorse Ranch and this house with his boyfriend at the time. Then they broke up, and now Ren and Colt are together. They wanted to start fresh by building their own home on the property, and Ren decided the best use of this place was to let his year-round employees live here."

"That's incredibly generous."

"It is. He's a great guy, and so's his nephew Beck. They run the resort together."

The inside of the house was as impressive as the outside. We cut through a huge living room, which reminded me of a nightclub, then went down two flights of stairs. When Gabriel opened the door to his room, I murmured, "This is amazing." He'd transformed a fairly small room into something magical by hanging jewel-toned, sparkly fabrics from the ceiling and over the walls, creating the illusion of a tent. It was like something out of *Aladdin*.

He found a towel and spread it out over his plum-colored comforter, and then we both took off our shoes and sat on the bed, facing each other with the pie between us.

When he handed me a soup spoon, I asked, "What's the plan of attack here?" He grinned as he pierced the crumb topping with his spoon, scooped up some of the cherry filling, and ate a big bite. I did the same, and then I told him, "This is delicious. I didn't know you could bake."

"I've been teaching myself over the last year. The people who live on-site are big on communal meals, and I wanted to be able to contribute. I don't really like to cook, but baking is pretty fun."

I ate another big spoonful of pie before saying, "This room is great. You need to come and help me decorate my apartment."

"Where do you live?"

"I rent a tiny studio in West Hollywood. It has plain white walls and a view of a parking lot and a dumpster. I'm not allowed to paint it, but the landlord never said anything about draping it in fabric."

"I'd be happy to help you decorate." I wanted to do a fist pump when I realized I'd just made plans to see him again after this weekend. He licked his spoon, and then he said, "So, tell me about your job. It must be so exciting to be a Hollywood makeup artist."

"It's pretty great, but it's not the steadiest job in the world. To make ends meet, I do makeup for several drag queens who perform around Los Angeles, which is a lot of fun. But neither of those are my dream job."

"What is?"

I pulled my phone from the pocket of my jeans and accessed my photos, and then I turned the screen to face him and said, "This is."

Gabriel murmured, "Oh wow," and put down his spoon before taking my phone with both hands.

On the screen was a selfie of me wearing bluish green makeup and prosthetic pieces that looked like scales and gills. "I started out trying for a merman, but I overshot and ended up with more of a swamp creature," I said with a self-conscious grin. "If you flip through that album, you'll see some other things I've done. I've been trying to build up my portfolio, so I can get a job doing special effects makeup."

As he scrolled through the photos, he told me, "These are incredible, Riley. How'd you learn to do this?"

"I watched a few videos online, but mostly I taught myself through a lot of trial and error."

"Isn't it hard to make yourself up?"

"It's not ideal. These transformations take hours though, so it's hard to find people who are willing to sit still that long."

He handed my phone back to me and said, "I'd be happy to let you make me over."

"Wow, really?" When he nodded, I exclaimed, "That would be amazing! I have a bunch of ideas for a series of fae characters that are really gorgeous and otherworldly, and you'd be the perfect model."

He seemed unsure of himself as he asked, "Do you think you

might want costumes to go with your makeup? I like to sew, and I'm pretty good at it. But you don't have to say yes or anything. It was just an idea."

"I'd love that! It would be so much fun to work together and come up with ideas."

Gabriel smiled at me and said, "It makes me happy to see you like this. I always hoped you'd come out of rehab with a new lease on life, and it's so great that you found something you're passionate about."

"It's all because of you."

He shook his head. "All I did was put you on a bus."

"You did a hell of a lot more than that."

"But you had to do the hard work of getting through rehab and then keeping yourself on track, which you've obviously done."

I told him, "You've done the same thing."

He glanced at me, and then he turned his gaze to the bedspread and asked, "How many times did you have to go through rehab?"

"Just that one time. How about you?"

"It took three attempts at rehab, an overdose that landed me in the hospital, and years of counseling and support groups to finally get to this point. I haven't used for almost two years now, but I don't fully trust myself. I don't know if I ever will."

I said, "You're doing great, and I'm proud of you."

"Thank you. I need to hear that sometimes." He still wasn't looking at me.

"Anytime you need someone to talk to, I want you to know I'm here for you. It's not like I have profound words of wisdom or anything, but I understand what you've been through and I'm a pretty good listener."

"I appreciate that." Gabriel hesitated for a few moments, and then he moved around to my side of the bed and leaned against me. When I put my arm around him, he rested his head on my shoulder.

I said quietly, "I'm also here whenever you need this."

After a pause, he murmured, "It's funny, you look so different, but your voice is exactly the same as it was all those years ago."

"Is it?"

He nodded. "It's also amazing how familiar this feels. We must have held each other like this a hundred times back then."

"Except our positions were reversed. You were always the one holding me." It was different too because it used to happen through a haze of drugs. This time, I got to experience all of it, from the softness of his hair against my cheek to the clean scent of his skin and the warmth of his body. It felt unbelievably good.

"You're right. I didn't think of that."

"You tried so hard to take care of me." After another pause, I said, "That entire year, when I was so sad and miserable with that sadist who called himself a Dom, do you remember how you'd cheer me up?"

He whispered, "I'd do your makeup, or I'd let you do mine. It seems dumb now, but it was all I had with me, just a bag with a few cosmetics. I didn't know what else to do to take your mind off things."

"Those times with you were a light in the darkness, and they meant everything. It's no wonder I have such a positive association with makeup, and why I gravitated to it as a career. It always reminded me of you."

His voice broke. "I'm so fucking sorry, Riley."

"For what?"

"For not getting you out of there sooner. It was a terrible situation, and that man was a psychopath."

"You tried," I said, as I held him more securely. "Don't you remember? You spent months trying to convince me to leave, but I wouldn't do it. That's how lost I was to my addiction. As long as Mason Simeck kept supplying me with drugs, I stayed and let him do whatever he wanted to me. I wouldn't let you help me until I terrified myself by nearly overdosing."

"I always wondered if you stayed because you had a relationship with Simeck and he meant something to you."

"That wasn't it at all," I said. "It was a business arrangement. One of his flunkies would bring me food or drugs or alcohol, whatever I needed, and I almost always stayed in that upstairs bedroom.

The only time I saw Simeck was when he summoned me to his basement dungeon. He didn't even provide aftercare. I think the reason he started sending you up to my room was because he didn't want the responsibility of actually taking care of me."

Gabriel sounded heartbroken when he whispered, "It's even worse than I thought. I should have tried harder to get you out of there."

"Like I said, you really tried, but you couldn't force me to go until I was ready. I shouldn't have left San Francisco without you, though. I was so scared I'd never find you again, but here you are. It feels like a miracle."

"It does."

I told him, "I went back and tried to find you a few months after I finished rehab, but you'd totally disappeared."

He tilted his head to meet my gaze and asked, "You went to San Francisco?" When I nodded, he sat up and exclaimed, "I told you never to do that, Riley, because it's not safe for you there! Simeck promised to find you and beat the hell out of you if you ever left. Don't you remember the armed thugs he kept at his beck and call? They tracked me down months after you went away and tried to bring me to him, probably because his security cameras caught me sneaking you out of his house. I barely escaped, and then I went into hiding. Later on, I tried to go back to San Francisco and just lay low, but the city never felt safe after that."

"I'm so sorry, Gabriel."

"Why are you apologizing?"

"All of that happened because of me. I should have been strong enough to get out on my own, without involving you."

He said, "You can't blame yourself for the choices you made when you were struggling with addiction."

"That's good advice. You should take it too, and stop feeling guilty about not getting me out of there before I was willing to leave."

A smile tugged the corner of his lips. "I'll work on it." It disappeared quickly though, and he said, "Wait a minute. Will's about to go to San Francisco for three weeks. Are you planning to go too, since you're working on the same film?"

"Actually, I'll be there for six weeks. His part wraps earlier than the others, and I'm under contract until the end of the production."

"You can't go, Riley."

"I have to, because I need this job," I said. "Besides, it's been four years. There's no way Simeck's still searching for me after all this time."

"No, I'm sure he's not actively looking for you, but you may still run into him or one of his cronies. The fact that you found me here on Catalina is proof it could happen."

"It could, but San Francisco is a big place so there's a pretty slim chance of that. Plus, even if our paths crossed through some weird coincidence, I bet I could walk right past him and he wouldn't recognize me. You said it yourself, I've changed a lot."

"That's true, but this still makes me nervous," he said. Then he surprised me by asking, "Can I come along to San Francisco? It might seem silly, but if I'm there with you and know you're okay, I won't have to worry so much."

"Of course you can, but is that the only reason you want to come with me? Because I'm sure I'm going to be fine."

"It's definitely not the only reason," he told me. "We just found each other, and you always meant the world to me, Riley. I don't want to say goodbye to you two days from now."

"I'm glad you want to come along. Just so you know though, I had no intention of saying goodbye to you in two days, or ever again."

That made him smile, and he said, "I like this plan of never saying goodbye."

Chapter 2

After talking late into the night, we ended up falling asleep together. At some point, each of us half-woke and discarded some of our clothes to make ourselves more comfortable, and then we climbed under the covers and went right back to sleep.

Finding Gabriel curled up in my arms the next morning was the best thing I could ever imagine. I closed my eyes and let myself enjoy his warmth and the feeling of his hair against my cheek. After a while, he stirred and raised an eyelid. A big grin spread over his face as he murmured, "Good morning."

"Hi." My grin was as wide as his. "That was the best night's sleep ever."

"It was." He slipped out of bed and said, "I'll be right back. Don't go anywhere." I watched as he hurried to the bathroom dressed in just his black sweater, which covered him to mid-thigh.

He returned a few minutes later wearing a grayish blue robe, and I took a turn in the bathroom. I didn't have my toiletry bag with me, so the best I could do was finger-comb my hair, rub some toothpaste on my teeth, and rinse my mouth with water. Then I looked down at myself and sighed. My slightly baggy blue briefs were about as sexy as cutting two holes in a grocery sack and sticking my legs through them, but it couldn't be helped.

When I returned to the bedroom, I found he'd made the bed and was sitting on top of the comforter with his phone. I put on my jeans and joined him, and then I ran a fingertip over the thin lace inset on the cuff of his robe and said, "This is pretty."

"Thank you. I made it."

"Did you really?"

He nodded. "I taught myself to sew because I love lingerie, but it was tough to find things cut for a man's body. This was made to match my favorite briefs." He got up and opened the robe, revealing sexy, lace-trimmed underwear in the same grayish blue color and soft-looking knit fabric.

I whispered, "My God, Gabriel. Look at you." His lean, strong body was perfectly accentuated by those sweet and sexy briefs, and by a gorgeous black tattoo of lilies that ran down the side of his hip and thigh. The tiny silver ring in his belly button matched my nose ring, but that seemed like a weird observation so I kept it to myself.

He grew self-conscious under my gaze and muttered, "I'm a mess," as he reached up and tried to fix his hair.

"No, you're not. You're absolutely beautiful."

"It's sweet of you to say that." He moved closer and ran his hand over the saturated black tattoo that covered my shoulder and upper arm. It was a compilation of gothic and fantasy images, including a winding staircase, a labyrinth, a dragon, and a dark forest, among other things. "I really like the way you represented addiction and your journey to leave it behind."

I told him, "You're the first person who's ever understood my tattoo without any explanations."

"Maybe it only makes sense to people who've traveled the same path."

I sat on the edge of the mattress and looked up at him, and he met my gaze. For just a moment, something that felt an awful lot like anticipation passed between us. He ran his fingertips along my cheek as my hand brushed his hip.

We both pulled back when someone knocked on the door.

Gabriel fumbled with the sash of his robe as he said, "That's probably my friend Tracy. He messaged me a few minutes ago and offered to bring me some breakfast. I told him I had a guest, so he said he'd bring enough for two."

Tracy turned out to be a scowling mountain of muscle. I knew at a glance he was ex-military, because he just had that look about him. He was probably six-foot-six, and since I was five-eleven on a good day, it was more than a little intimidating when he filled the doorway and glared at me. I was sure he'd offered to bring us breakfast for the sole purpose of seeing who'd spent the night with his friend.

"Riley Palma, meet Tracy Garcia." The sudden tension in the room wasn't lost on Gabriel, who seemed flustered as he continued, "Tracy's a good friend. In fact, he came here with me from San Francisco, because I was worried about making the move on my own. Tracy, remember me telling you about Riley?"

I got up and crossed my arms over my chest, and he ran an appraising gaze down the length of me as he told his friend, "You always made it sound like he was a fragile little kid." Okay, that definitely wasn't my favorite description of me.

"We were both fragile," Gabriel said, as he took a tray from Tracy's hands, "and he was nineteen the last time I saw him, but I don't think I ever described him as a kid." Tracy's look made it clear he didn't even sort of trust me, and after an awkward pause, Gabriel added, "Thanks for bringing us some breakfast. I owe you one."

"No problem. Call me if you need anything, I'll be right upstairs."

Tracy frowned at me one last time before he turned and left. Once the door shut behind him, I relaxed a bit and muttered, "He seemed fun."

"He's always been protective of me for some reason. Please don't take it personally." Gabriel placed the tray on the bed, then pulled two black pieces of clothing from a shelf in his closet and traded the robe for leggings and another long sweater. While he did that, I found my T-shirt and sweater and pulled them on, and he asked, "Want to eat on the balcony? It's probably a little cold out, but we could bundle up."

When I agreed, he found a pair of throw blankets, and I picked up the tray and followed him out a pair of glass doors to an absolutely stunning oasis. Potted succulents were clustered at each end of the balcony. There was also a wrought iron table with two chairs, and a big satellite chair loaded with cushions. I took in the panoramic view of Avalon and its sapphire blue harbor far below us as I said, "This is fantastic."

"I think so, too. Whenever I'm not working, I'm usually out here with a book or a sketch pad."

"I didn't know you draw."

"I'm not very good, but I like to sketch ideas for the lingerie I want to make."

As I placed the tray on the table and we sat down across from each other, I said, "I always have random makeup ideas bouncing around in my head, and I sketch them out, too. That's the only way I'll ever keep track of them."

He handed me one of the blankets, then draped the other over his legs as he said, "Maybe we can sketch together after we eat. I've been thinking about costumes ever since you mentioned wanting some to go with your fantasy makeup, and I'd love to see what you have in mind so I can plan my designs around it."

"That sounds great."

Our meal consisted of coffee, muffins, and breakfast burritos that came wrapped in foil with sides of fresh salsa. When I asked if they were from a restaurant, Gabriel explained that two of the guys made a huge batch of burritos every Friday morning. Then he said, "Maybe I shouldn't have assumed you wanted to eat in my room. I know you're here with friends, and I've been monopolizing your time."

"Phoenix came here with a stack of work, and since Will and Lorenzo just got engaged, I'm guessing they're going to spend this weekend totally wrapped up in each other. But even if all of that wasn't true, I'd still want to spend every single moment with you." That earned me the sweetest smile.

After we ate, Gabriel went and found a large sketchpad and a Mason jar full of colored pencils, and we curled up together beneath the blankets in that round satellite chair. I drew the fantasy makeup looks I'd been working on, and he talked excitedly and sketched some costumes to go with them. His designs were pretty and delicate with great details. When I told him that, he turned to me and asked, "Are they really okay? If not, I can change them."

I said, "They're perfect," and a smile lit up his face.

He rested his head on my shoulder as he colored his drawings. Once he'd designed costumes for each of the five makeups I was planning, we worked together to design a merman, because I knew I could do better than my last attempt. As Gabriel drew long, flowing hair onto our shared creation, I said, "I'm going to call one of my friends who does drag to see if he can lend us a couple of wigs. They'll really round out these looks when we go to photograph them."

"Good idea." He added a streak of blue to the hair and said, "I'm so excited about these costumes. It's been a long time since I've gotten to do anything this fun and creative. I mean, there's my lingerie, but it's different working alone versus collaborating with someone."

"Speaking of your lingerie, I'd love to see more of what you've made."

"Sure. I actually just finished a piece a couple of days ago, and I'd love to get your opinion on it." We went inside, and I sat cross-legged on the bed while he pulled a delicate creation of red silk and lace from his closet. "I usually make stuff to be comfortable and wearable, but with this one, I just let my imagination run free. It's totally impractical, but I wanted to see if I had enough skill to pull it off."

The strapless, corseted bodysuit had a delicate red framework that jutted out from both hips. "It's stunning," I said. "I can imagine it with a Marie Antoinette-style white wig, pale, powdery makeup, and red lipstick."

"That's exactly what inspired me," he said. "It's meant to mimic the undergarment women used to wear to give their skirts volume in the eighteenth century. I'm thinking of making a long, sheer robe to go with it, like Marie Antoinette might wear in her boudoir."

"That would be perfect."

As I ran my fingers down the decorative clasps along the front of the corset, he said, "It would have been fun back when I was doing burlesque, but aside from that, there's really no place to wear something like this."

"I didn't know you did burlesque."

"It was just for a few months, back when I was living in San Francisco."

I asked, "Did you like it?"

"There were some things I loved about it, like the costumes. The tips were nice too, but I was always nervous performing in front of an audience."

"Even so, I bet you were great at it."

He tried to shrug it off, but then he grinned and admitted, "I was pretty good."

"I would have loved to see you perform."

His grin turned teasing. "I'll give you a private show sometime." He turned back to the closet and traded the red garment for a black, strappy one. "This doesn't look like much on the hanger, but it's meant to mimic a bondage harness. I wanted to play with the idea of hard and soft, so it's made of silk ribbon instead of leather. There's a black silk jockstrap that goes with it."

"That sounds unbelievably sexy."

He hung it back in the closet. "It's not very practical, though. With all those straps, it takes forever to put it on. I'll simplify the design if I make another one." Gabriel moved to his dresser and opened the top drawer. "Here's some stuff that's actually wearable."

I got up to take a look. The drawer was filled with neat rows of underwear in a range of styles and colors, and I asked, "Did you make all of these?"

"Yeah, every last one."

"Wow, that's fantastic."

He glanced at me from under his lashes. "You don't think it's silly that I do this?"

"You're creating beautiful things that make you happy. There's nothing silly about it." When he leaned in and kissed my cheek, I smiled at him and asked, "What was that for?"

"For making me feel like my quirky little hobby isn't ridiculous."

"It's brilliant, actually. In fact, you should turn it into a business. I'll bet it's hard for anyone besides cisgender women to find lingerie that fits right."

"I've thought about that for years, but do you really think people would want to buy my designs?"

"Absolutely."

He said, "That would be a dream come true, but I don't have the first clue about how to run a business."

"Me neither, but we could learn. I'd be happy to help you."

"You really are sweet." He closed the drawer and changed the subject by asking, "Do you feel like going for a walk? You're probably tired of being cooped up in here."

I wasn't just going to forget about the idea of turning his passion into a business, but for now I said, "I'd love to take a walk with you, not that I feel cooped up. Can we go and see the horses? Lorenzo mentioned there are a few of them here at the resort."

"Sure. We can even go riding if you want."

"Or not. I've just always wanted to see one up close. As far as climbing on its back, hanging on for dear life, and bouncing around for a while, that actually sounds horrible."

He pulled a pair of black ankle boots from his closet and asked, "You've never seen a horse up close before?"

"Nope." I sat on the edge of the bed and put on my socks and shoes as I said, "The closest I've come to being in the country is watching it roll past my window on the drive from L.A. to San Francisco."

"You grew up in Southern California, right?"

"Yeah, in a working-class neighborhood in Torrance."

"They never took you on a field trip to a farm or anything like that?"

"No, but when I was in the fourth grade, they paid some guy to bring a cow to our school. Her name was Bernadette, and three kids got called on to try milking her. Sadly, I was one of those kids. Then she took a big dump on the hopscotch. I was nine, so obviously all of this made a huge impression on me."

He chuckled and said, "That all sounds very educational."

"Right? I don't know what we were supposed to learn from the visiting cow, but it was actually one of the best school days ever because we got to go outside and do something different for an hour. I always got in trouble in school because I had a hard time sitting still and paying attention, so anything to break up the routine was welcome."

"I used to get in trouble for not paying attention too, but in my case it was because I was always daydreaming."

While he put on a pair of socks and the boots, I asked him, "What would you daydream about?"

"It's silly."

"Tell me anyway."

Gabriel glanced at me, and after a pause he admitted, "A lot of times, I'd fantasize about what my life would be like once I was a grown up. It was all very innocent and totally unrealistic."

"How did you imagine it?"

"I grew up watching a lot of old movies, so I basically pictured a Doris Day film. I'd have an exciting job in a big city, a swanky apartment, and of course a handsome boyfriend who looked a lot like Rock Hudson."

I asked, "Did you watch those movies with your mom?"

"No. She had to work two jobs to make ends meet since she was a single parent, so this little old lady in our apartment building would babysit me after school. Her name was Miss Eleanor, and she was wonderful. We'd watch her favorite musicals over and over, and we'd both sing along while I tried to mimic the dance routines."

"Miss Eleanor sounds terrific."

"She really was. It broke my heart when she died during my freshman year of high school, but I'm lucky she was a part of my life for fourteen years," he said. "In fact, she was the first person I came out to when I was twelve, and she was so kind and accepting."

"I'm glad you had that support."

"Me too. I needed it desperately back then, and I really wasn't going to get it from my super religious family." As I followed him out of his room and up the stairs, he asked, "How old were you when you came out?"

"The first time I told anyone I was gay, I was sixteen and had just left home. She was an eighteen-year-old girl I met on the bus to San Francisco, and we just randomly struck up a conversation. I figured she was a safe person to tell, because if she ended up rejecting me it didn't really matter. She was nice about it, though."

He asked, "You never told your mom?"

"We didn't have that type of relationship. One where we actually talked, I mean."

As we cut through the living room, Gabriel glanced at me with sadness in his dark eyes. "I'm sorry, Riley. I should have known not to ask."

"It's fine. I made peace with it a long time ago."

"Were you afraid of coming out to your friends because you thought they'd reject you?"

"I didn't have any friends at that point. I was in a dark place when I was in high school, so I put up walls between myself and the rest of the world. Plus, I'd always planned on leaving as soon as I could manage it, so I never bothered trying to let anyone in." We paused when we reached the open, modern kitchen, and I muttered, "Moving to San Francisco was supposed to be a fresh start, but I was so naïve. I thought I could just find a job and an apartment, and everything would be great. Talk about a harsh wake-up call."

"It was like that for me too when I first moved there. I thought I was making all my dreams come true. Little did I know how hard it would be just to survive."

It was obvious neither of us really felt like delving into the past right then, so we let the subject drop. After a moment, he handed me a couple of apples from a bowl on the counter and took two for himself. As he led the way to the door, I asked, "What's with the fruit?"

"It's a bribe. Give a horse an apple, and they adore you for life."

When we got outside, we circled the resort's two main buildings, which formed an 'L' around the courtyard, and soon reached the equestrian center. It consisted of a large stable, a pair of corrals, and a couple of smaller buildings, all of which were tidy and perfectly maintained.

There were two horses in the first corral we came to, and Gabriel climbed up on the wooden fence and called, "Hi Luna, you beautiful girl. Come on over here and say hello." A gray horse with a white mane and tail actually did as he asked. He fed her an apple before stroking the white stripe in the center of her long face and cooing, "Look how pretty you are."

I said, "I never knew you were such an animal lover."

"I definitely am. Want to come over and say hello?"

"In a minute."

An even larger brown horse had wandered over, and Gabriel fed him the other apple as he said, "Hi there, handsome." Then he glanced at me over his shoulder. "There's nothing to worry about. They're both sweethearts."

"I'm sure they are. They're also huge though, especially that brown one. I don't know why I always assumed horses were smaller than that."

"A lot of them are. Old Linus here is just statuesque, aren't you, boy?" The horse nuzzled his hand, and Gabriel patted the side of the animal's neck.

The last thing I wanted was to seem cowardly in front of Gabriel, so I pushed aside my worries and approached the corral. Linus lowered his head and watched me as his nostrils flared. I started to hold out the apple, and Gabriel said, "Keep your hand flat and offer it to him on your palm. He'd never bite you on purpose, but he might do it accidentally."

I followed his instructions and stuck my hand and the apple into the corral, which immediately resulted in great big slobbery horse lips all over my palm. While the huge animal chomped on his treat, I wiped my hand on my jeans. Then I hesitantly touched the top of his nose, which turned out to be soft and velvety. He watched me closely as he allowed me to run my hand over his cheek.

I followed Gabriel's lead and climbed onto the bottom rung of the wood fence, which put the horse and me at eye level. "He reminds me of a giant dog," I said, "but he seems a lot mellower."

While I was distracted by the conversation, Linus took the opportunity to pluck the second apple out of my hand. The gray horse seemed annoyed and tossed her head while he calmly chewed his stolen prize. I started laughing and said, "I really like this horse."

"He's definitely a character." He stepped off the fence, then climbed through it and patted the horse's neck. "Aren't you, Linus?" Luna butted his shoulder with her nose, so he patted her, too.

I rested my elbows on the top of the fence and watched Gabriel as he had a completely adorable one-sided conversation with the horses. He'd always seemed so sophisticated and cosmopolitan, but he was perfectly at home in this setting, too. It showed me there was a lot more to learn about the man I'd thought about every day for the last four years. It was kind of like having an all-time favorite album, then discovering a bunch of new songs beyond the part you'd always listened to.

He glanced at me over his shoulder, and then he grinned and said, "You have the sweetest expression on your face right now. What are you thinking about?"

"How much I'm looking forward to getting to know you."

"You already know me, Riley. In fact, you probably know me better than anyone."

I climbed through the fence and went to stand right in front of him. "I do. But there's still so much more to discover, and that's incredibly exciting."

His gaze met mine, and there it was again, that feeling of anticipation hovering between us. My heart started to race. Even though I knew I shouldn't rush it, I wanted to kiss him more than anything, so I took a chance.

When my lips brushed his, he pulled back with a question in his eyes. I started to worry I'd moved too fast and totally blown it. But then he took my face between his palms and kissed me, and it was passionate and urgent and absolutely everything.

He seemed to surprise himself, because he stepped back after a few moments and mumbled, "What are we doing?"

"Something I've wanted to do for a very long time."

"You have?" When I nodded, he said, "I never thought of you like this."

"But there's a mutual attraction here. I know there is."

"You're right, but it's confusing," he said. "Back then, you were almost like a little brother to me."

"I'm not that broken nineteen-year-old anymore."

"No, you're really not. But you're still a lot younger than me, and—"

I interrupted him by saying, "You're only six years older, and really, what difference does it make? You know I had to grow up fast, so I'm not some typical twenty-three-year-old." I moved closer to him, and I was so happy when he closed the gap and put his arms around me.

"You're right, but there are still a million reasons why this probably won't work."

I slipped my hands around his waist and nuzzled his cheek. "But just imagine if it does."

At that point, Linus got tired of being ignored and leaned against us. We both laughed as we almost lost our balance, and Gabriel told the horse, "Message received, buddy. I'll go get the grooming kit so I can brush you." To me, he added, "The horses always seem to enjoy that."

He started to leave the corral, but I caught his hand and he turned to look at me. "Just give me a chance, Gabriel. That's all I ask."

I held my breath while he searched my face for a long moment. There was vulnerability in his eyes, which made me want to hold him and never let go. Finally, he said, "Okay, but we have to take this slowly."

"I can do that." Maybe.

He smiled at me, and then he climbed through the fence and went into the stable. When he was out of sight, I broke into a little dance, which made both horses turn and stare at me. I whispered to them, "Did you hear that? He's giving me a chance."

We spent a couple of hours at the equestrian center, keeping our conversation light and upbeat while we brushed several of the horses. After that, we decided we both needed a shower, so he went to his room and I went to mine. We'd agreed to meet in the lobby in half an hour, but it only took me about ten minutes to shower and change, so I was very early when I went downstairs.

I found Will, Lorenzo, Phoenix, and Beck lounging in front of a stone fireplace, along with Will's fluffy gray cat, who'd made herself comfortable on Beck's lap. The guys were drinking beer and engaged in an animated conversation, and Phoenix's laptop sat forgotten on the coffee table. When they saw me, Will called, "Get over here, Riley, and tell us everything!"

I sat beside Phoenix on one of the stylish orange couches and said, "Okay, but first congratulations again, you two. I can't believe you spontaneously got engaged last night!"

Will and Lorenzo were curled up together on the couch across from mine, and they exchanged lovesick grins as Will said, "Thanks. I can't quite believe it myself."

I asked, "Have you talked about the wedding?"

"A little. We both agreed we want to get married here at the ranch, since it's where we met. Beck and his husband had their gorgeous wedding here last November, and it was this perfect balance of elegant, but still fun and relaxed. That's what we're shooting for," Lorenzo said, as he lovingly brushed back a lock of hair that had fallen into his fiancé's eyes.

"It goes without saying you're invited," Will told me. "We're trying to pin down a date, so we'll let you know as soon as we figure it out."

Beck grinned at me and added, "From what I've been hearing, it sounds like you know exactly who you'll be bringing as your date to this wedding."

I grinned, too. "Yeah, I do."

Phoenix asked, "So, what's going on with you and Gabriel?"

"Well, we've been getting reacquainted, and he's coming with me to San Francisco. Since I was going to hitch a ride with you, do you think there's room for one more in your Bronco?"

"Sure," he said. "There's plenty of room, as long as you don't mind getting cozy with Will and Lorenzo and Madame Leota." The cat shot him a look when he said her name.

"That's fine with me. Also, Gabriel messaged some friends who live in San Francisco last night, and they're letting us use their apartment while they're visiting the UK. He says you're welcome to stay with us." Phoenix and I had been planning to share a hotel room to save money and I'd invited Gabriel to join us, but he'd had a much better idea.

"You two are going to want some privacy, so I'll fend for myself," Phoenix said.

"Are you sure?"

"Definitely."

I turned to Beck and said, "I just realized we're getting ahead of ourselves, because he hasn't had a chance to talk to you about getting some time off yet."

Apparently Beck was the most laid-back boss ever, because he just shrugged and said, "He can take as much time off as he needs, it's no problem. The resort won't even reopen until the first week of April, because we're redesigning the spa and didn't want to annoy our guests with a bunch of noise and construction mess." The blue-eyed brunet, who was wearing plaid shorts and a neon yellow T-shirt with a cartoon fish on it, didn't seem old enough to be running a high-end resort, but from what I'd heard he was actually turning the place into a huge success.

Just then, Gabriel's enormous friend Tracy came in through the door at the back of the lobby, carrying a box. He scowled when he spotted me and kept going. Once he'd exited through the door at the front of the building, I muttered, "What's with that guy? When he saw me in Gabriel's room this morning, he acted like I was a criminal or something."

"To be honest, I've never understood their relationship," Beck admitted. "He and Gabriel came here together from San Francisco, and I get that they're good friends. But it seems like Tracy assigned himself the role of Gabriel's protector when there's really no need for that."

I asked, "Do you think Tracy has a crush on him?"

"That's what I assumed at first," Beck said, "but now I don't think so. It's more like Tracy needed a project, and he chose to focus his time and energy on Gabriel. I get the impression he's been a bit lost since he left the Army. He's thrown himself into his job looking after the horses, but I just don't think it's enough for him."

I admitted, "Even though it's a bit odd, I guess it's not a bad thing that Gabriel has someone looking out for him."

Beck's phone beeped, and he picked it up from the coffee table and read the screen before saying, "Speak of the devil." A moment later, Gabriel entered the lobby holding his phone, and Beck called, "Of course! Take as much time off as you need."

Gabriel looked so sexy. Once again, he'd dressed all in black, which seemed elegant and sophisticated on him. His slightly cropped, long-sleeved sweater revealed his pierced belly button, and his slim-fitting pants and boots with a bit of a heel emphasized his long legs. Red lipstick drew my eyes directly to his gorgeous, full lips.

He asked his boss, "Even if it's six weeks?"

"That's totally fine," Beck said.

Gabriel settled in on my right and told me, "In that case, we're all set. My friends that are letting us use their apartment will be home in about three weeks, but they're totally fine with us staying until you're finished with the movie."

I smiled at him and said, "This is going to be great."

We were joined a few moments later by three more guys who worked at the resort. I'd met Vee the night before, and he greeted me like we were old friends. The other two were a slim Asian-American guy named Ezra and a big blond named Isaac, who looked like a Viking. Ezra parked his wheelchair in front of the fireplace, and Isaac sat at his feet and looked up at him with pure adoration in his eyes.

Everyone started talking about the resort, which I found out was becoming well-known for its summer camps for grown-ups. While they brainstormed some new ideas for the upcoming season,

Gabriel took my hand and put his head on my shoulder. At that point, I totally lost track of the conversation. All that mattered was the beautiful man sitting beside me, who smelled like soap and tangerines and everything good in the world.

It still felt like an absolute miracle that I'd actually found Gabriel again. In fact, I could barely believe he was right here beside me. More than anything, I just wanted to enjoy the moment, but worry began creeping in, and I sent a silent plea into the universe—*please don't let me screw this up.* I'd never had so much to lose before.

Chapter 3

On Sunday morning, I woke up pinned down in Gabriel's bed. An arm and a leg were flung across me, and the blankets were so tangled around us that it seemed like a miniature tornado had touched down during the night. All of that made me grin, and I kissed the top of his head and made myself comfortable, since I wasn't about to wake him.

When he shifted slightly, his thigh grazed my cock. I tried to ignore the fact that I instantly started to get hard, just like I'd ignored it the night before. We'd spent some time kissing and cuddling, but as soon as we'd started to get turned on, both of us had backed off. We just weren't ready to go there, maybe in part because we knew sex was going to be an issue.

Even though my natural tendency was to be submissive, I figured I could probably deal with that when we finally decided to have sex. But I really couldn't be anything but a bottom. I'd tried to top in the past, at the request of whatever random hookup I'd been with at the time, and I'd absolutely hated it. I knew he felt the same way about topping. We'd talked about sex in the past, and we'd been on exactly the same page when it came to what we not only liked, but needed.

Sure, that still left us with oral sex and a lot of other ways to pleasure each other, but I was worried about never being able to fully satisfy him. I knew sex wasn't everything in a relationship, but it was important. For now, we were both content to just kiss and cuddle, but sooner or later, the disconnect of two bottoms trying to make it work was going to be an issue. I knew that for a fact.

After a few minutes, Gabriel woke up and stretched as he grinned at me. He looked adorably rumpled in his baby blue flannel pajamas and what was left of a short ponytail on the crown of his head. I wrapped my arms around him, and he put his head on my chest as I murmured, "It's so nice to wake up with you."

"I was just about to say that." He burrowed into my arms and murmured, "I wish we could stay in bed all day. Since we can't though, I propose going straight to bed once we get to San Francisco."

"Works for me."

"I just realized I never asked how we're getting there."

"We can hitch a ride with Phoenix," I said, "who's also driving Will, Lorenzo, and Will's cat. He's sure we'll all fit in his SUV. It might be a bit cramped though, so we could take my car if you're more comfortable with that. Be forewarned—it's a loud, slow, and truly ancient VW bug, so it won't be very luxurious. I'm fine with whichever you prefer."

"Would your bug make it that far without breaking down?"

"Probably not, but I'm good at fixing it. I always keep a huge tool kit and some spare parts in the backseat."

He grinned at me and said, "I think we should probably carpool with Phoenix." I nodded in agreement, and he kissed my cheek before climbing out of bed and heading to the bathroom.

When he came back a few minutes later, he smelled minty and his hair was combed. I took a turn in the bathroom and used my toothbrush, since I'd had the foresight to move my stuff to his room the night before.

He'd already started packing by the time I returned to the bedroom. "I really want to work on the costumes to go with your fantasy makeup when we're in San Francisco," he said, "but is it crazy to bring along my sewing machine? It's portable, but the carrying case is pretty big and I don't want to take up every bit of space in your friend's SUV."

"Don't worry about that. I'll hold it on my lap if there's no room in the back."

"For six hours?"

"Sure."

"That's very sweet, but I'd never ask you to do that."

"You're not asking," I said, "I'm volunteering. It might not come to that anyway, but definitely bring it."

"Okay. I know you'll be at work a lot of the time, so it'll be nice to have a way to keep busy." He glanced at me and asked, "Do you think it'd be alright if I visited you on the movie set? I'd love to watch you work, even if it's just for an hour or two."

"I'd love that."

"Are you sure? I don't want to get in the way or anything."

"You absolutely won't be in the way," I assured him, "and I'm flattered that you want to see what I do."

"I'm so proud of you, Riley. Look how far you've come in just four years! It's amazing that you're a Hollywood makeup artist."

"Like I said before though, I was just hired as an assistant. The only reason I'm doing Will's makeup is because he and I met through Phoenix and hit it off, so he asked to work with me exclusively. There's a whole hierarchy in the makeup department, and I was at the very bottom of it. But stars are allowed to bring in their own makeup artists or make special requests, and that's literally the only reason I'm doing more than fetching coffee and catering to the whims of the lead makeup artist."

"You're selling yourself short. If you weren't good at what you do, Will wouldn't have asked you to do his screen makeup, and the lead artist wouldn't have signed off on it."

I grinned and said, "I'm great at what I do, no false modesty there. I just don't want to mislead you into thinking I'm super successful or anything. After this movie wraps, I'm going to go right back to the bottom of the hierarchy, assuming I can even find another job in the field."

"The experience you're gaining on this movie will help, won't it?"

"Oh, for sure. This'll look great on my resume. But the fact is, there are only so many jobs to go around, and a hell of a lot of makeup artists are constantly trying to break into the movie business."

As he folded some pajamas and placed them in a suitcase that was open on the bed, he asked, "How'd you get your first movie job?"

"When I was in cosmetology school, a guest speaker came to talk to us about careers in the film industry. I struck up a conversation with him after class, and we ended up going out for coffee. He's a friend of mine now and got me my first job, which led to the next two. It's definitely a field where it pays to know people."

Gabriel studied me as he folded a pair of black pants. "I used to think you were an introvert, same as me, but I was wrong about that. You're actually very outgoing."

"Oh no, you were right the first time. I can be social, but afterwards I totally need to go hide in my makeup cave and recharge."

He grinned and asked, "Makeup cave?"

"I once heard a scriptwriter refer to her home office as her writing cave, so for lack of a better idea I borrowed the name. You'll see what I mean in a few hours. We're going to stop by my apartment before getting on the road to San Francisco, so I can pick up a few things." I frowned and added, "I obviously never imagined I'd be taking you to see my home when I left for Catalina, and the place is a huge mess. Please don't hold that against me. I was only home for a day after filming wrapped at the first location, and I pretty much just threw my stuff everywhere."

"That's fine," he said with a smile. "It'll give me a chance to see you in your natural habitat."

He was joking, but I started to worry about what kind of impression my cluttered home was going to make on him. I wanted to convince Gabriel I had my shit together, and my apartment really wasn't going to sell that message. There was nothing I could do about it, though. It wasn't like I could ask him to wait in the car while I went inside to pack my stuff.

I changed the subject with, "I'll go get us some coffee while you pack. Is it okay to just help myself to stuff upstairs?"

He nodded. "All the food and drinks in that kitchen are shared. By the way, some of the guys do a big brunch for all of us every Sunday morning, so we should plan on joining them in about an hour. Since the resort's closed, that'll be happening in the main building."

"Sounds good."

I started to leave the room, and he called after me, "I take my coffee with—"

"A ton of milk and a little sugar." I grinned at him over my shoulder and said, "I was paying attention yesterday." He was grinning too as the door swung shut behind me.

My smile faded when I reached the main floor and spotted Tracy Garcia. He was sitting by himself, drinking coffee at the counter that fronted the open kitchen. I hated the fact that we were dressed identically in white tank tops and gray sweatpants. Normally, I felt pretty good about my body, but next to this behemoth I looked like his mini-me.

We frowned at each other as I stepped into the kitchen, and then I ignored him while I opened a few cabinets and searched for mugs. After I found them, I discovered the coffee pot was nearly empty, so I poured the half cup that was left and started brewing a fresh pot.

My back was to Tracy, and I could feel his eyes boring into me. Once I started the coffee maker, I turned to him and blurted, "You know, I'm not the enemy. I want the same thing you do, for Gabriel to be happy."

His voice was a low growl when he said, "You just fucking went off and left him behind."

It took me a minute to process that, and then I asked, "Are you talking about four years ago, when he put me on a bus to Reno?"

Tracy's scowl deepened. "Were there other times you abandoned him?"

"I don't know what the hell you think happened four years ago, but let me paint you a picture. I was starting to go through with-drawal, and I couldn't stop shaking. I was sick and dizzy and trying not to puke, and with the last of my strength I begged Gabriel to come with me to Nevada. I fucking *begged him*. He wouldn't do it, though. He said I didn't need a junkie like him dragging me down. He wouldn't even give me a way to contact him after I got out of rehab.

"He literally carried me onto that bus because I was too weak to make it up the stairs. Then he took off, and before I could go after him and try again to get him to come with me, I ended up passing out. By the time I came to, the bus was outside San Francisco, and I had absolutely no way of finding him again. If you want to hate me for leaving him behind, get in line. I spent the past four years hating myself for it, even though I know for a fact there wasn't a single thing I could have done differently."

Tracy's dark expression wavered for a moment. I could tell he was doubting his version of the truth, which I was sure he'd twisted around and misinterpreted from whatever Gabriel had told him about the day I left. After a pause, he said, "So how the hell did you find him here?"

"Call it dumb luck, a random coincidence, or fate, but it was a total surprise to run into him again after all these years. To me, it says we were meant to be together."

"You're really not."

I frowned at him and asked, "What are you basing that on?"

"You've been back in his life for two days, and what's the first thing you're doing? Taking him back to San Francisco! What the hell's the matter with you?"

"It was his idea to come along."

He snapped, "You could have refused to take him with you."

"He's not a child, Garcia. If he wants to go to San Francisco, it's his choice."

"So, you're fine with the fact that he's putting himself at risk, just because he thinks he has to babysit you?"

I asked, "How is he putting himself at risk? Don't tell me it's because my former 'Dom' is still holding a grudge after all this time and will magically find us in a city of almost a million people, because that's pretty unlikely."

I hadn't thought it was possible for Tracy's scowl to deepen, but it did as he growled, "That just shows how totally fucking ignorant you are."

I crossed my arms over my chest. "Then please enlighten me with your great wisdom."

"It's not just because that sociopath would fuck you both up if he happened to cross your path. You proved it could happen, by the way, by randomly stumbling across Gabriel this weekend."

He wasn't wrong about that last part. I asked, "Okay, so what else is wrong with taking him with me to San Francisco?"

"That city is toxic to him! He relapsed over and over again when he was living there. It wasn't until we moved here, to this relatively controlled environment, that he was finally able to get a handle on his addiction. Now you're about to take him back to a place that's loaded with triggers. You've dealt with these same issues, so don't you see why this is a huge problem?"

"I get what you're saying, but Gabriel gets to decide where he goes. This trip was his idea, and it's insulting to treat him like a helpless little waif who can't think for himself." Tracy looked away, and after a few moments I said, "Even though you've been acting like a douche, I'm glad you brought this up. I'll definitely talk to him about it. And I get that you're worried about him, but just so you know, acting like I'm the enemy isn't doing your friend any favors."

He remained silent as I turned my back to him again and prepared two cups of coffee. I was on my way back to the stairs and almost out of earshot when Tracy muttered, "I was just trying to take care of him."

I paused and glanced at him over my shoulder. "I know, and I'm glad he has a friend who cares about him." I actually felt bad for the guy as I left him alone in that big, empty kitchen.

When I got back to Gabriel's room, his suitcase was piled high with clothes, and he said, "This is never going to close."

"Sure it is. We'll gang up on it."

He grinned at me and took the mug I offered him. After tasting it, he said, "Thank you. This is perfect."

"I'm glad I got it right." I sat on a corner of the bed and drank some coffee before saying, "So, I just had a little chat with your pal Tracy."

A frown line appeared between his dark brows. "Was he rude to you?"

"Nah, not really. He's just worried about you going to San Francisco, because he thinks it might set you back in your recovery. What do you think about that?"

"I can see why he's worried. Being back there could potentially stir up a lot of emotions, and I'm not always great at dealing with that. The years I spent in San Francisco were really awful at times, but I also made some amazing friends there, so it's not like I want to avoid it forever. You already know some of my story—the drug abuse, obviously, and the fact that I worked as a prostitute. I don't know if I ever really explained how I got there, though."

I said softly, "You don't have to talk about this if you don't want to."

Gabriel held the coffee mug in both hands and leaned against his dresser. "I want you to understand this about me, though." After a pause, he said, "When I first moved to San Francisco, I ended up homeless. It was a constant struggle just to find someplace safe to sleep every night and to afford my next meal." He shifted his gaze to a spot somewhere beyond the open balcony door before saying, "I turned to prostitution because it was the only way I could earn enough to keep a roof over my head. When I started, I swore it was just until I landed a job with a steady income. I also told myself it was just my body and it didn't mean anything, but it took a huge emotional toll on me."

He paused again before saying, "The first time someone offered me drugs, it seemed like a way to escape from my depressing situation for a while. No one ever plans on becoming an addict, but soon all I cared about was my next fix. It didn't matter what I had to do to get it. I know a million junkies tell that exact same story, but I still need to take ownership of it."

I could only imagine the memories he was grappling with as he exhaled slowly. Then he said, "The best and worst parts of my life are all tangled up in that city. I reached points lower than I ever thought possible, but I also made some absolutely wonderful friends, and they became the supportive, loving family I'd always wanted."

He was still staring at a spot off in the distance, through that open door as he continued, "Being here at this resort has kind of been like living in a bubble. There's been very little in the way of stress, triggers, or temptation, but I can't hide from myself forever. I think this trip to San Francisco will be a good way to start easing myself back out into the real world."

I asked, "Are you sure? Maybe it'd be easier if you started by spending time in L.A., or anyplace else that doesn't have so many bad memories."

"But I think it's important to face my demons. I also really want to spend time with you, and I want to see my friends. It would mean everything to me to reclaim San Francisco, and I think this trip will be the perfect opportunity to totally drown out those bad memories with good ones."

"How can I help you while we're there?"

"Just keep talking to me," he said. "Ask questions. If I get quiet or start to withdraw, call me on it."

"I absolutely will. What about counseling? Would you like me to help you find someone while we're there?"

"Actually, I already have a counselor," he said. "He's on the mainland, so we do phone sessions every other week."

"Okay, that's good." His gaze had shifted to the floor, and after a few moments I asked, "Why aren't you looking at me?"

"Because I'm embarrassed. It's so hard to talk about the fact that I used to be a prostitute."

"Please don't be embarrassed," I said. "I was in the same position you were, so I totally understand how you got there."

"But you never resorted to prostitution."

"Sure I did. That's what I meant when I called my time with Mason Simeck a business arrangement. He might not have paid me in cash, but he supplied me with drugs and gave me a place to stay, and in return I let him fuck me, torture me, and basically do whatever he wanted to get his rocks off. Looking back now, it's horrifying that I allowed those things to happen. But at the time, it was what I felt I needed to do to survive and get my next fix."

He whispered, "Fuck," and put down his coffee cup. Then he climbed onto the bed with me and grabbed me in a hug. After a while, he said, "You might have some concerns about dating an ex-prostitute, so I want you to know I've been tested repeatedly and by some miracle, my results were always negative. I just thought I should put that out there."

"For future reference, I've been tested too, and my results were negative. I really don't know how I dodged that bullet, given some of the choices I made when I was using."

Gabriel said, "I'm glad we got this conversation out of the way. I was worried it'd be really awkward."

"Nah. We can talk about anything. I think we just proved that."

He kissed my forehead and climbed off the bed, then changed the subject by saying, "I should keep packing. I don't know what time your friend is planning to leave, but I don't want to keep him waiting."

Between the two of us, we managed to get the suitcase zipped. Next, he packed his sewing machine in its plastic case and gathered some spools of thread and other supplies in a floral tote. There wasn't enough room for a sketch pad, so I put one in my backpack for him.

Once he finished packing, he went to take a shower. When he returned, he was dressed in his blue robe, and he was carrying an overflowing cosmetics bag, along with an armload of bottles. A cloud of steam and the sweet smell of his shampoo wafted through the bathroom door. He dropped his supplies on the bed and sat down with them as he said, "I'm going to see if I can pare this down to just the essentials."

"I'll get my shower while you do that."

By the time I returned from the bathroom with a towel around my hips, Gabriel had piled a lot of makeup onto his nightstand. Lined up in front of him were a few basic cosmetics, along with his grooming supplies, and he muttered, "I'm terrible at traveling light, but I think this'll do." It was gratifying when he glanced at me, then looked again and ran his gaze down my body.

"I'm going to have two huge makeup kits with me, one for the set and the other for my fantasy makeup. You're welcome to use anything you want."

"Thanks. That'll be fun."

He looked up at me when I came over and stood in front of him, and I ran my fingers over his freshly shaved cheek as I asked, "Can I do your makeup?"

"Today, you mean?" When I nodded, he said, "I'd love it if you did that for me once we're in San Francisco, but I'm not going to wear any today. It's just not the day for it."

"What do you mean?"

"It's one thing to be femme here at work where everyone knows me, and San Francisco is an open-minded place overall. But between here and there is a big stretch of the kind of place I grew up in—rural, small-town America. Some days, I feel strong enough to weather the stares and disparaging comments I usually get in places like that. Other days, like today, I just want to fly under the radar."

I muttered, "I hate the fact that you can't be yourself wherever you go."

"That's on me, though. There will always be plenty of haters in the world. All I can do is get myself to a point where I feel strong and confident no matter where I am," he said.

"If you ever want me to beat up any of those haters for you, just let me know."

He grinned and said, "You'd make a great knight in shining armor, but I don't think we'll have to go there." Then he went back to packing his toiletry kit, so I found my backpack and pulled out my last clean outfit. I hung my towel over the back of a chair and took a few moments to try to shake the wrinkles out of my T-shirt.

It surprised me when Gabriel's hands slid over my shoulders and down my back. When I tossed my shirt aside and turned to look at him, his hands traced my pecs, then skimmed my torso before circling my hips. He met my gaze as he said, "You're so beautiful, Riley."

My voice sounded rough when I told him, "No one's ever called me that before."

He traced my lower lip, then cupped my face between his palms and kissed me. My heart raced as he deepened the kiss. I tasted his mouth and felt the dampness in his freshly washed hair when I ran my fingers into it.

I was overcome—by desire and emotion and sensation, by all of that and all of him. My cock swelled as we tumbled onto the bed. His robe had fallen open, and I kissed his exposed shoulder, his chest, and his stomach before taking his cock between my lips. He drew a sharp breath as he sprawled out on the bed—as much as he could beside his big suitcase—and parted his legs.

I'd thought about that moment, the one where we transitioned from 'just friends' to lovers, so many times. I figured we'd probably have to ease into it, but then it just happened, driven by lust and longing and a mutual attraction that was intense and undeniable. I wrapped my hands around his hips as I sucked his cock, and it was so gratifying to feel him writhe beneath me and to hear the primal sounds that slipped from his lips.

My hard-on throbbed, aching for attention, but I kept my focus on pleasuring him. It paid off, because in just a few minutes he muttered, "I'm going to come, Riley." A tremor rolled through his body as I sucked him harder and faster, and then he arched off the bed and cried out as he came.

Afterwards, I gathered him in my arms and he wrapped himself around me. As soon as he caught his breath, he slid his hand between my legs and grasped my cock. Then he started jerking me off, and I moaned softly as I draped my leg over his hip to give him better access.

It felt wonderful, and I was so desperate for release that I came in just a few minutes. Now it was my turn to gasp for breath and wait for my heartbeat to gradually return to normal. Meanwhile, he cleaned me up with some tissues and gathered me in his arms. I grinned and said, "So, that happened."

"Yes it did," he said with a smile. "You looked so damn sexy that I couldn't help myself."

"Really? You thought I looked sexy?"

"Why do you sound so surprised?"

"I just never thought of myself that way."

He lightly caressed my cheek. "But you must hear it all the time from the men you date."

"Actually, I don't date."

He asked, "Why not?"

"Because you were the only man I wanted, and I didn't know where to find you."

He totally thought I was kidding, and for now, I decided to just leave it at that. Gabriel grinned at me and kissed my forehead, and then he sat up and said, "We should get dressed. Our friends will probably want to leave soon."

Once we were ready, I sent a text to Phoenix and helped Gabriel with his luggage. Then we joined everyone for brunch in the resort's main building. Phoenix came over to us and said, "Hey, good timing. We need to leave in about twenty minutes, because Will has a meeting with his agent to talk about his next movie. It shouldn't take long, and we'll get on the road after that."

The meal had been set up buffet-style, and we filled our plates and joined about a dozen people at a long table. The conversation was loud, animated, and punctuated with laughter. I mostly just paid attention to Gabriel, who seemed happy as he watched what was going on around him and ate his breakfast.

Sometime later, Will got up and told everyone, "We need to get going if we're going to catch the next ferry, but Lorie and I will be back in three weeks. We love you guys, and we'll miss you."

As our little group prepared to leave, Beck grabbed me in a back-slapping hug and said, "You're always welcome here, Riley, and you need to come back soon." I promised I would. While that was happening, I noticed Tracy and Gabriel hugging each other while Tracy whispered something to him.

Beck pulled one of the resort's trolleys into the circular drive. Then he and his husband, a tall, handsome Greek man named

Leonidas, helped us load our luggage before we all climbed onboard. It was a gorgeous, sunny day, and Avalon looked postcard-perfect as Beck drove us through town. I was totally fine with the fact that I'd seen almost none of it during this visit, because how I'd spent my time instead was so much better.

Once we were all standing on the ferry dock, Will shifted Madame Leota in his arms and muttered, "Okay, this is going to suck. Can you guys help me?" Lorenzo picked up the pink plastic cat carrier while Leonidas held its door open, and Will tried to slip the cat inside. "Come on, girl," Will said, as the cat braced all four feet around the opening. "You can't board the ferry if you're not inside this thing. Please just cooperate."

Beck suggested, "Try putting her in backwards."

Will flipped the cat around and tried to load her butt first, but her back legs shot out and she anchored her paws on either side of the opening. I grinned and said, "I can't help but admire her total commitment to stubbornness."

It took a while, but eventually they managed to wrestle the cat into the carrier. Will pushed his dark curls out of his blue eyes as he caught his breath, and Madame Leota glared at all of us through the wire door. The ferry's horn sounded, which let us know it was departing in just a few minutes, and Leonidas told us, "You'd better get going."

Will grabbed his friend Beck in a hug and muttered, "This weekend absolutely flew by."

"It really did," Beck said. "Continue to knock 'em dead, my friend, and I'll see you when this movie wraps."

After we all said our goodbyes, we boarded the first ferry of the day heading to the mainland, which was almost empty. We selected some benches on the open top deck, and Gabriel curled up right beside me and put on a baseball cap and sunglasses before taking my hand. His all-black outfit also included canvas slip-ons and a long cardigan over a fitted V-neck T-shirt and skinny jeans. He'd definitely toned down his feminine side, and it made me sad that he didn't feel he could totally be himself, but at least there were still elements of his personal style in what he was wearing.

He said, "This is exciting. It's been a while since I've been off the island."

"Did Tracy make you promise to check in a lot?"

"He did." Gabriel glanced at my profile as I put on a pair of sunglasses and tilted my face toward the sun. "Are you okay with that?"

"Sure. Why wouldn't I be?"

"Some people are the jealous type, like the last guy I dated."

I grinned at him and said, "I'm not jealous of Tracy, but I'm definitely jealous of this guy you dated."

"Don't be. Roger and I were terrible together. We only lasted a few months before we decided we were much better off as friends."

"You dated a guy named Roger? I'm picturing a skinny math teacher."

He laughed at that and said, "Not quite. You'll see for yourself as soon as we get to San Francisco."

"Because the first thing you're planning to do is introduce me to your ex-boyfriend?"

"Roger works for Sawyer and Alastair, the couple who's letting us use their apartment. He's bringing us the keys."

That was going to be interesting.

After the fairly quick ferry ride, we stuffed our luggage into Phoenix's SUV and he drove us to my apartment in West Hollywood. As Gabriel and I climbed out of the dark blue Bronco, Will told us, "The meeting with my agent should take less than an hour. I'll message you when we're on our way back to pick you up."

I lived on the second floor of a nondescript building that dated from the 1960s. It had a chipped stucco exterior, and the long hallway always smelled like fried food. I didn't know why. As I unlocked the deadbolt and opened the door, I said, "I'm sorry it's such a cluttered mess."

Gabriel followed me inside, and when I turned on the light, he murmured, "Oh wow."

The studio apartment was a rectangle with white walls, and its one small window looked out over the parking lot and a dumpster. My twin-size bed was just inside the door, and it was piled with the two loads of laundry I'd washed right before I went to Catalina. There was a tiny kitchen in the corner and an even tinier bathroom, and every square inch of what was left had been turned into my makeup studio.

Gabriel wandered into the apartment and looked all around him as he said, "This is amazing." The walls were completely covered with sketches of makeup ideas, pages from magazines, and random inspiration photos. Three six-foot-long folding tables formed a squared-off 'U' at one end of the apartment, filling the narrow space wall-to-wall. The tables were crowded with makeup, wigs, masks, facial prosthetics, and other tools of the trade.

An office chair was positioned in the center of the 'U', and Gabriel sat down in it and turned slowly as he took it all in. Meanwhile, I pushed aside the laundry so I could sit on the bed and murmured, "I know it looks like a jumble, but I actually have it organized in a way that makes sense to me."

"I absolutely love this."

"You do?"

"Definitely. You have so many great ideas in these sketches. Look at that merman! He's breathtaking." He indicated a large drawing in colored pencil that showed a head-to-toe look for one of my fantasy makeups. "If I find the right fabric, I think I can sew that tail for you."

It was shimmering, iridescent, and covered with long, delicate streamers, which extended past the fin at the bottom. "I was trying to do something different, so I thought about combining the type of mermaid tail most people think of with a jellyfish's arms, or tentacles, or whatever they're called."

"I love that idea. I've never seen anything like it."

He seemed as fascinated by all the stuff on the tables as he was by the drawings. While he picked up and examined one thing after another, I folded my laundry and packed my duffle bag. Once I finished, I asked Gabriel, "Can I get you anything to drink? I should have asked you that when we first got here. I'm a terrible host."

"No thanks, I'm fine," he said, as he opened a jar of cream and sniffed it. I loved his curiosity.

I slipped off my sneakers and sat on the bed as I watched him look with his hands. When he opened a glittery eyeshadow palette, he whispered, "Ooooh." Then he picked up a Q-tip, swept it over a deep purple color, and smeared a line onto the back of his hand. He did that with three more Q-tips, using a clean end for each color. Then he stuck his hand into the patch of sunlight filtering in through the window and turned it this way and that, so the lines of color sparkled.

I crossed the room to him and said, "You can make me up if you want."

"Are you sure?"

"Absolutely."

You would have thought it was Christmas morning by the way his face lit up. I knelt down, then sat back on my heels, and he got to work with the eyeshadow palette, holding my chin in one hand as he concentrated on coloring my lids. "Just so you know, I'm doing a terrible job and will absolutely insist that you wash your face before we drive to San Francisco," he said. "Don't even think about trying to humor me by wearing this out of here." He added some black eyeliner, then asked, "I don't trust myself to apply mascara without poking you in the eye, so can you put it on for me?"

I took the mascara and the hand mirror he offered me and did as he asked, pausing to admire the glittery ombre effect on my eyelids as I said, "You did a great job. It's not easy to blend from pale pink to deep purple, but you totally pulled it off."

He smiled at me before opening a big makeup tote and exclaiming, "I just hit the motherlode! Look at all this fun stuff." Among other things, there were several types of false eyelashes, stick-on rhinestones, little pots of glitter, and even more eyeshadow in a rainbow of colors.

"I use that kit for my drag queens."

"It must be so much fun to make them up."

"It really is, especially because they're usually willing to let me experiment and take their look over the top. I also love it when I get to work with someone who's new to drag. I've actually had people burst into happy tears the first time they see themselves in full make-up." I grinned and added, "Of course, that means I have to immediately fix the makeup job, but it's totally worth it."

He smiled at me as he brushed my hair from my forehead. "I love how passionate you are about your craft. And that's what all of this is," he said, as he gestured around him, "passion, not clutter. I'm also impressed by how much time and effort you've obviously put into it."

"I'm determined to make something of myself. That's why I'm always trying to learn new techniques and build my skill set." I looked up at him, and after a moment I said, "I didn't know when you and I would find each other again. I was sure it would happen though, and when it did I wanted to be a man you could be proud of. I'm still a work in progress, but I'm really trying to get there."

He caressed my cheek and said, "I'm already so proud of you for a million reasons, Riley."

I never cried anymore. I'd done too much of it in the past, and now I needed to be stronger than that. But when he said he was proud of me, I had to blink back tears. Gabriel whispered, "Sweetness, are you okay?"

I looked away and muttered, "I don't want to be that boy anymore. I've tried so hard to outgrow him."

"What do you mean?"

"You just called me 'sweetness'. It's what you used to say back when I was that broken nineteen-year-old. You'd hold me and rock me and call me that name while I cried myself to sleep. I can't stand the thought that you still see me that way."

"I don't, but it's not a bad thing that I still see traces of him in you. I've always adored that boy."

There was a question I'd been carrying with me for years, and after a pause I said, "I know you didn't want to come with me to Reno because you thought you'd derail my recovery. But once you got a handle on your addiction, why didn't you call my aunt and uncle and ask them where I was?"

"I called them the day after you left to make sure you'd made it to Reno, and they told me they'd gotten you into rehab. Once I knew you were safe, I threw away their contact information to make sure I didn't have a way to find you."

I met his gaze and asked, "Why would you do that?"

"Because I thought I'd never be anything but an addict, and the last thing people in recovery need is to be around someone who's still using." His voice was rough with emotion when he told me, "I'm so sorry I failed you."

"You didn't fail me, Gabriel."

"Yes, I did. You needed a friend after you got out of the treatment facility. I know that because I sure as hell did, but I wasn't strong enough to kick my addiction and be there for you. Now that I know your aunt and uncle weren't there for you either, I feel even guiltier than I already did for abandoning you like that."

I took his hand and said, "You have to stop doing this to yourself. Instead of focusing on the fact that you saved my life, you're letting yourself feel bad about things that were never in your control. I know what it means to be an addict, so I know exactly what you were struggling with back then. I don't blame you for not having more to give me while you were going through that, and you can't blame yourself either. We both have to forgive ourselves for what happened in the past if we're ever going to move forward."

He knelt down in front of me and grabbed me in a hug. As I rubbed his back, he whispered, "I love you so much, Riley."

He didn't mean it the same way I did. I knew that for a fact. Loving someone and being in love with them were two very different things, but it still felt good to hear those words. I kissed his forehead and said, "I love you, too." If only he knew how much I meant it.

We shifted to the bed and curled up with each other for a while. When a text alert beeped I ignored it, but he murmured, "That's probably Will."

I took the phone from my pocket and read the screen before

saying, "You're right. They're leaving his agent's office now and will be here in about twenty minutes."

We both got up, and Gabriel said, "I'll help you finish packing." After we worked together to assemble my fantasy makeup kit, he caught my hand to get me to hold still and used a cleansing cloth to wipe off my eye makeup.

Then we still had a few minutes before our friends arrived, so we sat side-by-side on the bed to wait. After a pause, he asked, "Do you think we'll ever be able to talk about that time in our lives without getting upset?"

"Definitely. It's just a lot to process right now, because finding each other again brought all kinds of emotions to the surface."

"I really need to get my guilt under control," he muttered.

"I need to do the same thing with my embarrassment. I just really want you to see me as the man I am now and not the boy I was then, because I can't stand how weak I used to be."

"You were never weak," he said. "Far from it."

I glanced at him and asked, "Do you really think so?"

"I know that for a fact. You went through hell and survived. There's no way you could have done that if you were weak."

"That's a totally different perspective than the one I've been carrying with me all these years."

He laced his fingers with mine and said, "Sometimes it helps to see yourself through someone else's eyes."

Chapter 4

It was almost nine o'clock when we arrived in San Francisco, after what turned out to be a fun road trip. Will needed to memorize his lines for the scenes he was shooting over the next few days, so for the last half of the drive we each chose one of the five main characters and rehearsed the scenes over and over again. To keep it interesting, we added different accents and funny voices and played up the drama, with hilarious results. By the time we reached our destination, all five of us had the lines memorized forward and backward.

When we pulled up in front of the white art deco, high-rise apartment building where Gabriel and I would be staying, Phoenix said, "Wow, this is nice."

It really was. We climbed out of the SUV, and while our friends helped us unload our luggage, I asked Phoenix, "Are you sure you don't want to stay with us?"

"I'm sure. I moved my reservation to a cute bed and breakfast for the next three weeks, and I'm looking forward to it." Phoenix put my duffle bag on the sidewalk and told me, "Will has to be on-set at nine tomorrow morning for a meeting with the director, so I'm picking him up at his hotel at eight-thirty. I know you're not scheduled until ten, but if you want a ride and don't mind going in early, I can swing by and pick you up first. My B and B is just a few blocks from here."

"That'd be great. I'd love some time to get set up and check out the new location."

We thanked Phoenix for the ride, and after we all said goodnight and our friends drove off, Gabriel sent a text. Then he told me, "I just messaged Roger, and he'll be right down. He said he was airing out the apartment, since it's been closed up for the last month."

I didn't know why that name made me picture a skinny little nerd, but I couldn't have been more wrong. A tall guy whose dark suit barely contained his giant shoulders, chest, and arms stepped out of the building after a minute, and Gabriel exclaimed, "There he is!"

I asked, "What exactly does he do for your friends?"

"He's Alastair's former bodyguard and their head of security."

Before I could ask why his friends needed either of those things, Gabriel rushed to meet him. Roger grabbed him in a hug and said, "'Ello gorgeous," as he lifted him off his feet. Gabriel and I were the same height, and since he looked tiny compared to this guy, I knew right away I was going to suffer by comparison.

Even so, I tried to stand tall as Gabriel led his ex-boyfriend over to me and said, "Roger Foster, meet Riley Palma." Close up, I realized this guy only had about three inches on me, but he also had the mass of a small planet.

Roger crushed my hand as he shook it and said, with a thick British accent, "Pleasure to meet you, mate." Even though his tone was friendly, I couldn't help but notice he sized me up carefully. That was probably his bodyguard training coming into play.

Between the three of us, we managed to get all the luggage inside and onto the elevator in one trip. Gabriel punched in a code to access our floor, and when I glanced at him, he explained, "I lived here for a while."

Once we reached the apartment, Roger unlocked the door, then handed Gabriel a set of keys. We dropped our stuff in the foyer, and I wandered into the living room and muttered, "Holy shit."

The massive apartment was like something out of a movie with its open and modern layout, expensive-looking artwork, and elegant furnishings. Instead of lingering and taking it in, I went straight to the open glass door at the far side of the living room and stepped out onto the wide balcony. The view of San Francisco's iconic skyline took my breath away.

Gabriel joined me a few moments later and said, "It's beautiful, isn't it?"

He stood right beside me and leaned against the railing as I muttered, "There are no words."

"It's funny that you went right to this. The balcony was always my favorite spot when I lived here."

"I can see why." San Francisco was notoriously expensive, and an apartment like this would be, what? A million dollars? Probably a lot more. I just had to ask, "How can your friends afford a place like this?" How could *anyone* afford it?

"Alastair's family is loaded. They own a department store in London, along with several manufacturing facilities. That probably makes him sound like he's spoiled, but he works hard to run the family business, and his husband Sawyer runs a very successful chain of coffee houses."

"Wait. Is Sawyer's last name MacNeil?" When Gabriel nodded, I said, "A Sawyer MacNeil's opened in West Hollywood last year, and it's one of my favorite hangouts. How on earth do you know these people?"

"I met Sawyer back before the coffee houses and the rich husband. We hit it off right away, since we have a lot in common. He did burlesque with me for a while, and we used to visit thrift shops together looking for costumes and vintage lingerie."

"And now he's a coffee mogul."

"Basically."

I asked, "Has the money changed him?"

"Not at all. He's always been a genuinely kind person, and so is Alastair." He grinned and added, "Well, Sawyer has changed in one way. He buys his lingerie in Paris now, instead of the thrift store. Can't say I blame him."

"I can't believe they're letting us stay here. I mean you, sure. You're their friend. But they don't know me at all."

"Any friend of mine is a friend of theirs, as far as Sawyer and Alastair are concerned," he said.

"They sound nice."

"They really are. They're both very open and trusting, almost to a fault. That's why Roger is so important to them. He's overly cautious, which is exactly what they need."

"I can imagine. Rich people must be magnets for all kinds of scammers and con artists."

"Exactly." After a minute, he leaned into me and said, "Roger's leaving soon, so come with me to say goodbye."

We joined his ex in the pristine kitchen, which was white and stainless steel and looked like a display in a designer showroom. At one end of the room was a huge, shiny machine, and after a moment I realized it was the kind of professional, high-end espresso maker you'd usually find in a restaurant or coffee house. I really hoped there was a Mr. Coffee or something hidden away in a cupboard, because my chances of brewing anything on that beast were pretty much nonexistent.

Roger was drinking tea and reading something on the screen of a thin laptop, which he closed when we approached. Now that I got a look at him in better lighting, I saw he was probably in his early thirties, and his brown hair was buzzed off in a cut chosen for ease, not style. He had a square jaw, and there was a scar on his right cheek, which could have made him seem like a tough guy. But there was also an unmistakable spark of amusement in his eyes, which made him seem more like an overgrown boy.

He turned to me with a smirk and asked, with an accent that was more chimney sweep than Mary Poppins, "Recovered from the shock, 'ave you? I don't think I've ever seen anyone's mouth literally fall open from surprise before. Made you look like one of those inflatable sex dolls." He opened his mouth in a wide oval to demonstrate, then laughed at his own joke.

Gabriel put two mugs on the kitchen island and playfully slapped Roger's huge bicep. "Don't tease, Ro. You know this apartment is ridiculously nice, so who wouldn't be impressed by it?"

I sat down across the kitchen island from Roger and frowned at the easy rapport between the two of them. They laughed and teased each other as Gabriel dropped teabags into the mugs and added hot water. Then he put a cup in front of me with a spoon and a bowl of sugar cubes. I'd never actually seen a sugar cube before, but it was pretty far down the list of things to gawk at in this place.

Roger said, "Before I forget, here are a couple of numbers for you." He slid a neatly printed notecard over to Gabriel. "At the top is the car service I use. I put your name on my account, so if you need a lift and I'm not around to drive you, call that number. I took the liberty of stocking the fridge and pantry so you'll be set for a while, but the next number is for a local market that delivers. Your name's on that account, too."

I had to bite my tongue to keep from telling him taking care of Gabriel was my job, not his. Fortunately, Gabriel handled it for me by sliding the card back to Roger and saying, "I appreciate it, Ro. I really do. But I can handle this stuff myself."

Roger tried to look repentant. "Forgive me. I didn't mean to overstep."

Gabriel said, "Let me know how much I owe you for the groceries you bought, and I'll go by an ATM tomorrow."

"There's not a chance in hell of me taking your money, love, so consider it a gift." Roger finished his tea, got up, and put his cup in the dishwasher. Then he picked up his laptop and tucked it under his arm as he said, "I'll let you get some rest, since you must be knackered after your drive. Call me tomorrow." He turned to me and added, "Pleasure to meet you, Riley. I'm sure I'll be seeing you soon." I couldn't help but notice he left the notecard on the counter.

Gabriel walked him out. When he returned to the kitchen a couple of minutes later, he said, "He means well, but he tends to overdo the whole caretaker thing. Part of the reason we didn't last as a couple is because Roger was always treating me like a child, and I got tired of him acting like I couldn't do anything for myself. You just got a little taste of that with the groceries and the car service."

"If I had as much money as Roger, I'd fuck up in exactly the same way," I admitted. "I wish to God I had the means to make sure you always had a full refrigerator and a car and driver to safely take you anywhere you wanted to go."

Gabriel circled the kitchen island and draped his arms over my shoulders. "It'd be different coming from you."

"Why is that?"

He shrugged and said, "It just feels more balanced between you and me. We take care of each other."

I kissed the tip of his nose before asking, "Are you hungry?" When he nodded, I said, "Let's see what your enormous, muscle-bound ex-boyfriend bought us."

The answer to that was pretty much the entire supermarket, because the fridge was packed solid. We decided to keep it simple with sandwiches and deli-made potato salad, which we ate at the kitchen island. Once we finished the meal and cleaned up, Gabriel said, "Let's move our luggage out of the entryway."

The apartment had three bedrooms, and the way Gabriel carried his sewing machine directly to one of them suggested it must have been his room at one point. Like the rest of the apartment, it had a neutral color palette of white, sand, and shades of gray. I wondered if he'd draped it in jewel-toned fabrics when he lived here, to make it feel like home.

He put the machine on a desk in the corner while I heaped our luggage beside the bed. Then he stretched his arms over his head and muttered, "I could really use a hot bath after all those hours in the car."

I hung my leather jacket over the back of a chair and asked, "Can I join you?"

That earned me a flirtatious smile. "Definitely."

I told him I'd fill the tub and grabbed my toiletry case on the way to the adjoining gray and white bathroom. A bubble bath seemed like a good idea, so after I got the water running I found my body wash and squirted some into the large tub. It didn't do much, so I took off the lid and dumped in half the bottle, but it was still pretty lackluster. After I took off my clothes and wrapped a towel around my hips, I turned on the tub's jets to see if that would stir up the bubbles a bit. Then I returned to the bedroom, since a tub that big would take a while to fill.

Gabriel was sitting on the bed, dressed in a silky pale blue robe with a delicate pattern of pink cherry blossoms. I sat beside him and ran my hand down his sleeve as I said, "This is beautiful. Did you make it?"

"I did, and thank you for the compliment." He slid closer and brushed his lips to mine. We sort of got lost in each other for a while, before we finally decided we should check the tub.

Both of us started laughing when we went into the bathroom. The jets had stirred up the body wash so much that at least two feet of billowy white foam extended above the rim of the tub. I turned off the jets and the tap as I said, "This wasn't exactly what I had in mind when I decided on a bubble bath."

"It looks so fun, though!"

Gabriel hung his robe on a hook, stepped into the tub, and disappeared into the foam. I called, "You okay in there?"

"Yup. Come find me."

I grinned as I hung up my towel and waded into the froth. I had to tunnel through it with my hands, and I soon found Gabriel in a little den he'd hollowed out amid the bubbles. He kissed me when I reached him, then blew at the top of my head, which sent a dollop of foam floating upward.

I leaned against the back of the tub, and he put his head on my chest. "It's like being in a cloud," he murmured, as he played with the bubbles. They formed a golden, glowing shell around us as they reflected the soft bathroom light.

We soaked for a while, and then I found the soap and combined washing him with a light massage. When I ran my hand over the perfect curve of his ass, then swept back over it a second and third time, he looked up at me with a mischievous glint in his eye.

Gabriel straddled me and rubbed his cock against mine, which made both of us rock hard. He kissed me before whispering, "Maybe we should move this to dry land."

I flipped the lever to drain the bath, and we went from the tub to the shower to quickly rinse off the suds that clung to our skin. We'd barely gotten dried off when I tossed my towel aside, drew Gabriel into my arms, and kissed him. His entire body responded, melting into mine as he parted his lips for me.

When we both started to get hard again, he dropped to his knees on the white bath mat and looked up at me. I knew exactly what he wanted. He was submissive through and through, and he was asking me to take control. His arousal was written all over him, not just in his stiff cock, but in the flush of his skin and the longing in his gaze, which was locked with mine.

He needed this. I knew it for a fact. I also knew exactly what to do, because I knew what I would want if I was the one on my knees. I ran through the entire scenario in my head—all I had to do was tangle my fingers in his hair and fuck his mouth. Then I could put him on my lap and edge him while he begged for release, only allowing him to come when I said so. He'd absolutely love that.

My heart raced as the seconds ticked by. *Just fucking do it,* I told myself. *Take charge. Give him what he needs.*

But I remained rooted to the spot as something dangerously close to panic welled up in me. I didn't know if I had the confidence to take charge. The thought of trying and failing was beyond embarrassing, and I couldn't stand the thought of making things awkward between us. And when it became painfully obvious I couldn't give him what he needed, would we revert back to being just friends?

I had to get through this in a way that didn't ruin everything, so I dropped to my knees, cupped his face between my palms, and kissed him. It wasn't what he'd wanted, but it was so much better than the only other alternative I could come up with, which was bolting from the room.

He returned the kiss, tenderly instead of passionately, and then he drew me into an embrace. I wondered what was going through his mind, but I was too scared to ask. He stroked my damp hair, and after a while he said gently, "You have to be up early tomorrow, so we should get some sleep."

I nodded, and we both stood up and got ready for bed. While he brushed his teeth and dried his hair, I put on sweats and a T-shirt, then got a few things organized for the next morning. After that, I took a turn in the bathroom while he got dressed in plum-colored flannel pajamas.

We got comfortable under the thick, white duvet, and he gave me a chaste kiss goodnight. He fell asleep minutes later, and I watched him for a while before slipping out of bed. On my way through the living room, I scooped up a throw blanket that was draped over the couch, and I wrapped myself in it before curling up on a chair out on the balcony.

I stared at that million-dollar view without really seeing it. A lot of emotions churned in me, but more than anything I was disappointed in myself. I'd always known we were far too similar when it came to sex and that it was going to be a problem, but I thought we'd have more time to figure it out. Whenever I'd imagined finding Gabriel again, I always assumed it would be a while before our relationship turned sexual.

Not that I wanted us to slow down. I'd waited such a long time for this, and I wanted him with every part of me. The powerful physical attraction between us was more than I'd dared to hope for, and if it meant everything was happening faster than I'd expected, so be it.

It just meant I needed to pull myself together and find the confidence to give Gabriel what he needed. Losing him again was not an option.

~

The next morning, Gabriel cooked us breakfast while I got ready for work. As we sat down to heaping plates of blueberry pancakes, I asked, "Are you sure you don't want to come with me today?"

"You're going to be busy, so I'll come along in a few days when you've settled in. Today I'm planning to visit some fabric and thrift shops, because I really want to get started on the costumes to go with your fantasy makeup."

"I'll pay for it, since it's for my project."

"It's our project," he corrected with a grin, "so you pay for the makeup, I'll pay for the costumes."

"But isn't fabric expensive?"

"Nah. I'm the king of bargain hunting."

I wanted to insist, but that seemed like something his ex would do. Instead, I let it go and said, "Okay then. I'm looking forward to seeing what you find."

After we ate and cleaned up the kitchen together, he walked me to the door. I put down my makeup kit and gave him a hug, and he kissed my cheek and said, "I hope today goes great."

"Thanks, I'm sure it will. I'll be back around six. Can I take you out to dinner tonight?"

"I'd like that."

As I left the apartment and made my way to the elevator, worry nagged at me. I couldn't quite decide if I was imagining it, but it seemed like we'd taken a step back from becoming a couple and returned to 'just friends' territory. Or maybe I was reading too much into a kiss on the cheek.

I tried to put my worry aside as I loaded my makeup case in the back of Phoenix's SUV, then climbed into the passenger seat. After we exchanged greetings and he pulled away from the curb, he said, "I'm clearly off my game as a personal assistant. I should have told you to leave that huge case in the Bronco last night, instead of hauling it in and out of the apartment."

"I didn't think of it, either."

He glanced at me and asked, "Are you okay? You seem sort of down this morning."

So much for my attempt at a poker face. "I'm fine. I just have some stuff on my mind."

"I'm surprised. I expected to find you giddy with happiness after an entire weekend with your precious Gabriel."

I glanced at his profile and said, "I would be, except that I'm screwing it up already."

"I highly doubt that."

"I'd explain, but you probably really don't want to hear about my sex life, especially first thing on a Monday morning."

Phoenix shrugged and told me, "If you think it'll help to talk about it, go ahead."

"Okay. Well, without going into graphic detail, Gabriel wanted me to take charge last night, and I froze up. I knew exactly what he wanted, but I just couldn't do it."

"Since you told me you're submissive, is that surprising? It seems like taking charge is the last thing you'd want," he said.

"It's not like I'm totally disgusted by the idea of taking control. In fact, the only part that makes me uncomfortable is Gabriel watching me awkwardly flail my way through it while I try to gain some confidence."

Phoenix asked, "Have you talked to him about this?"

"I can't. Not yet, anyway. I'm trying so hard to get him to think of me as more than the insecure kid he used to know, and this would definitely send the wrong message."

He glanced at me and said, "You know what sends the message that you're a mature adult? Communicating openly and honestly with your partner."

I couldn't help but grin, because sometimes Phoenix seemed like my own personal Ted Talk. "I know you're right, but it's much easier to say than do. When you've been in relationships, did you feel comfortable telling your partner about your anxiety and self-doubt?"

"No, I really didn't."

"See? It's tough to make yourself that vulnerable."

"You're not wrong." After a pause, he asked, "Have you thought about visiting a BDSM club? You wouldn't have to participate, but it'd probably give you some ideas."

"That's the thing though, I already know what to do. Gabriel and I talked about this a long time ago, so I know he's not into the hardcore stuff. He doesn't need me to tie him up and deliver forty lashes with a bullwhip, thankfully. All he needs is for his partner to be confident and in charge. I should be able to do that! I fake confidence all the time, like whenever I go on a job interview. But I just couldn't manage it last night, and now I'm worried about derailing our relationship before it even has a chance to get off the ground."

"I think that's the real problem here," Phoenix said, as we rolled along slowly with the morning traffic. "You're afraid of making mistakes, and that fear is holding you back."

"It definitely is, but what do I do about that?"

"I have no clue. In fact, I really shouldn't be giving relationship advice when my own love life is a dumpster fire."

I pivoted in my seat a bit so I could look at him. "In the year I've known you, I don't think you've gone on a single date or even hooked up with anyone. You just put all your time and effort into your clients, going way above and beyond your job description to take care of them. But what about you? When are you going to take time for yourself?"

"Probably very soon, not by choice. I don't have another gig lined up when Will's part wraps in three weeks and my contract with his agent ends. He wants me to work for him again when his next movie starts filming this summer, but he really won't need me between now and then. I don't know what I'll do. I mean, financially I'll be fine. I have a lot of savings. But I like to be busy, so I'm not looking forward to a bunch of downtime."

I exclaimed, "It's the perfect time to get out there and date! Are you on any of the apps? I can help you take a sexy profile photo if you want. I'm thinking buck naked, except for a cowboy hat and a smile."

I was joking about that, because Phoenix was hardly the type to post a beefcake picture online. But he looked flustered as he blurted, "No! Definitely not."

"Okay, then you can keep the Levi's on. No shirt, though. I suspect there's a hot bod under all that flannel."

"No way. I'm not doing a dating app, and I'm fine with being single. I just need to find another client for the next few months until Will needs me again, because I'll go crazy if I'm totally idle."

"You're never idle," I pointed out. "Just look at all the stuff you brought along for a two-day getaway to Catalina. If you don't find work right away, how about focusing on your musical career? I think it's been eight or nine months since the last time you played a gig."

"That wasn't a gig, it was an open mic night."

"Well, whatever. You were still up on a stage performing, which is what you love and how you should be spending your time. You can't give up on your dream."

"I won't. It's discouraging to know I'll never achieve the kind of success my brother has, but I'll keep trying," he said. Then he added quietly, "That dream is all I have." His identical twin was selling out stadiums as a country-rock singer, and Phoenix had gotten into his current line of work by spending a few years as his brother's assistant. I could only imagine what it must feel like to watch someone that close living the dream that had eluded him for years.

"I'm glad you're not giving up. It breaks my heart when people abandon their dreams." When I spotted Will and Lorenzo waiting for us in front of a huge, grand hotel, I gestured at them and said, "Just look at Will. He tried to launch his acting career for ten years before finally landing this primo movie role. He's living proof that we have to keep trying."

Phoenix muttered, "I've been trying to launch my singing career a hell of a lot longer than that," as he swung the SUV into the circular driveway in front of the hotel and came to a stop.

Will loaded his cat into the backseat, and the two men followed. After we exchanged greetings, I told Will, "I can tell you're excited to get back to work. You're practically glowing."

He'd just had the last few weeks off while the rest of the crew kept working on location in Northern California. Even though he was playing the title character in the movie adaption of the best-seller *Alex and After*, it was actually a smaller role than that of the four lead actors, since his character died partway through the movie.

"I really am excited to return to the production," he said, "but I need to calm down and get back in Alex's mindset. He's anything but upbeat."

"Well, at least these flashback scenes in San Francisco are pretty lighthearted," I said, "although it feels super weird to me. I know all movies are filmed out of order, but I've been on this emotional journey with your character, and it was devastating when you filmed his death scene a few weeks ago. Now it's like, hey look, there he is and he's happy. Although obviously these scenes take place months before he dies."

"It did feel odd to film his death scene in the middle of the production," Will said, as Phoenix merged back onto the busy street and Lorenzo held the cat up so she could look out the window. "But having the last few weeks off was even more disorienting. Somehow, I have to find Alex again before the cameras start rolling. Otherwise, Lang's going to make us do a million takes until I get back in the groove." Gage Lang, the director, was notorious for asking his actors to do a huge number of takes even at the best of times, let alone when something felt a bit off.

When we arrived at our location for the day about fifteen minutes later, I muttered, "This is wild."

The film was set in the mid-1990s, and a residential street in one of San Francisco's upscale neighborhoods had been turned into a time capsule of that era. Two dozen cars parked along the street were all from about 1992 or older. They'd also turned it into fall with pumpkins and Halloween decorations. I watched as crew members spread dry leaves on the street and sidewalk, then arranged them into natural-looking drifts. I assumed they'd have to deal with those pesky green trees lining the street in post-production, since they weren't blasting the leaves off of them or spray painting them with fall colors.

Phoenix dropped off Will and Lorenzo near the mobile production office, and then he rolled forward about ten feet before getting stuck behind a catering truck. He asked me, "Do you want to hop out here? I'm not sure where hair and makeup is, but I don't think I can get much farther down this street."

I thanked him for the ride and grabbed the makeup case from the back of his SUV. Then he made a three-point turn and drove past the street that was blocked off at both ends for filming. A small crowd of onlookers had already gathered at the barricades, and I heard one of them exclaim, "Oh my God, I think Dallas Jaymes was in that Bronco!" A buzz of excitement went through the crowd, and I sighed on Phoenix's behalf. It must be a total pain in the ass to look exactly like a celebrity. He basically got all the inconvenience and none of the perks of being famous.

I hung my crew I.D. around my neck and lugged my makeup case through the temporary village of trailers and RVs until I found the one reserved for hair and makeup. Since I was the first to arrive, I got to work turning on lights and setting up folding chairs at each of the four workstations inside the RV. Then I went around and opened all the windows, because it was musty and smelled a bit like dirty socks.

When Gina, the lead makeup artist and my boss, arrived maybe half an hour later, she frowned and said, "It smells like a used jock-strap in here." That, too.

"I've been trying to air it out. It's either slightly better now, or I've just gotten used to it."

She put her huge case on the table at the first makeup station and shot me a look over her blinged-out sunglasses. "You're early. If you're trying to suck up to me, keep doing that. I like it."

Gina was pretty awesome. She was probably in her mid-fifties and had been in this business about thirty years, which basically meant she had zero fucks left to give and didn't take shit from anyone. She was nice to me though, and I liked her. When Will requested me as his personal makeup artist for this film, she could have refused, since I was jumping ranks in a big way by actually being allowed to make up one of the lead actors. But she'd chosen to give me a chance, and she really didn't have to do that.

"I got a ride with Will Kandinsky's assistant," I explained. "He needed to get his client here for a nine a.m. meeting with the director."

I tried to downplay the fact that Will and I were friends, although not much got past Gina. It seemed like a cheesy way to get ahead in this business, by exploiting friendships, but Will and I had actually met for the first time at the start of this production. We were friends now, but I didn't want her to think that was why he'd asked to work with me exclusively.

Then again, Gina was going to reach her own conclusions. There wasn't much I could do about that.

She paused to check her short auburn hair in the mirror, and as she went to work setting up her station, I asked, "Can I bring you some coffee, or something to eat from craft services?"

"Nah, I'm good. Thanks, though. You're not actually scheduled to start for another hour, so just relax. Or maybe look around the set and get familiar with the layout, up to you. We're only at this location today, just long enough for them to film three outdoor scenes. You know how to find tomorrow's location, right?"

"Yeah, I have a map, and I think I will take a look around," I said, as I headed for the door. "I want to check out the vintage cars they brought in for today's shoot."

Gina grinned a little and said, "You make me feel old, kid. This film is set about ten years after I graduated from high school, but sure. I suppose they are 'vintage' cars. At least you didn't call them antiques."

The first thing I did when I left the RV was make sure I knew where the makeup crew would be standing by during filming. It was our job to do touch-ups between takes, and Will was my responsibility. According to the production schedule, in the first scene of the day he'd be walking down the sidewalk and having a conversation with two of the lead actors. Given the director's love of multiple retakes, it would probably take half the day to shoot what would end up as two minutes of the movie.

After I determined where I'd be while the cameras were rolling, I strolled down the center of the street where filming would take place. I wondered what it took to get the permits to close off a city block like this, and how they got the local residents to actually agree to it.

After I snapped a few photos, I sat on the curb and sent them to Gabriel with the caption 'Happy Halloween, circa 1994'. He replied a minute later with: *That's really cool. How's it going so far?*

I wrote: *Great, just waiting for things to get rolling. What are you up to?*

He responded with: *Roger is here. He brought chocolate croissants from my favorite local bakery, and we're having coffee and catching up.*

It was a good thing he couldn't hear me, because I sighed dramatically. Then it took me four tries to compose a message that didn't seem sarcastic. I ended up with: *Enjoy*. After I hit send, I muttered, "Fuck." That could totally be read like it was dripping with sarcasm.

Why was I so threatened by his ex? Okay, yes, he was built like Jason Momoa, but Gabriel had broken up with him. The whole jealousy thing was immature and ridiculous, and I really didn't want to be that guy. Well, except for the part of me that was pure caveman and wanted to yell that Gabriel was mine, snarl at Roger, and chase him away with a wooden club. But that part of me had some serious issues, and it was best to keep a lid on that possessive little fucker.

I was still sitting on the curb a few minutes later when Phoenix showed up with the cat under his arm. He was also carrying a bulging tote bag, and he was wearing dark glasses and a baseball cap, which made me say, "You know, that's not much of a disguise. How many people asked for your autograph between wherever you parked and here?"

"Six. I hate it when movies film on location and draw out all the star-seekers. What's wrong with a nice, secure movie lot, far from gawking onlookers?"

I got up and asked, "Have you ever considered changing your look, so people stop thinking you're Dallas?"

"I spent several years clean-shaven with short, bleached blond hair. During that time, I was almost never mistaken for my twin, but I felt like I'd lost my identity. Eventually, I decided I wasn't going to let Dallas take that from me."

I couldn't help but grin. "I'd love to see photos of you with that hair."

Phoenix grinned too and started walking toward the trailers at the end of the block. "No chance."

We noticed a commotion among a group of onlookers, and I glanced over to see Harper Royce had arrived on set. Harper was a lead actor on this film and one of the hottest young stars in Hollywood. He was tall, handsome, and loved by everyone—except his former assistant, Phoenix Jaymes. As Harper went right up to the wooden barricade, then started signing autographs and posing for photos with fans, I said, "It seems not everyone hates filming on location."

Phoenix scowled and kept walking as he muttered, "It's a dream come true for an attention whore like Royce."

When we reached hair and makeup, Phoenix said he'd look for me at lunchtime and went to find Will's trailer. I climbed back into the RV, which now contained half a dozen crew members. They were happily gossiping about the latest Hollywood scandal while Gina ignored them and scrolled through her phone.

A little while later, Harper Royce joined us. He smiled at Gina and said, "Can you believe it? I'm actually early for once," as he took a seat at her workstation. Then he waved at me and said, "Hey, Riley. Did you have a good weekend?"

I couldn't help it, I was a fan even if my friend hated his guts, and it secretly thrilled me that Harper Royce knew my name. "It was epic. How was yours?"

"Super low-key. I went home to L.A. and just chilled. I didn't even get out of my pajamas on Sunday." He flashed me the disarming, dimpled smile that had helped make him a star, and then he asked, "What made yours epic?"

"I went to Catalina and found the long-lost love of my life."

He nodded his approval and said, "That's epic, alright."

Gina went to work on Harper's makeup, which was pretty minimal. The green-eyed blond was absolutely gorgeous, so all she really had to do was even out his tanned complexion and play up his eyes with an extremely subtle application of liner and mascara. When she was finished, it didn't look like he was wearing any makeup at all, but he seemed younger, well-rested, and even more radiant than usual.

There were only three actors on set that day. In addition to Will and Harper, the third was Emma Rosen. She was arguably the biggest star on this picture, and she traveled with her own makeup artist and hair stylist. That meant it was a pretty low-pressure day in our department, but I still felt a little nervous.

A few minutes before Will joined us, Gina called me over and said, "So, you get what we're going for today, right? Your makeup needs to be more subtle than what we were doing a few weeks ago."

Will was close to thirty and absolutely beautiful, with big blue eyes, porcelain skin, and a flawless smile. He was portraying a twenty-two-year-old drug addict, so as his makeup artist, it was my job to make him look paler, thinner, and younger. I also had to show the signs of addiction on his face in a way that wasn't obvious or cartoonish. Those signs had been more pronounced in the scenes we'd filmed a few weeks ago in Northern California, to show the character was deteriorating shortly before he killed himself. But the upcoming scenes were flashbacks to happier times, so everything I'd been doing had to be dialed back, while still transforming the actor into the character.

I assured Gina I knew what to do, but deep down I was doubting myself. She'd obviously be checking my work and walking me through any adjustments before Will stepped in front of the camera, and I really wanted to impress her. I always felt like I had a lot to prove, now more than ever.

When Will joined us in the RV a few minutes later, he was practically bubbling over with excitement. He greeted Harper with a hug, and when he sat down in front of me, I said, "I can tell your meeting with the director went well."

"It did. I'll be signing the contract for the lead role in his next movie on Friday. It's a fantastic part, and I'm really looking forward to it." I handed him a headband, and as he used it to push his dark curls from his face, he added, "We also talked about our expectations for Alex over these next three weeks. The character's obviously in a better place emotionally in these scenes, as opposed to the ones we already filmed, but he's still struggling. We were talking about how best to convey that."

It was going to be a challenge for both of us. What I needed to do as a makeup artist was the same as what Will needed to do as an actor. I had to transform him into someone else, and I had to do it subtly and with a lot of finesse.

The next several minutes were spent reshaping his face to make him look even leaner than he already was. This was accomplished with contours and highlights that had to merge seamlessly with the light foundation makeup. A natural-looking blush also had to be applied strategically. Even though he needed to look pale, a sheer wash of color was still needed to keep his makeup from looking flat.

After I set his face with translucent powder, I turned my attention to his eyes. This was going to be the real test of my ability. I picked up a tiny brush and an eyeshadow palette, and then I chewed my lip for a few moments while trying to decide exactly how I should approach this.

Out of the corner of my eye, I saw Gina pause what she was doing to watch me. *Do something even if it's wrong*, I told myself. It was important to make her think I had this under control, otherwise she'd absolutely take over for me and I'd lose this incredible opportunity.

Will closed his eyes for me, and I swept a sheer, pale gray color near his lash line. That shade was the right call, and it gave me the confidence to press on. I knit my brows as I concentrated on creating a tiny, subtle composition of light and shadow around and just beneath his eyes.

It needed one more thing, so I added a paper-thin red line above his lower lashes and smeared it, which created the illusion that his eyes were slightly bloodshot. Will held perfectly still, looking up at the ceiling while I did that, and he murmured, "It's a good thing I trust you. Otherwise, I'd probably be flinching like crazy right now."

As I added just a bit of red right in the inner corners of his eyes, I joked, "Tell you what, you keep not flinching, and I'll keep not stabbing you in the eye."

He grinned at that and said, "Deal."

Finally, I stepped back and said, "Look at me, please." When Will did as I asked, I couldn't help but smile. Alex looked back at me, young and fragile with wide, haunted eyes, his beauty marred ever-so-slightly by the addiction that was slowly killing him from the inside-out.

When Gina came over to check my work, she actually said, "I'm impressed, kid." That was a huge compliment coming from her.

She went back to the front of the RV and chatted with two of the hairstylists while I pulled my phone from my pocket and took a few photos. It was important to document what I'd done, so I'd be able to precisely recreate that makeup. Then I stepped aside and indicated the mirror as I said, "Take a look, Will."

He pulled the headband from his hair and finger-combed his curls, and then he smiled at his reflection and said, "There he is. I knew Alex was in there somewhere."

I snapped one more photo and whispered, so Gina wouldn't overhear, "I gotta be honest, I wasn't sure if I could pull this off. I felt confident in the makeup we were doing before, but I didn't know if I could dial it back and still make you look like Alex."

Will got up and squeezed my shoulder as he said, "I never had any doubt."

A production assistant arrived and told the actors they needed to be on set in ten minutes. Will told me he'd see me out there, and the RV emptied while I went to work packing a kit with the makeup I'd need for touchups between takes.

Before I left for the set, I sent the last photo I'd taken to Gabriel with a message that said: *Just wanted to show you the makeup I did for Will this morning. I'm pretty proud of it.* Then I stood there and chewed my lip while I waited for his reply. A few moments later, he messaged me with: *It looks incredible! Great job, Riley.*

That was all I needed to hear. The positive reinforcement from Will and Gina felt good, but his opinion meant everything to me.

As predicted, the cast and crew spent hours filming a two-minute scene. Will, Harper, and Emma strolled down the same stretch of sidewalk over and over again, telling the same story, until the director inevitably cut the scene and started from the top. I swooped in and touched up Will's makeup as needed, but mostly I just sat idly by and tried not to get so lost in my thoughts that I missed the call to get up and do my job.

Eventually, an hour-long break was called. Will went off with Lorenzo, who'd been watching the filming with rapt attention, and a couple of crew members invited me to join them for lunch. I politely turned them down and headed to the RV with the hope of having a few quiet minutes to myself. I could be social when I needed to, but the introvert in me always ended up craving down time during these full days on set.

It startled the hell out of me when Roger Foster fell into step with me and said, "'Ello Riley."

I didn't break my stride as I asked, "What are you doing here?"

"I thought you could use a cuppa." He was carrying two paper cups, which were emblazoned with the sophisticated 'Sawyer MacNeil's' logo.

"I somehow doubt you came all this way to bring me coffee." He was wearing a visitor pass on a lanyard around his neck, and I gestured at it and asked, "How'd you get onto the set? They don't give those things to just anybody."

"I sweet-talked my way in." He looked pleased with himself.

"I highly doubt that."

Roger chuckled and asked, "You don't think I'm capable of sweet-talking?"

"I don't think our security team is that stupid."

"They're not rocket scientists, either. The truth is, I asked one of them the name of your head of security, then went around the corner and told another bloke I had a meeting with the man whose name I'd just been given. They let me right in." He shook his head, as if he was disappointed in them.

"I can't believe that worked."

"Never underestimate the power of a sharp-looking suit and a flashy business card."

I muttered, "I'll remember that next time I need to trespass someplace I don't belong." We reached the RV, and I turned to him and asked, "So, what are you doing here, Roger? And don't go with the bullshit answer about bringing me coffee this time."

"I wanted the opportunity to talk man-to-man."

"Why?"

"Because you're dating someone who means the world to me,

and I want to let you know I intend to beat you to a bloody pulp if you hurt him."

I mulled that over for a few moments, then said, "I respect that. Did you really bring me coffee?"

He handed over one of the cups and said, "Seemed the least I could do, what with my plan to threaten you and all."

"That's classy." I took a sip of what turned out to be a perfect latte, then held the door of the RV for him and said, "After you."

Roger preceded me into the Winnebago and observed, "It smells like an armpit."

"You're not wrong. We'll be back in a decent trailer tomorrow. Filming on city streets is a pain in the ass, for many reasons."

"I can imagine."

I tossed my leather jacket over the back of a chair, and we sat down facing each other. He crossed his ankle over his knee, and I gestured toward him with my coffee cup and said, "That really is a sharp-looking suit. The security game must pay well."

"It can, if you're willing to make certain sacrifices."

"Like what?"

"Like working constantly, including nights, weekends, and holidays, and letting your relationships suffer. To do it right, the job always has to come first."

I took another sip of coffee and asked, "Is that what you think went wrong between you and Gabriel?"

"What reason did he give you for ending our relationship?"

"He said you treated him like a child, and he got tired of you trying to do everything for him."

"That's what I do, I take care of people. I thought he understood that going in. I also thought it was what he liked about me. Shows what I know." I was surprised by the vulnerability I glimpsed in his eyes, but he quickly pulled his guard up and said, "Anyway, I suppose this is me continuing to look out for him, even if he doesn't want me to. Gabriel's one in a million, and I've got to be honest, you're about the last thing I expected when he mentioned he was bringing a new man around."

"What were you expecting?"

"Someone more…"

He drew a circle in the air with one hand while looking for the right word, and I tried to help him out. "Suave and sophisticated? Older? More refined? Successful? Someone like you, basically?"

"I suppose that's exactly what I expected."

"But instead you got a poor twenty-three-year-old ex-junkie who quite obviously isn't good enough for a man like Gabriel." He frowned a little, and I continued, "That's what you were thinking, right? I look like a bum, so that's what I must be. No way could someone with tattoos and thrift shop clothes turn out to be a good person who fully intends to treat Gabriel like the absolute treasure he is."

"You're making me feel like an arsehole for judging you based on appearance."

"Good. It's a shitty thing to do," I said. "Also, please stop showing up with groceries and chocolate croissants and trying to worm your way into Gabriel's good graces. Put yourself in my shoes. How would you feel if you were totally crazy about someone, and his giant, British, well-dressed ex kept coming around and doing things for him you couldn't afford, like paying for a car service?"

He grinned and tried to lighten the mood with, "Thanks for noticing I'm well-dressed."

"I hate the fact that your suit costs more than my car."

"What do you drive?"

"A rusted-out vintage VW bug."

"Fucking hell, mate, those things are collectibles now. You might be sitting on a gold mine."

"Yeah, no. I managed to find one so shitty that nobody in their right mind would want it." I drank some more coffee, and after a moment I asked, "How long did you and Gabriel date?"

"About seven months in all, but I was gone for a lot of that. It was right when Sawyer and Alastair were scouting locations to expand the coffee house chain, and I was still traveling with them at that point. Looking back, it was a huge mistake not to make Gabriel a priority."

"Why aren't you with your employers on this trip to the UK?"

He said, "After my relationship with Gabriel crashed and burned, I realized I had to make some changes if I was ever going to build a life for myself. I ended up hiring a team of four men to replace me as Alastair and Sawyer's bodyguards, which should tell you something about the hours I used to work. Of course, it was too late for Gabriel and me by then. He'd moved on, literally and figuratively, and taken that job on Catalina."

I studied Roger for a few moments before asking, "Are you still in love with him?"

"It wasn't love. I think it could have grown into that, given a chance, but we never got there. I have a great deal of affection for him, and I always will. But that's not the same thing."

"Are you going to try to steal him from me while he's in San Francisco for the next six weeks?"

Roger chuckled and said, "You're extremely direct. I like that."

"You didn't answer my question."

"I'm not immoral enough to actively try to sabotage your relationship. But if you fuck it up and Gabriel dumps you, I might ask him to give me another chance."

"I don't have a problem with that. Know why?" When he shook his head, I grinned and said, "Because I have no intention of fucking this up."

Roger grinned too and got to his feet. "I'm finally starting to understand what he sees in you." As he made his way to the door, he added, "Take care of him for me and remember, I meant what I said about beating the hell out of you if you hurt him."

"Taking care of him has always been the plan."

Once he was gone, I exhaled slowly and relaxed a little. I actually liked Roger, despite myself, but he was definitely intimidating.

<h1 align="center">Chapter 5</h1>

The rest of that afternoon was pretty uneventful. The cast and crew managed to film all three of the outdoor scenes, while I sat through take after take and did occasional touch-ups to Will's makeup. Shortly after five, we were back in Phoenix's SUV and once again rolling through traffic. The cat's back feet dug into my thigh as she stood up and looked out the passenger window, and Lorenzo asked, "Would you guys like to have dinner with us? We're thinking about heading to North Beach for some Italian food."

Phoenix made some excuse, probably because he didn't want to feel like a third wheel, and I said, "Thanks for the offer, but I'm taking Gabriel on a date tonight. I'm not sure where we should go, though. I looked online during my break and couldn't find a restaurant that was both romantic and actually affordable."

"Maybe a restaurant isn't the way to go," Will said. "You're a creative guy, so I'm sure you can think of a fun alternative."

I pivoted around as much as I could without knocking the cat over, so I could look at Will in the backseat. "This is technically my first date, and I really don't want to mess it up. If I think too far outside the box, he might not even be sure if it's a date at all. Also, it'd be one thing if we were in L.A. and I could take him to one of my favorite hangouts, but I barely know San Francisco anymore."

Will looked confused. "You mean it's *your* first date, yours and Gabriel's?"

"It's that too, but I meant what I said. I've never gone on a date before."

Phoenix asked, "How is that possible?"

"My life can basically be divided into two halves—before and after Gabriel. As a teen, all I cared about was partying, so dating was the last thing on my mind. I was a huge mess when he and I met and became friends, and that was followed by him shipping me off to rehab. With sobriety came clarity. I realized Gabriel was all I wanted, and I had no interest in random hookups or dating anyone else."

Lorenzo asked, "But what if you'd never found him again?"

"I just had to keep believing it would happen. There were days in rehab when the hope of seeing him again was all that kept me going. Now that it's actually happened though, I feel like I'm blowing it. All my focus was on finding him again, instead of figuring out what I should do after that."

"Don't worry, you've got this." Phoenix pulled to the curb and said, "Let me help. To start with, how about getting him some flowers?" He gestured past me to a small florist's shop, with containers of brightly colored blooms lining the sidewalk. "While you're doing that, I'll come up with some possible locations for dinner."

"We'll help, too," Lorenzo said, as all three guys grabbed their phones. "Between the four of us, I know we can work some magic."

"That's really nice of you, but you guys don't have to do this," I said. "I'm sure you want to get on with your evening, instead of helping me with mine."

"Come on, this is totally fun. I've always wanted to 'Queer Eye' the hell out of somebody," Will said with a grin. "Lorie, see if you can find a nearby barber who can do a quick drop-in while Phoenix figures out a location for the date, and I'll see about a wardrobe intervention. Riley, all you have to do is pick out some nice flowers, then put yourself in our hands."

I thanked them before handing off the cat and climbing out of the SUV. Then I just stood there for a while staring at the flowers. Given all that variety, I decided against roses. They seemed too obvious, and I wanted Gabriel to know I'd put some thought into this.

Finally, I selected an exotic mixed bouquet in deep, dark jewel tones. I didn't even know what most of the flowers were called, but it made me think of the way Gabriel had decorated his room at the resort, so I thought he might like it. I took it into the shop to pay for it, and the woman behind the counter wrapped it in dark purple paper and tied it with a black ribbon. I didn't hate that.

By the time I returned to the Bronco, my friends had apparently made a lot of progress on Operation 'Queer Eye' Riley. "Can you message Gabriel and tell him you'll pick him up at six-thirty? We have two more stops to make," Phoenix said, as he pulled back into traffic.

"Sure. Anything else I should tell him?"

"You can tell him the dress code is dressy casual," Will said.

I turned to look at him and raised a brow. "Isn't that an oxymoron?"

"He'll know what it means."

"Okay, but I don't think I can pull off whatever that is," I told him.

"Leave it to me," he said. "I've got you covered."

Since Will was one of the best-dressed people I knew, I decided to trust him and sent the following message: *Hey Gabriel. I'm planning to pick you up for our date in an hour. I've fallen into the clutches of Will, Lorenzo, and Phoenix, who've become my fairy godmothers for tonight. I'm not sure what to expect, but I've been informed the dress code is 'dressy casual'. I'm totally lost, but I bet you know what to do.*

Gabriel wrote back a few moments later: *Sounds great! I love excuses to get dressed up. Should I meet you in the lobby?*

I replied that I'd come upstairs to get him, and then I glanced at Will again and said, "He's getting dressed up. It's nice that he's excited about it, but unless we're about to go out and buy me a suit,

I'm definitely going to suffer by comparison. Also, you know I can't afford a suit, right?"

"You don't need one. Just leave it to me."

Phoenix took the next right, while Lorenzo placed a call and began speaking to someone in Spanish. His tone was light and cheerful, and he ended up laughing and joking with whoever was on the line. When he disconnected the call, he told me, "You're all set for a haircut in thirty minutes. This guy's squeezing you in, so you and Will have to shop fast."

His fiancé looked confident as he flashed us a big smile. "Challenge accepted."

Maybe five minutes later, Phoenix pulled up in front of a discount department store and took the flowers from me as he said, "I'll keep these safe. Also, you went pretty goth with this bouquet, but I kind of like it. They look like you put some thought into them. Good luck shopping. Lorenzo and I will wait here, so we don't slow you down."

When we walked into the store through a pair of sliding doors, which were flanked with theft detectors, Will paused and did a quick scan. Then he led me to the men's department and flipped through the longest rack of shirts I'd ever seen. "There's a little of everything in these places, from trash to treasure," he explained. "I'm focusing on finding quality fabrics, and we'll do the best we can with the fit since there's obviously no time for alterations." He grabbed a black button-down shirt and thrust it at me while he continued to sort through the rack with his other hand. "Try this on over your T-shirt. I'm guessing at your size, and this'll help me narrow it down."

I awkwardly clutched my leather jacket between my knees because I didn't know where else to put it, then did as he asked. The first shirt was too big, so we moved down about six feet and he started flipping through the rack again. The next shirt he produced actually fit pretty well, but then he handed me four more and insisted I try them all. Within minutes, he'd selected three shirts and began striding across the store. An oddly jumbled selection of housewares was dead ahead, but he hung a right when we reached the aisle. I asked, "Wouldn't pants be back there in the men's department?"

"We're going with the jeans you're already wearing and one of these button-downs," he said, as we came to a stop at the perfume counter. A few men's colognes were mixed in among the samples. He sniffed each one before pointing a blue bottle at me and spritzing it five times. He returned the bottle to the counter, and I coughed as he grabbed my hand and towed me toward the register. "I know that seems like too much cologne," he said, "but you're going to change your shirt and a lot of the scent will go with it."

When we got in line at the register, I asked, "Why three shirts? I just need one for tonight."

"You're a handsome guy, Riley, but you hide it under baggy, worn out T-shirts and shaggy hair. Besides having something to wear tonight, these are meant to upgrade your wardrobe overall. Keep rocking the jeans, because they look great and fit well. The vintage leather jacket and black Converse sneakers are good too, because they show your style. But switching from the oversized tees to a nice button-down is going to make all the difference."

"I'm not sure if I can afford three shirts right now, though." The one price tag I could see was marked thirty-nine dollars.

"I'm buying these for you." When I started to protest, he grinned and actually pressed his index finger to my lips to shut me up. "Don't even think about arguing. Also, I'd love to take you shopping again when we have more time, because this is a lot of fun."

I knew it was impossible to talk him out of anything, so I left it at, "Thanks. I owe you one."

"No you don't, and you're welcome."

He paid with a credit card when it was our turn at the register, and I winced when it came to over a hundred and twenty dollars. "I thought this place would be cheaper," I said, once we'd checked out and were heading for the exit.

"There were definitely less expensive shirts on the rack, but the goal here wasn't to spend the least amount possible. It was to buy stuff that looks good and is well-made. I would have taken you somewhere nicer, by the way, but this was the closest and fastest place I found when I searched online."

"This is nice in my book. I'm usually a thrift shop kind of guy, not so much by choice, but out of necessity."

He turned to me with a sympathetic expression when we reached the SUV. "I know what it's like to worry about money. I grew up so poor that the church used to give my family care packages with hand-me-down clothes. That's probably why I overcompensate now," he said, as he touched the lapel of the obviously expensive light gray suit jacket he wore with a white button-down and dark gray jeans. "But I really believe the right clothes change us. They can give us confidence and make us carry ourselves differently. They also change the way people perceive us. Maybe that sounds shallow, but I think the way we present ourselves to the world matters."

"It's not shallow, and Gabriel will appreciate the fact that I'm making an effort, so thank you again."

His blue eyes crinkled at the corners as he smiled at me and said, "It's my absolute pleasure." When we climbed into the SUV, Will asked his fiancé, "How did we do?"

Lorenzo glanced at his phone and told him, "Seventeen minutes. Impressive."

Our next stop was a tiny barbershop maybe seven blocks from the department store. "That's one of the great things about San Francisco," Phoenix said. "Everything's all crammed together. Not like L.A., where you might need to take three freeways to reach your destination."

He waited in the car with the cat and resumed his search for date ideas while the rest of us went inside. Lorenzo and the silver-haired gentleman who owned the place greeted each other like old friends, though that was based solely on their earlier phone conversation.

As I hung up my jacket and sat in the only barber chair in the tiny shop, the man asked, "So tell me, what can I do for you?"

I gestured at my friends and said, "I'll go with whatever they suggest."

Will asked the barber to trim the sides and back while keeping a little length on the top. "Then we'll see about cleaning up that almost-beard," he added.

The barber misted my hair with water as I told my friend, "A shave is a bad idea. I don't want to look like a twelve-year-old."

"We're not going for clean-shaven," Will explained. "But we can definitely trim your facial hair and make it look neater."

I relaxed a bit and said, "Okay. I trust you."

Maybe half an hour later, I exchanged my T-shirt for a new, black button-down, then turned to study my reflection in the mirror. My hair had some shape and style to it for a change, and there was just enough of a beard left to stop me from looking like a kid. I actually liked what I saw, which wasn't always the case.

Lorenzo insisted on paying, no matter what I did to try to convince him otherwise, and we all thanked the barber before returning to the SUV. As Phoenix cut across town, he said, "I had a pretty inspired idea for tonight, if I say so myself. The bed and breakfast where I'm staying has a gorgeous backyard, so I called the woman who owns the place and asked if you could use it for your date. She was all for it. I'm her only guest right now, and she says she's glad the garden will get some use."

I said, "Thank you, that sounds nice."

"That just leaves dinner, and I texted you a list of options," he said. "There are a few affordable local restaurants that sound good and offer free delivery, and there's also a food truck court about two blocks from the B and B. It just depends on what you and Gabriel are in the mood for."

I browsed through the links he'd sent me for a few minutes, and when we pulled up in front of Will and Lorenzo's hotel, I turned to my friends and said, "Thank you again for everything. I've never been taken care of like this."

Will shifted the cat in his arms and smiled at me as he squeezed my shoulder. "Thank you too for letting us be the pit crew for your first date, and good luck tonight." Lorenzo handed me the flowers, which had somehow ended up in his care, and they both said goodnight to Phoenix and me before heading into the hotel.

I fell silent as Phoenix pointed the SUV toward the apartment, and after a while he asked, "Are you nervous?"

"Yeah, and I wish I wasn't."

"I know it's easier said than done, but try not to put too much pressure on yourself. He already likes you, and he's not expecting you to prove your worth or anything like that. He just wants to have a nice evening with you." He was absolutely right.

Once we reached the apartment building, Phoenix parked in the loading zone and said, "Don't feel like you have to hurry, seriously. I'll sort through my in-box while I'm waiting." He turned his attention to his phone while I went inside.

When I got to the apartment I had to knock since Gabriel had the only set of keys, and when he opened the door, I whispered, "Wow."

He was dressed all in black in a button-down shirt, slim-fitting pants, a sexy pair of stilettos, and a tailored knee-length jacket that corseted his waist. His glossy hair hung from a side part and partly covered one eye, and red lipstick emphasized his gorgeous mouth, which curved into a smile as he blurted, "You look amazing!"

"You took the words right out of my mouth. My God, Gabriel, look at you. You're absolutely breathtaking."

He murmured a thank you and seemed pleased by the compliment. After a beat, he gestured at what I was holding and asked, "Are those for me?"

I handed over the flowers as I stammered, "Oh! Yeah. I forgot about them."

"Let me put them in water before we go." I dropped my shopping bag just inside the front door and followed him to the kitchen, and he asked, "When did you go shopping?"

"On the way home. Will, Lorenzo, and Phoenix helped me get ready for tonight. I think they took pity on me, because I'm always such a mess." It wasn't the most flattering thing to admit to, but it was honest. Plus, he couldn't have failed to notice that about me.

He filled a vase with water, and as he transferred the flowers into it he said, "These are spectacular and exactly what I would have chosen for myself. Thank you."

"I'm glad you like them."

"I love them, and this, too." He turned to me and slid his hands over the sides of my head as he said, "This haircut is perfect for you."

I grinned as I tilted my head to look up at him. "I'm glad you think so. Also, this change in perspective is going to take some getting used to."

He slipped one foot out of his shoe and dropped down to my height. As he ran his fingertips along my jaw, he asked, "Better?"

"Only because I can do this now." I kissed him before saying, "The shoes are very sexy, though."

"I love them, but are we going to be doing much walking? I can only last about an hour in heels, but I can change them depending on our plans."

"We have the choice of walking a couple of blocks or not at all, depending on what you prefer for dinner. I'll tell you about our options on the way downstairs. Phoenix is waiting to give us a ride."

By the time we climbed into the SUV, we'd decided to visit the food trucks and Gabriel seemed excited about our plans. Phoenix dropped us off at our destination after giving us the address of the B and B, and Gabriel held my hand as we walked around and read all the menus. Nine trucks were crammed at various angles into the parking lot of a funky vintage bowling alley, and a lot of people were lined up waiting to order or eating at some picnic tables. Gabriel said, "It all smells wonderful. I don't know how we're going to pick one."

"There's no rule that says we have to."

We ended up buying something from almost all of the trucks, and then we carried our bounty two blocks to the bed and breakfast. Phoenix and an adorable magenta-haired little old lady were sipping wine on the front porch when we reached the charming pink Victorian. He introduced her as Miss Pearl, and I juggled several boxes and bags so I could shake her hand as I said, "Thank you for letting us use your garden, ma'am. We really appreciate it."

"It's my pleasure," she said, as she smoothed her floral caftan. "That garden was my Mel's pride and joy, so it makes me happy when people enjoy it. We used to be a stop on the botanical society's annual tour, back in the day. Mel's been gone a few years now, but I do my best to keep the garden up to snuff."

I said, "I'm sorry about the loss of your husband."

She smiled at me with a sparkle in her dark eyes. "Melanie was my wife. We were together forty-two years and finally got to legally marry three months before she passed."

"I'm sorry you had to wait that long," Gabriel said.

Miss Pearl told us, "At least it happened in her lifetime. Mel liked to joke about me finally making an honest woman of her."

I sorted through the items I was carrying and said, "We brought you both some pasta and dessert to thank you for tonight. Would you like to join us for dinner?"

I handed four white boxes to Phoenix as Miss Pearl said, "From what I've heard, you've got some wooing to do with this gorgeous young man right here, so you don't need us hanging around. Go on ahead and cut through the house, everything's all set up for you out back. I do appreciate the offer and the treats, though."

We thanked her and stepped through the front door with its elaborate stained-glass window. On our way through the pink floral interior, Gabriel smiled at me and asked, "Is that what's on your agenda? Wooing me?"

That made me smile too, and I said, "Absolutely."

Both of us were awestruck when we stepped through the French doors at the back of the house. The garden was an overgrown oasis of flowering plants, punctuated by a big, fluffy-looking tree and a graceful white gazebo. Dozens of string lights in all sorts of shapes and colors added to the magic.

Miss Pearl had thoughtfully set the table in the gazebo with floral china and a cluster of candles in various glass containers. She'd even included throw blankets on the chairs and a silver wine bucket with nonalcoholic sparkling cider, probably with Phoenix's input. We both piled our parcels on the table, and as we sat down Gabriel said, "This is just incredible. Thank you, Riley."

"I can't take credit. All I did was get help from the right people." While he organized the bags and boxes containing our dinner, I opened the bottle and filled our wine glasses. Then I gestured at a nearby plant with huge, yellowish, cone-shaped blossoms and said, "That looks like something from an alien planet."

Gabriel glanced over his shoulder and said, "It's called Angel's Trumpet. Fun fact, it's actually poisonous. I've always loved it, though. There used to be a big clump of it beside the apartment building I grew up in." He looked around and grinned. "Actually, almost all the plants in this yard are poisonous. That can't be a coincidence, and it makes me think I would've liked Mel. She was obviously a quirky individual."

"Or a serial killer."

"Nah. There's love and care in this yard, so maybe she just found beauty in things others didn't understand. Also, talk about an inefficient way to kill people. You'd have to chase down your victims and be like, 'hey, could you drink this gallon of oleander tea for me? Why? Oh, no reason'."

I chuckled at that and said, "You have a point."

"So, what's the plan of attack with dinner? We ended up with some pretty random stuff."

"I'm having my dessert first, because why not?"

"Good idea." We picked up our caramel apple empanadas, and he tapped his to mine as he said, "Cheers."

After dessert, we worked our way through two kinds of sushi and a tapas sampler, then split a Vietnamese banh mi sandwich, a fancy grilled cheese, a carton of spicy lentil curry, and a basket of seasoned fries. While we ate, I asked, "So, how was your day?"

"It was good. I was bummed to discover one of my favorite fabric stores had gone out of business, but then I totally scored at the thrift store. I found a pair of sheer curtains with an iridescent sheen to them, and they're going to be perfect for the mermaid costume."

"That sounds great."

"I'm excited. I made a pattern when I got home, and I'm looking forward to sewing it."

I asked, "Were you concerned about running into Simeck or one of his cronies when you were out running errands?"

"It's definitely been in the back of my mind, but he lives clear across town, and he wouldn't go near the types of places I visited today. There's a difference between being cautious and being paranoid, and I don't want to let fear stop us from enjoying our time here."

"I agree."

He refilled our glasses, and after a few moments he said, "So, tell me about work today."

"It was a bit odd, since we were filming on a city street and working out of an RV. There were crowds of fans and a lot of security to keep them under control. It all went off without a hitch, but I'll be glad when we're settled in at our next location." I wiped my mouth with a cloth napkin before saying, "I almost forgot to tell you. Roger slipped past security and came to visit me at work today."

A crease appeared between Gabriel's dark brows, and he asked, "What did he want?"

"To make sure you're okay, basically."

"He came to ask you if I'm alright?"

"Well, no. I think he wanted to get a sense of who I was, and he also threatened to beat me up if I hurt you." Gabriel swore under his breath, and I said, "It's okay. He meant well."

"I'm surprised you're defending him."

I shrugged and said, "How can I fault someone for wanting to take care of you?"

"He threatened to beat you up!"

"I'd deserve it if I ever hurt you. By the same token, I'd go medieval on anyone who tried to cause you harm."

Gabriel tried to hide his grin as he muttered, "Why am I always attracted to cavemen?"

I knew I shouldn't be, but I was secretly thrilled to be lumped into the same category as his big, tough, former bodyguard of an ex-boyfriend. Then again, Gabriel had actually dumped him, so I knew I shouldn't follow Roger's example too closely.

When we finished eating, he said, "All of that was delicious, but I'm so full. The hammock under the tree is calling my name."

He left his shoes under the table, and we brought our blankets with us to the hammock. Once we both settled in comfortably, I closed my eyes and listened to the accordion music that drifted to us from one of the neighboring houses. "There's a lot I've missed about San Francisco," he said after a while. His head was on my shoulder, and he idly played with the open zipper on my leather jacket. "More than anything, I've missed the people. Not just my friends, but the quirky individuals who tend to gravitate to this place. I know the population is changing as housing prices keep skyrocketing, but I love the fact that there are still people like Miss Pearl with her pink hair and poisonous yard, and whoever's absolutely killing it on the accordion right now. I even love the fact that all the houses are crammed together, so we can be out here by ourselves, but there's all this life around us. It makes me feel like I'm part of something bigger than myself."

"That's what I imagined it would be like when I moved here at sixteen. I thought I'd find a home and a community, maybe even a family. You know how that turned out."

He said, "I'm glad we have the next six weeks here. Hopefully you'll get to replace those bad memories with some good ones."

When I noticed he was tapping his foot in time to the accordion music, I climbed out of the hammock and held out my hand. "Here's a perfect opportunity. Dance with me, Gabriel."

He let me help him up, and we put our arms around each other and swayed to a song that felt like it belonged to another place and time. I decided to get fancy and spun him before saying, "Fair warning, I'm going in for the dip. This might end badly, but every romantic movie I've ever seen tells me I have to give it a shot." He let me tip him back, sweep him around, and pull him upright again, and I exclaimed, "Hey, we did it!"

That made both of us laugh. Then he draped his arms around my shoulders and met my gaze as he murmured, "You just keep surprising me, Riley."

"In a good way, I hope."

"In the best possible way." He kissed me before saying, "My turn." Gabriel put a hand on my lower back and dipped me, then pulled me upright and flashed me a big smile. "You're not the only one with some tricks up your sleeve."

"So I see. What else can you do?"

"I'm glad you asked. I've never done this to accordion music before, but let's see how it goes."

He retrieved his heels and put them on, then brought a chair over and indicated it with a flourish as he said, "Please take a seat."

I did as he asked, and he called, "Excuse me person with the accordion, could you please play something I can strip to? I want to put on a show for my date." The music stopped abruptly. A few moments later, our hidden musician started to play a pretty great rendition of 'Lady Marmalade'. Gabriel grinned and called, "Thank you, that's perfect," as he crossed the brick patio.

He started to dance to the music with his back to me. When he unbuttoned his jacket and dropped it off his shoulders, I realized the black button-down shirt was backless. He swung his hips from side to side, then pulled up the jacket, turned, and strode toward me. My breath caught as he pushed my legs apart and dropped into a crouch with his hands on my knees.

He locked eyes with me and licked his lips. A moment later, he stood up and strode across the patio as he took off his jacket and tossed it aside. When he came to a stop, he widened his stance and bent at the waist, putting all of the focus on his ass. I whispered, "Holy shit."

He snapped upright, spun around, and crossed the patio again, approaching me like a panther stalking its prey as he unbuttoned his shirt. Then he ran a hand up his body and pushed aside the fabric to reveal one of his shoulders. He made that little peek of skin the sexiest thing I could ever imagine.

The slow, seductive striptease went on another minute or two, until the song ended. Gabriel and I both cheered and applauded the accordionist, and I kept applauding as Gabriel turned to me and took a bow. "That was a little taste of my short-lived burlesque career," he said, as he straddled my thighs and sat on my lap while buttoning his shirt. "I'd usually strip down to lingerie, but I thought I should probably keep my pants on in Miss Pearl's yard."

"That was incredibly sexy."

"I used to do a slower, more seductive strip tease when I was working at the burlesque club, but that song called for something a bit more down-and-dirty."

"It was so hot." I slid my hands over his shoulders and down his exposed back as I murmured, "This shirt is amazing, too. Where did you find something like this?"

"I made it. Well, kind of. I have several black button-downs in my wardrobe, and one day I decided to make them more interesting. This one was easy. I just had to cut out the back panel beneath the yoke and refinish the seams."

"What's a yoke?"

He touched the fabric that covered his shoulders and spanned the upper part of his back. "I cropped another shirt, and I cut the top of the sleeves off a third one, which gives a little peek of skin, right here." He cupped the sides of my shoulders as he said that. "I like shirts that look normal under jackets, but then have an element of surprise."

"You're brilliant. You know that?"

He chuckled and said, "Hardly."

"I'm serious."

Even though he murmured, "You're biased," he seemed flattered. The accordion player had started up again, and Gabriel climbed off my lap and kicked his shoes off. Then he held his hand out to me and said, "Let's take another spin around the dance floor."

We danced through three songs, and then our anonymous accordion player finished off his set by playing a good night lullaby and falling silent. We applauded again, and then Gabriel said, "I suppose we should get going. Miss Pearl might want to retire for the night."

We cleaned up the table, gathered the dishes, and carried them into the house, where we found Miss Pearl and Phoenix enjoying another bottle of wine. Phoenix got up from the kitchen table and loaded the dishwasher for our hostess while we chatted for a few minutes. We found out the accordion player was a little old man who used to be a bus driver, and who practiced the instrument every night for two hours. "The accordion music used to drive me nuts," our hostess admitted, "but then one day I decided to look at it as a positive and just enjoy it. Like a lot of things in life, sometimes it's just a matter of changing your perspective."

When he finished with the dishes, Phoenix handed me his keys and said, "I've overdone it with the wine, so you'll have to drive yourself." I told him we could just call a Lyft, but he said, "No need. I won't be going anywhere tonight."

We made plans to pick him up the next morning, and after we said goodnight, Gabriel and I went out to the driveaway by a side door. When he asked if he could drive, I handed over the keys, and he said, "It's still early. Do you think it'd be okay if we drove around a bit?"

"Sure. I really don't think Phoenix would mind."

He turned right when we left the neighborhood, heading toward the city center as he said, "I miss having a car. I only had one for a short time, but I loved that sense of freedom and being able go anywhere I wanted on a whim."

"What happened to your car?"

"I gave it to my mom when I moved to Catalina, so she wouldn't have to take the bus to work anymore. First though, I tried to give it back to my friend Zachary, who bought it for me. But he didn't really need it and thought my mom would get a lot of use out of it."

I asked, "Are all your friends rich?"

"He isn't rich, he's just really generous. After my overdose, I moved back in with my mom for a while. Zachary was worried about me because I was so isolated out in the country, so he found an old Subaru Brat and had a mechanic friend fix it up. It was one of the nicest things anyone's ever done for me."

"He sounds like a great guy," I said.

"He really is. I'm looking forward to introducing you to him and his husband. He was stunned when I told him you and I had found each other again, and they're both excited to meet you."

I glanced at his profile and asked, "Does that mean you told him about me before our reunion?"

"Zachary knows everything about me, and we share a lot of history. He and I both quit using around the same time, although I relapsed and he didn't. To say he's seen me at my absolute worst is putting it mildly. He was actually the one who called the ambulance when I overdosed at our drug dealer's house."

"He saved your life."

Gabriel said, "He not only saved it, he helped me build the life I have now. It's because of him that I know Sawyer, Roger, Tracy— the list goes on."

A shadow passed over his features, and I asked, "What's wrong?"

"I can't help but think about the friends who aren't in my life anymore. There are a few people I was close to when I was an addict, like my former roommate Scottie. I really tried, but I just couldn't convince him to get help. Eventually, I had to distance myself, and it breaks my heart. I feel like I failed him."

"I know you did everything you could, because that's the kind of person you are. But some people just don't want to be saved," I said. "I also know you did the right thing by walking away, because being around people who are still using definitely would have undermined your recovery."

"I know. But I still feel guilty."

"Even if you couldn't save everyone, you did save me. Don't forget that."

He whispered, "Thank God."

Eventually, we ended up in a part of San Francisco that never appeared in travel brochures. Homeless people settled in for the night in the doorways of graffiti-covered buildings while a drug deal went down in plain sight, and a group of prostitutes tried to catch the attention of people driving by. Gabriel said softly, "This is my old neighborhood. Scottie and I lived in that decaying building across the street, and I used to work that corner. It looks like it hasn't changed at all."

"Before Simeck took me in, I lived in an abandoned building two blocks over. It was a nightmare."

Gabriel pulled to the curb and turned to look at me. "I'm sorry

Riley, I didn't realize you'd lived in this same neighborhood. The last thing I wanted was to stir up a bunch of bad memories for you."

"I actually believe in confronting my past. If we leave things in the dark, they just keep growing until they start to seem monstrous. But if we drag them into the light, we can see them for what they are, and they don't seem so scary anymore."

He whispered, "I wish I was strong like you."

"You're so much stronger than you realize, Gabriel. You were strong enough to save both of us."

"But there's still so much I struggle with, and I feel like I should have made a lot more progress by now."

"That doesn't make you weak," I said. "In fact, every day that you get up and keep trying is a testament to your strength. And who says you should have made more progress? As long as you're moving forward, no matter the speed, that's a total win."

When Gabriel grinned a little, I asked, "Am I being too clichéd? When I was in rehab, I had a counselor who was super positive all the time, and who'd basically talk in bumper stickers. She'd say stuff like 'all progress is good progress' and 'just keep putting one foot in front of the other'. It was annoying, and I think I just did the same thing to you."

"Did she help you, though?"

"She did, actually. Whenever things get tough, I find myself repeating her little catch phrases, and I can practically hear her cheering me on."

"Just keep being my cheerleader, Riley," he said, as he put the SUV in gear and pulled away from the curb. "I like it."

It was still pretty early when we got back to the apartment. Gabriel took off his heels first thing, and on our way through the living room, he muttered, "What a huge contrast between this place and our old neighborhood. It's hard to believe we're in the same city."

"It feels odd to me to be surrounded by this much luxury. This just isn't the world I live in, and it never will be."

As we continued to the bedroom, he said, "Honestly, I felt more at home back in that rough neighborhood than I ever did here, even though Sawyer and Alastair were so welcoming all those months I lived with them. It just always felt like playing dress-up in someone else's closet, if you know what I mean."

"I can see why."

"It's actually the same at Seahorse Ranch. I'm staying in a lavish house that isn't mine, and I'm working at a resort I'd never be able to afford as a guest. Even though I absolutely love the friends I've made there, it doesn't feel like home any more than this place ever did."

When we reached the guestroom, he sat down on the edge of the bed and looked up at me. I brushed his hair back as I said, "You just need a place to call your own. It'll happen."

"Will it, though? I'm turning thirty this year. That means I've been on my own for well over a decade, and I feel like I have nothing to show for it."

I knelt down in front of him and took his hand. "You have me, Gabriel, and a lot of people who absolutely love you and care about you. Plus, you battled addiction and won, so it's not true that you have nothing to show for the last few years."

He flashed me a lopsided smile. "Way to turn it into a positive."

"Were you serious when you said you'd love to turn your lingerie into a business?"

"Definitely."

"In that case, we're going to make it happen." I asked, "Did you bring some with you?"

"Yeah, I brought as much lingerie as I could cram into my suitcase."

"Perfect. Starting this weekend, we're launching phase one of your brand. Once we get the business to turn a profit, you'll have enough money to find a place you can call home."

His smile got wider. "I love it when you're like this."

"Like what?"

"You're so confident you can make this happen. It makes me believe it, too."

"Oh, it's happening," I told him. "One question: how do you

feel about posing for some fairly risqué photos in your lingerie, then posting them on social media?"

He shrugged and said, "It's not much different than when I was dancing burlesque, which made me feel sexy."

"Okay, good." I got to my feet and kissed his forehead. "This is going to be the start of great things. You'll see." I was determined to make that the absolute truth.

Chapter 6

Saturday morning, Gabriel rolled over in bed, raised an eyelid, and muttered, "What're you doing?"

"Getting design ideas for your company's website." I was sitting up in bed with my old laptop, and he put his head on my chest so he could see the screen.

"My company that doesn't actually exist?"

"It will, and I want to set up a website for you as soon as possible. It's a pretty easy first step to making this dream a reality."

He asked, "Do you know how to do that?"

"Sort of. I took a web design class last year and built myself a website to showcase my fantasy makeup. That was a piece of cake. The difference is that yours will have an online shop, so I'll have to find a professional web developer to make sure it's set up in the right way and scalable. The last thing we want is for your site to crash when traffic picks up."

Gabriel grinned and nuzzled my bare chest. "I love your optimism. I have no inventory and haven't sold a single thing yet, but you're anticipating this huge run on lingerie for guys."

"I looked online, and there are very few companies doing this."

"Maybe there's a reason for that."

"It's a growing market." I pushed his hair from his face and asked, "Do you want to give the company your name, in the style of Andrew Christian?"

"Definitely not."

"Okay. Did you have another company name in mind?" When he shook his head, I suggested, "What about something with 'angel' in it? Angel wings? Guardian angel? Angel soft?"

"At least one of those is a brand of toilet paper."

I chuckled and said, "Okay, so scratch that one."

"This is too much to think about before coffee." He kissed my chest, then slid out from under my arm and said, "I'm going to take a shower. Then after breakfast, we can do that photo shoot, if you still want to."

"Definitely." After a beat, I called after him, "Angel food? Like the cake? I totally suck at naming things, if you hadn't noticed."

He laughed at that, then paused in the bathroom doorway and turned to me, looking adorably rumpled in his midnight blue cotton pajamas. "What do you think about Fallen Angel Lingerie?"

"I love it."

"Actually, I do, too."

"I'm going to see if the domain name is available." I started to do a quick search on my laptop.

"Hey, Riley?" When I looked at him, Gabriel said, "Thank you."

"Anything for you."

He spent a long time in the bathroom, and when he finally emerged, he told me, "Every inch of me is shaved and moisturized, and I did the best I could on my hair. I can really only straighten it to a point before it starts to look like doll hair."

He climbed onto the bed wearing his blue-gray robe as I told him, "You look perfect."

"Doubtful." He took a look at the laptop's screen and exclaimed, "Oh wow, I love that!"

I'd drawn a stylized pair of black angel wings and paired them with the company name in a simple but elegant font. "It's just meant to be a place holder until we find an affordable graphic designer."

"No, that's perfect. I want to use it for my logo."

"I can clean it up a bit if you want," I said. "I didn't spend a lot of time on it."

"Don't change a thing. I love the fact that it's a little rough."

"Well, great. There's something we can cross off our to-do list. Also, the domain name was available, so I went ahead and registered it. Then I set up an Instagram account for Fallen Angel Lingerie, and I added a link to sign up for an email newsletter. It's a good idea to start building a mailing list, so when your online shop opens you'll already have a customer base."

Gabriel asked, "How do you know this stuff?"

"For a while, I wanted to open my own special effects makeup studio, so I did a bunch of research. It didn't work out, but now I can use what I learned to help you launch your company." I set aside the laptop and kissed his forehead. "Right now though, you need breakfast."

We both climbed out of bed, and as he followed me to the kitchen he asked, "Why did you decide against starting your own company?"

"It was decided for me when I couldn't get the capital I needed. Every bank basically laughed in my face when I tried to take out a loan. I mean, I knew it was a long shot. I'm young and inexperienced with zero collateral, so why would they trust me with their money? I had to try, though. I really wanted to make my own opportunities instead of waiting for an established studio to take a chance on me, but it wasn't very realistic."

While I got a pot of coffee brewing with one of our hosts' many coffee makers, Gabriel said, "I'm sorry it didn't work out."

"It's okay. Sooner or later, someone will give me a chance. Maybe the new fantasy looks we're going to shoot this afternoon will finally get me noticed."

The first order of business though was to take some photos of Gabriel modeling his lingerie for his new Instagram page. After a light breakfast, he sorted through his collection while I took a quick shower. When I returned to the bedroom, my cock instantly started to get hard and I had to adjust the front of my jeans. He'd changed into an all-black outfit, including a sheer robe with lace trim and a pair of black silk and lace panties. The underwear hugged his body and was cut high in the back, exposing a lot of his absolutely perfect ass. As if that wasn't hot enough, he'd also put on a pair of thigh-high black stockings and his stilettos.

He fidgeted with the robe as he checked his reflection in a full-length mirror. Then he turned to me and asked, "Do I look okay?"

There were two very different sides to Gabriel—the one that could strut around in heels and dance burlesque, and the shy, quiet boy who doubted himself and craved reassurance. The second one looked at me from beneath his dark lashes, and I drew him close and said, "You're so beautiful, Gabriel. Look what you do to me." I took his hand and pressed it to my racing heart. "I'm in awe of you. I wish I had the words to tell you how absolutely breathtaking you are."

He said, "You're so sweet. Every other guy I've ever known would have put my hand on his hard-on right then, not his heart." He meant it as a compliment, but it made me feel like a harmless little kitten, when he was used to panthers.

I stretched up and kissed him, and then I stepped back and murmured, "We should probably get to those photos. The balcony is sunny right now, but it'll be in shadow before too long."

As he followed me out of the bedroom, he asked, "Are you sure this look isn't too much? There's a line between sexy and trashy, and I'm worried I crossed it."

"You haven't. We'll keep it that way by making sure your poses aren't too suggestive."

"Okay. I trust you."

I stopped off in the kitchen and made him a fresh cup of coffee, which I brought along to the balcony. "You know what? Don't even pose," I said, as I handed him the mug. "Just enjoy the coffee and the view, and let's see what we get."

Gabriel leaned against the railing while I took pictures with my phone. After a while, he glanced at me over his shoulder and said, "We'd talked about leaving my face out of the shots for anonymity's sake, but somehow that doesn't feel right. I want men to feel sexy in the stuff I design, but it's not just about that. It's also about helping them explore and express their feminine side. If I hide my face, I feel like it's sending the message that we need to keep our femininity a secret."

I leaned against the lounge chair and said, "I definitely get what you're saying, but one reason you decided to hide your face was because you were worried about Mason Simeck. I guess we need to ask ourselves what the chances are of him actually seeing these photos, then somehow using them to track us down."

"Maybe the real question is, how long do I keep letting fear influence my decisions? It scared the shit out of me when Simeck's men found me and tried to abduct me. I've had a hard time letting go of that fear, even after all this time. But maybe he really doesn't give a shit about us anymore. Even if he does, how's he going to use these pictures to find us? It's not like we're publishing our home address or anything."

"It's your call," I said. "I totally get what you're saying about why it's important to show a face with the lingerie. We don't want to treat it like a dirty little secret. But we can always find someone to model for us if you want to remain anonymous."

"The thing is though, this is really personal to me. The more I think about it, the more I realize I want to be the face of my brand. I also want to stop living in fear because of things that happened in the past."

"Okay. I totally support that."

He put down his coffee mug and said, "I'll be right back. I want some makeup."

While he was gone, I took some photos of the view. He returned a few minutes later, dressed in a demure purple camisole with lace at the neckline and matching briefs. Both pieces fit him like a glove. "Let's not use those first photos," he said, as he sat on the lounge chair and tucked his bare feet under him. "I feel like that last outfit was just a bit too much."

He flipped his hair over to one side as he dug through his cosmetic bag. Then he pulled out a compact and a tube of lip gloss with a subtle tint to it. As he held up the mirror and applied the gloss to his lips, I took several pictures. He looked up at me and grinned, and I snapped another photo.

I kept photographing him through five more outfit changes, before he decided we were done for the day. We went to our room and climbed onto the unmade bed, and he tucked an arm behind his head and grinned at me. He'd changed into his favorite grayish blue lace-trimmed underwear and a matching camisole for the last set of photos, and I murmured, "You're the most beautiful person in all the world, Gabriel."

He grinned at me. "What an overstatement."

"Nope, it's a fact."

I jumped up and stood on the foot of the bed. Then I held the phone above him and snapped a photo as he laughed and asked, "What are you doing?"

"Trying to show you what I see."

I almost lost my balance, and he said, "Come back. You're going to fall off the bed."

"Just one more."

He was still laughing as I bounced from one foot to the other, and he threw his arm over his eyes and said, "You've taken a million pictures today. Be done already!"

I snapped one final photo, then stretched out beside him. "Here's actual proof of how beautiful you are." When I showed him the screen he sighed and shook his head, but he was smiling. After I put the phone on the nightstand, I gathered him into my arms and said, "That was a lot of fun, and I think we got some great shots."

It made me sad when his smile faded. "I had fun too, but I can't help but think it's all a bit pointless."

"What makes you say that?"

"I just don't see how I'll ever be able to afford actually getting a company off the ground. I have about six thousand dollars in the bank, which I was able to save because I had free room and board at the resort for the last year. I'm willing to spend every cent of that, but I know it's not enough. Even if we somehow manage to produce some inventory, there are a million other expenses that go into starting a business."

"So, maybe what you need is an investor. Your friend Sawyer is the obvious choice, since you mentioned he likes lingerie. Plus, his husband's family owns a department store and several manufacturing facilities in the UK. I bet they'd know exactly where to go to get your lingerie made at a good price."

He sat up and shook his head. "There's no way I'd ever ask Sawyer for money. He and his husband have already done so much by opening their home to me, both when I needed a place to stay and again for this visit. I'd feel like I was taking advantage of their friendship."

"You wouldn't be going to him for a handout. You'd be asking him to invest in your company, which would end up making him a profit."

"Or not," he said. "This whole thing could crash and burn, and I'd feel terrible if my friend ended up losing money because of me."

"Then what's the alternative?"

He muttered, "To give up on this crazy idea."

"Already? We've barely gotten started."

"It's such a nice fantasy that I could turn my passion into a business, and this photoshoot felt like living a dream. But realistically, there's no way I can afford to do this."

I asked, "What if you scale it back and just make pieces to order?"

"I thought about that, but it isn't really what I want. The dream is an online shop with stuff people can actually afford. It's time-consuming to make custom pieces versus having them mass-produced. That means I'd have to jack up the price if I wanted to earn more than a dollar or two an hour by sewing everything myself."

He had some good points, but there was no way I was willing to give up so soon. "I get not wanting to involve Sawyer and Alastair, but what about asking Roger for some contact names? You said he's worked closely with Alastair's family for years, so he might know people in garment manufacturing who could answer our questions and give us some cost estimates. What if this is cheaper than we're assuming it is?"

Gabriel shook his head. "He probably would know who to contact, but I don't want to open that can of worms. The moment Roger even suspects I need something, he'll launch into full solve-all-my-problems mode."

"I bet you can reel him in, though," I said. "Just explain that all you need are some names and phone numbers, nothing more. What's the worst that could happen?"

He grinned at me. "People always ask that question right before disaster strikes."

"Roger might pleasantly surprise you, though."

"I doubt it."

"Okay. But I think we should still post some photos to the Instagram account and see what happens. It may catch the eye of a potential investor, or even another designer who might want to partner with you. It doesn't cost anything to try, so why not?"

"Might as well," he said, even though he didn't seem very hopeful. "We don't have anything to lose."

Later that afternoon, my friend Emory joined us for lunch. He was carrying two wig forms with a long, brunette wig and an even longer white one. He put them on the table in the entryway, grabbed me in a hug, and exclaimed, "It's been too long, Riley!"

"That's because your 'weekend getaway' to San Francisco has lasted three months," I said. "Are you ever going back to Southern California?"

"I'll have to sooner or later. My dad hasn't figured out yet that I took a leave of absence from UCLA. Once he does, I'm sure he'll guilt me into returning to grad school."

"I forget, what were you studying?"

"I was working on my PhD in engineering."

When he let go of me, Emory pushed his thick glasses further up the bridge of his nose and flashed me a shy smile. He was a skinny African-American guy of about twenty-five, who most people wrote off as a quiet, introverted geek. But somehow, he also transformed into an absolutely fierce and drop-dead gorgeous drag queen.

As I led him through the living room, I said, "That must mean he doesn't know you're performing at a local drag club five nights a week."

"God no. He doesn't even know I do drag." Emory looked around and said, "Um, are we going to talk about the million-dollar apartment?"

"It belongs to a freakishly successful gay couple. You know I could never afford a place like this."

"You and me both," he muttered.

We reached the kitchen just as Gabriel pulled an apple pie from the oven, and I said, "Emory Townsend, meet Gabriel Moriarty."

Emory's big, brown eyes lit up, and he said, "Oh cool, like the bad guy in the Sherlock Holmes books." When Gabriel took off his oven mitt and stuck his hand out, Emory shook it vigorously. Then he asked, "Just so I don't screw it up, what are your pronouns?"

I'd never actually heard anyone ask Gabriel that, but I realized it probably wasn't uncommon, given the way he dressed. At the moment, he was wearing a long, off-the-shoulder black tunic and leggings, along with a bit of red lipstick. "He and him," Gabriel said. "Thanks for asking."

Emory sat on one of the stools at the kitchen island and pushed back the sleeves of his oversized gray sweatshirt as he said, "I'm not so great in social situations. Like, if there's a way to be awkward, I'll probably find it. But at some point I realized it was better to ask about pronouns when I was unsure, instead of making assumptions. My first thought was that you were gender fluid and might use they and them, but see, I was wrong about that."

"I was excited when I first heard the term 'gender fluid' a few years ago, because I thought there might finally be a term that fit me," Gabriel said. "I wanted a better alternative than 'crossdresser', because that's such a catch-all term and tends to confuse more than explain. Eventually though, I realized being gender fluid is much different than what I am. I'm just a guy who feels most comfortable when I'm expressing my feminine side. The closest word that seems to fit is 'femme' but even that has more than one connotation."

"I know what you mean about the word 'crossdresser'," Emory said, as I began pulling sandwich ingredients from the refrigerator. "Sometimes people use that term for drag queens. But you choosing to dress a certain way in your day-to-day life, me performing on stage in drag, and men who dress in women's clothing as a fetish are very different things. It doesn't make sense to cram all of that under one label."

"I hope this doesn't sound ignorant," I said, as I turned to Gabriel, "but do you really want a label, whether it's femme or androgynous or anything else?"

"I guess I do sometimes, just because it would be nice to have a concise, easy way to explain myself to people. Not to everyone, obviously. I don't care what most people think, and not everyone needs or deserves an explanation about why I dress this way," Gabriel said. "But occasionally, when I'm meeting someone like a new coworker or a friend of a friend and they're obviously struggling to understand me, it would be nice to say 'I'm this' and be done with it. I can tell them the whole truth—that I dress like this because I like it, because it feels comfortable and natural, and because it's how I want to express myself—but somehow even that just leads to more questions."

I thought about that while I filled three glasses with ice and soda, and Emory said, "Maybe it's a copout, but I don't tell everyone I'm a drag queen. I just don't want to field a bunch of awkward questions or explain why I do it. Riley knows because that's how we met. About a year ago, I saw him doing makeup for another performer and asked him to do mine, because he was absolutely killing it." I put their drinks in front of them, and Gabriel and Emory clinked their glasses together in a toast.

They both took a drink, and Emory continued, "The one person I wish I could explain it to is my dad, but he'd never understand why I do drag." His hand brushed over his forehead and his very short hair, as if he was smoothing back locks that weren't there, and he said, "We might as well be from different planets. Just to give you an idea, he's a former defensive tackle who now works as a trainer for the Oakland Raiders. His whole world is about super macho men doing super macho shit. We already had nothing in common before I started doing drag, and now—honestly, I just don't even have the energy to try to make him understand." He sighed and shook his head.

"My mom will never understand me either," Gabriel said, "but I decided I'm okay with that. Well, not okay, exactly."

"But you're resigned to it." Gabriel nodded, and Emory turned to me and asked, "Are you close with your parents?"

"No. I haven't seen my mom since I was sixteen, and I never met my dad. He took off before I was born." While I was talking, I busied myself by taking a pasta salad from the refrigerator, then grabbing some sandwich rolls.

Emory asked, "Do you ever think about going to visit your mom?"

"Definitely not. In fact, I don't even know where she's living these days. All I ever heard from her was how she never wanted me and how worthless I was. It's taken seven years to undo some of the damage she did to me, so never seeing her again is a form of self-care."

I took some dishes from the cupboard, and when I turned to face Gabriel and Emory, they both looked upset. Gabriel said, "I'm so fucking sorry you had to go through that."

"You don't have to feel bad," I said. "I got out, and I learned to take care of myself. I'm going to be okay." I would have liked to say I *was* okay, but that wasn't entirely true. I was still a work in progress, since pain that deep took a long time to fade.

I tried to lighten the mood after that, and the three of us chatted about some of our favorite drag performers over lunch. When we finished eating, I invited Emory to join us while I applied Gabriel's fantasy merman makeup for the photoshoot we planned to do that afternoon. "Um, hell yes," my friend said. "I'd love to watch you work your magic."

All my materials were arranged on the balcony table. After Gabriel changed into a pair of gym shorts and tied his hair back, the three of us got comfortable and I went to work. Emory watched closely and asked a lot of questions as I glued several prosthetic pieces to Gabriel's skin, adding sharpness and definition to his brow line, cheekbones, and collarbones. Delicate, translucent pieces flared out and back from the sides of his face and from his shoulders, almost but not quite like fins, because I wanted this look to be above and beyond anything I'd seen before.

The next step was to airbrush all of him from the waist-up. I used a machine to spray on a sheer, iridescent white base, then went back in and strategically added shades of blue and green to create depth and shadow. Finally, we sat knee-to-knee as I applied the details, including sensual eyes and lips, and a scale effect just around the edges of his face and shoulders.

In all, the transformation took almost three hours. The three of us chatted while I worked, and Gabriel displayed the patience of a saint by sitting still for me.

Once I was finished, Emory teased his white wig with a comb so it would look wild and unkempt, and then he helped Gabriel put it on, carefully tucking it behind the extensions on the sides of his face. I snapped a test photo and finetuned the makeup a bit, and then I handed Gabriel a mirror and asked, "What do you think?"

He held the mirror close, then at arm's length and murmured, "Oh wow! This is just incredible. I look like I stepped out of a movie."

Emory said, "I'm already thinking about how to do a version of this look for drag. It'd knock the audience on its ass!"

"I forgot to ask," Gabriel said, "what's your drag name? Please tell me it's something like Gia Hardon, Claire Voyant, or Tess Tosterone."

I chuckled and said, "If you just came up with those off the top of your head, that's impressive."

"I just love a punny drag name," he told me with a smile.

"Okay, so in my defense, I came up with my drag name on the fly," Emory said, as his slender fingers gathered strands of Gabriel's wig and twisted them into curls. "This was about two years ago, when I finally scraped up the courage to enter a drag contest at a club in West Hollywood. Up until that point, I'd just been doing bedroom drag. That's where you secretly make yourself up in your room, then wash it off before your dad sees it."

"And he totally dodged the question," I said with a smile. "His drag name is Polly Swallows, which I actually love."

Emory frowned a little. "It could be better, but I'm stuck with it now."

"Yeah, because you're awesome and won that first drag contest," I pointed out.

Gabriel looked impressed. "You're Polly Swallows? No way!"

Emory's eyes went wide. "You've actually heard of me?"

"Don't sound so surprised," I said. "Polly has thousands of followers on social media, or hadn't you noticed?"

"Yeah, but it's one thing to be known within the drag community," Emory said, "and another to discover people outside of that world actually know your name."

Gabriel grinned. "I saw a music video you did for a song called 'Beach Blanket Bimbo'. It was hilarious."

Emory seemed simultaneously embarrassed and flattered. "Thanks. I had a lot of fun with that."

While I packed up my supplies, Gabriel told him, "I didn't even sort of recognize you without your makeup."

"No one ever does, partly because I never post photos of myself out of drag. I want my dad to find out about Polly on my terms, not because some random person sees a picture of me and goes running to tell him."

"Makes sense." Gabriel got up and told us, "I'm going to get my costume, be right back."

Once my makeup kit was packed up, Emory followed me inside and asked, "Are you going to the beach to take these photos?"

"We thought about that, but we decided it'd be more unexpected to photograph him in a bath tub. There's a huge, freestanding tub in the master bathroom, and the guys who own this place said we're welcome to use it."

"I like that idea."

I asked, "How soon do you need the wigs back? We're pulling

together a woodland nymph look for the brown one, but we still need to figure out where to photograph it."

"There's no hurry. I'm not currently using either of them in my act."

A minute later, Gabriel returned carrying the tail he'd made. It was beautifully constructed from iridescent material, with a wide, semi-transparent fin at the bottom and long, sheer, ruffled streamers that looked like a jellyfish's tentacles extending beyond it. In other words, he'd made it look exactly like the sketch I'd had on the wall of my apartment.

Gabriel fanned it out and held it to his waist to show us the full look, and Emory seemed impressed. "Okay, the makeup was already phenomenal," he said. "Now that I'm seeing this all together, it's a work of art."

"I was worried that I didn't really get it to look organic," Gabriel said, as his fingers skimmed the fabric he'd quilted to resemble scales.

"It's absolutely perfect," I said. "In fact, it elevates my makeup."

"I'd better get going," Emory said, as he glanced at the time on his phone. "I have an appointment in half an hour. Are these photos going on your website, Riley?"

"Yeah, they should be up by tonight," I told him. "Thank you again for loaning us the wigs, they're the perfect finishing touch." Before he took off, we promised to come to the club soon to watch him perform.

We walked him out, then went to the master bathroom and got set up for our photoshoot. I touched up Gabriel's face and body, then helped him with the tail, which wrapped around him and held together in the back with Velcro. We'd been discussing this shoot all week, so he knew just what to do as he got into position.

I shot several close-ups and portraits, first with him sitting on the edge of the tub, then inside it. We took some pictures without water, then filled the tub. For the final few shots, we turned it into a bubble bath. I climbed onto a chair and used a selfie stick to hold the phone above him. That let me capture some gorgeous full-length shots with him leaning back, looking right into the camera, and resting his elbows on the edge of the tub while the tail fanned out over the other end.

Finally, I stepped off the chair, checked my camera roll, and said, "Okay, I think we're done."

"You sure?"

"Yeah, I got some amazing shots. I can't wait to post them."

I helped him out of the tub, and he removed the tail, then dried off and pulled his gym shorts on. Next, I began carefully removing the prosthetic pieces from his skin. After a few moments, I said, "Can I ask you something?"

"Of course."

"Every day this past week, you had a different excuse for not coming with me to the movie set. You seemed really excited about it at first, so I'm wondering what changed."

He admitted, "I've been putting off going to the set because it's really intimidating. I'm trying to work up my nerve though, because I really would love to watch you work."

"Why are you intimidated?"

"Just look at the people you work with, the famous actors and that director. Hell, even your supervisor and coworkers intimidate me. They're all successful people at the top of their game, and I just won't fit in with them."

I said, "If I can fit in there, so can you."

"But you're not a failure like me, Riley. I don't think you realize how insanely talented you are. You've already come so far, and it's just a matter of time before you land your dream job, then go on to open your own studio and become wildly successful."

"You're not a failure," I insisted. "Not even close."

"Well, I feel like one." It broke my heart to see him so down on himself.

He ran his fingertips over his cheekbone, rubbing off some of the glue residue as I removed the final prosthetic. Then I said, "Why don't you go ahead and take a shower? That should all come off with some soap and warm water. I'll clean up in here."

"Okay."

"Thanks again for doing this, Gabriel. I really appreciate it."

As he left the master bathroom, he said, "Thanks for including me. It was nice to feel needed."

I hung the tail in the shower to drip-dry, and as I drained the tub I chewed my lower lip and tried to make up my mind about something. Finally, I took a business card from my wallet to look up a number, then sent a text, which said: *Hi Roger, this is Riley. Will you please meet me at my job one day next week? We have some things we need to discuss.*

He replied a few moments later with: *Sure mate, I'll be there on Monday at lunchtime. Can I ask what this is about?*

I sighed and wrote: *I need you to do what you do best—give Gabriel help he doesn't want but actually really needs.*

Roger asked: *Does he know you're contacting me?*

My next message said: *No, and he's not going to like it. But I just don't know how to help him get his lingerie company off the ground, and I'll bet you do. He doesn't want to involve Alastair and Sawyer, just so you know. Also, this isn't an invitation to go nuts and take over the entire project. I just need some general advice and some contacts in the garment manufacturing industry.*

He replied: *I can definitely help, but he's going to be angry when he finds out we've gone behind his back. Mostly with you—he expects this type of behavior from me.*

Gabriel probably would be mad, but hopefully he'd forgive me when he realized I had the best of intentions. He needed that company, for his own feelings of self-worth as much as anything else. I hated going behind his back, but all I was going to do was gather some information. As long as Roger didn't get carried away, this should be no big deal.

Chapter 7

The following Friday morning, Gabriel finally agreed to come to work with me. I was rolling back the sleeves of my royal blue button-down shirt—part of the 'Will collection'—when he joined me in the living room, and I knew at a glance he was feeling insecure. He'd opted for a simple button-down shirt and jeans, along with a long cardigan and canvas slip-ons, all in black. The fact that he was opting not to show his feminine side to the world spoke volumes.

He was fidgety as we rode the elevator downstairs, and I held his hand as we stood under the awning over the main entrance waiting for our ride. It was a typical San Francisco morning, foggy and breezy but beautiful at the same time. The city wore the color gray well.

After a while, I said, "Before we got here, we talked about what spending time in San Francisco might do to your recovery. So, this is me checking in to make sure you're okay."

"I'm fine. It probably helps that I've spent most of my time in my own little world in that apartment, working on my sewing projects. Except for that one night when we visited our old neighborhood, it's barely registered that we're in the city that used to be such a struggle for me."

I asked, "Even though you actually lived in this same apartment through part of your recovery?"

"The apartment always felt like an oasis, even back when I barely had a handle on my addiction. It just doesn't seem like real life. It's too perfect and beautiful up there, high above the city with nothing to worry about."

"I can understand that," I said. "It reminds me of how I felt in rehab. It was like it existed in a parallel universe, far from the real world and all my triggers."

He looked at me and asked, "Was it hard for you after you left the treatment center?"

"Yeah, at first. The thought of using was always in the back of my mind. But as time went on and I realized I was in control, I learned to trust myself."

"Why'd you choose to go back to L.A.? There must have been a lot of bad memories, since you grew up there."

"I wanted to go somewhere familiar," I said, "where I knew my way around and had some idea of what to expect. The only two places I'd ever lived were L.A. and San Francisco, and I knew I wasn't strong enough to come back here right away. It would have been way too easy to relapse. So I chose L.A., but not the part I grew up in. Torrance and West Hollywood might be a short drive from each other, but they're nothing alike."

"That makes sense."

"I wish I'd been stronger back then," I admitted. "What I wanted more than anything when I left rehab was to come and find you, but I needed to get myself together first. When I finally returned to San Francisco, nearly a year had passed and you'd vanished. I thought I'd made the biggest mistake of my life by waiting too long."

He turned to me and touched my cheek. "You did the right thing by staying away. It's what I told you to do. Between avoiding Simeck and the fact that I was still using, this was the last place you should have been."

"But it cost me four years with you. And what if I hadn't stumbled across you on Catalina? How many more years might have gone by?"

Gabriel wrapped his arms around me. "You found me at the right time, just when you were meant to. Who's to say this would have worked if you'd found me sooner? Maybe I wouldn't have been ready for a relationship, especially if I wasn't at a good place with my recovery." I'd never thought of it like that.

Phoenix pulled up and parked at the curb, and Gabriel kissed my cheek before taking my hand and leading me to the SUV. We said hello to our friend as we settled in, and as Phoenix pulled into traffic I asked him, "What are you doing this weekend?"

"I need to get serious about finding my next job," he said. "This is Will's last full day on set, followed by half-days next Monday through Thursday. This time next week, he and Lorenzo will be back on Catalina and taking some time off to plan their wedding. I'll go back to work for him in July when his next picture begins filming, so the tricky part is finding someone to hire me for the next four months. People usually want personal assistants who are going to be around a while."

I knew there was no point in suggesting again that he take some time off. Phoenix needed structure and a schedule, and more than anything he needed to be busy. That was just who he was. Even throwing himself into his music wasn't enough for him. He needed projects, the more challenging the better.

Will was feeling the upcoming transition, too. When we picked him up at his hotel, along with his fiancé and their cat, he seemed a little wistful. "I can't believe this is my last full day of filming," he said. "It's been such a great experience, but now it feels like my part is just sort of fading away, while the rest of the cast and crew still have almost a month of work ahead of them."

"I hope you're planning to come back for the wrap party in a few weeks," I said.

Lorenzo nodded. "We wouldn't miss it."

I leaned toward Gabriel, who was sitting in the passenger seat, and said, "I'm hoping you'll be my date to the party. It should be a lot of fun. They're renting out an entire Japanese restaurant here in the city, and after dinner there's going to be karaoke. I don't sing, but I'll gladly be your backup dancer if you feel like getting up on stage." I busted out a few awkward dance moves in my seat, and Gabriel grinned at me. He didn't actually say yes to attending the party, but I figured he'd decide if he wanted to go based on how today went.

When we arrived at our destination, Gabriel took it all in with wide eyes. Several trailers lined the street and filled the parking lot of a boarded-up building, which was going to be demolished to make way for a high-rise condo development. Directly across the street was a row of stately Victorians. For the last few days, filming had been taking place in the house on the corner, which was meant to be the home of Liam's family, the character played by Harper Royce. Funnily enough, a totally different house clear across town had been filmed for the home's exterior.

When Phoenix dropped us off and went to find parking, I took Gabriel's hand and led him to the production office, where I signed him in and got him a visitor pass to wear on a lanyard around his neck. Then I led him to the trailer shared by the hair and makeup departments. As usual, I was the first to arrive, since Phoenix always made a point of getting Will to the set early. I put my makeup kit on a table back in the corner, then went around flipping on the lights at each of the four workstations. While I got a pot of coffee going, Gabriel wandered around the trailer looking at everything, and I grinned at him and said, "It's not exactly glamorous, I know. After I do Will's makeup and make sure Gina doesn't need anything, I'll take you across to the set. We'll be spending most of the day in the yellow Victorian, which is where Will and Harper Royce will be filming two fairly long scenes."

When the coffee finished brewing, I fixed up a cup and brought it to Gabriel. He was standing at the window, and I stood right behind him and wrapped my arms around him. He thanked me for the coffee, then gestured at all the activity happening outside and said, "I can't believe how many people are working behind the scenes on this movie. It's like an entire village."

"Yeah, it's really something. Everyone has a very specific job to do, and somehow it all comes together into something that's pure magic. Hopefully someday, I'll be designing makeup for fantasy and science fiction films. But even as the least important person in the makeup department, I still feel like I'm a part of something special."

Gabriel put down his coffee cup and turned to me. "I'm already glad I came along today," he said, as he draped his arms over my shoulders. "You just gave me a lot of insight into what this job means to you."

I kissed him, and he deepened the kiss as he ran his hands down my back. For the last few days, we'd done plenty of kissing and cuddling but had avoided anything sexual. Even without talking about it, we both seemed to realize I needed some time to figure things out. But there was so much heat and longing in his kiss that I knew something had to give, and soon.

We parted quickly when the trailer door swung open, and Will announced, "It's just me. You can keep making out if you want to. I can come back later."

I murmured, "No, it's fine," as I went to my work station and hung up my leather jacket, then tried to be subtle about adjusting the front of my jeans.

Will had already stopped off in the wardrobe department and changed into an oversized Pearl Jam T-shirt with a flannel shirt over it, along with jeans and beat-up sneakers. Before I went to work, I tucked tissue into his collar to protect the clothes, then handed him a stretchy headband, which he used to restrain his unruly curls. He said, "You know the first thing I'm going to do when I'm done playing Alex?"

As Gabriel retrieved his coffee and sat in the folding chair beside my workstation, I guessed, "Get a haircut?"

Will dragged out the word, "Absolutely," and grinned at me. "Also, I'd be just fine with never, ever wearing another flannel shirt for the rest of my life. I've loved playing Alex, but his personal style and mine are worlds apart."

"Worlds and several decades," I said, as I unpacked my makeup kit. "I was born too late, because I probably would have felt right at home in the 1990s grunge scene."

As I began applying pale foundation to Will's face, Gabriel said, "It's been a while since I've read the book this movie is based on, but I'm curious, what scenes are you filming today?"

"These two scenes aren't actually in the book," Will said. "Not directly, anyway. In the novel *Alex and After,* Liam talks about all the time Alex spent at his house, and how he was practically a member of Liam's family. The screenwriter felt it was important to show more of their history, so he fleshed out what used to be Liam reminiscing and created what we're filming today. One scene is the two of us hanging out and talking in Liam's bedroom, and the other is dinner with Liam's parents and sister." He grinned and added, "The funny thing is, Harper and I are both older than the characters we're portraying, and the actor playing Harper's dad is only eleven years older than he is."

I chuckled and said, "That's both weird and awesome."

"How old is Alex in this scene? I remember he was twenty-two when he died," Gabriel said.

"This is a year before, so I'm trying to pass for twenty-one," Will said, as a frown line appeared between his brows. "I know I'm almost thirty, but I didn't think it was that much of a stretch. At least, not until I met the novel's author, who wasted no time telling me I was too old and dead-wrong for the part of Alex."

Gabriel said, "Oh wow. I thought the author was a total recluse who never granted interviews."

Will nodded. "He is. Phoenix and Lorenzo tried to do something nice for me by arranging a meeting through this guy's niece. It was actually really devastating, since I've adored *Alex and After* since I was a teen, and the author turned out to be such a jerk. But I still love the book despite who wrote it, and I'm still honored I got to play a character who meant a lot to me and countless other people."

I kept working on his makeup while he and Gabriel talked about the book. A few minutes later Gina arrived, wearing a big pair of sunglasses and carrying a trade publication and a cup of coffee. When I introduced her to Gabriel, she peered at him over the top of her glasses and said, "You're cute." Then she sat down at her station and began flipping through the magazine.

At about nine thirty-five, she said, "Don't tell me, let me guess. Royce is late again today."

"Yeah, I actually was supposed to meet him over half an hour ago to run lines," Will said, as I put the finishing touches on his makeup.

"Why the fuck can't he hire a decent personal assistant to whip him into shape? It's not like he can't afford it," Gina muttered.

Will looked at me and said, "He needs Phoenix."

"Except for the fact that Phoenix can't stand him." I leaned back to assess my work. "He worked for Harper for a year, remember? It didn't exactly go well."

"But I'll bet Harper was on time for everything that year," Will said.

"Probably." I put down the brush I was holding and told him, "You're all set."

Gabriel sounded impressed when he said, "That's a remarkable transformation. You don't look like yourself anymore, Will, but you also don't look like you're wearing any makeup."

Will grinned and told him, "That's because your boyfriend is a genius," which embarrassed me and made me feel good in equal measure.

A few minutes later, the lead hairstylist showed up and went to work on Will's dark curls while Gabriel and I stepped outside to get some air. "So, that was the most interesting part of my day," I told him, as we stepped back to let a member of the camera crew pass with a rolling dolly. "Gage Lang, the director, tends to have his actors do a huge number of takes for each scene, so the rest of the morning will be spent watching Will and Harper deliver the same lines over and over, then jumping in and touching up Will's makeup as needed. After lunch, I'll need to do a more thorough touch-up. Then we'll have three additional actors on set for the dinner scene, and I'll be assisting Gina and the other makeup artist as needed."

"You really did an amazing job with Will. I'd seen the before and after photos on his Instagram, but it was even more impressive up close. Not that he looks his age, but you shaved years off of him, and you made him look...almost fragile, I guess. That's exactly how I always imagined Alex."

"In person, the shadows around his eyes seem a little too blue, but they'll read correctly on film."

Gabriel grinned at me. "Just accept the compliment, Riley."

"Fine. Thank you for the compliment." I grinned too and kissed the tip of his nose. Then I gestured toward a tall African-American man with a shaved head near the production office and asked, "Want me to introduce you to Gage Lang? He's right over there."

"Maybe later. He looks angry."

"Probably because he just found out Harper is late for the third time this week."

Since everything was on hold until the actor showed up, Gabriel and I took a seat on the stairs leading up to the makeup trailer, and I pointed out some of the crew members and explained what they did. A few minutes later, Harper stuck his head around the edge of the trailer and asked, "How mad is Lang that I'm late?"

"Just short of fuming, from what I saw."

"Shit. I really tried to get here on time today, but my pet sitter canceled on me at the last minute and it took me a while to find a replacement." Harper looked around, then stepped out from behind the trailer. When he saw Gabriel sitting beside me, he immediately went into what I'd come to think of as his 'charming movie star mode'. He stuck his hand out and flashed his dimpled smile as he said, "Hi there. I'm Harper Royce."

Gabriel seemed a bit starstruck as he shook Harper's hand and mumbled his name. Then I asked, "Is it a cat? The pet you need a sitter for, I mean. Will always brings his to work and keeps her in his trailer. If you bring yours along next time the sitter bails on you, maybe his fiancé could watch both of them."

"Actually, it's a chicken, and she doesn't play well with others." I tried to decide if he was kidding, but Harper seemed perfectly serious. He ran a hand over his short, dark blond hair and said, "Man, am I dreading another of Lang's lectures. I know I've been screwing up a lot, but I really don't mean to."

"Don't you have a personal assistant to help with stuff like hiring pet sitters?"

"Not at the moment."

"You know what you need to do? Hire Phoenix Jaymes," I said. "I know he worked for you in the past, so I don't have to tell you how great he is."

Harper frowned and said, "He was the best P.A. I ever had, but he hates my guts."

"He's a professional though, so I bet he can put aside any past misunderstandings and get the job done. My suggestion is to throw money at him until he agrees to work for you again. He's available beginning a week from today."

"I guess it doesn't hurt to ask, and God knows I need his help." Harper looked around again and said, "I can't face Lang yet, so I'm going to go to wardrobe. Please tell Gina I'll be with her in about ten minutes, or longer if Lang intercepts me on the way back here."

I promised I would, and once he was gone Gabriel asked, "Why would you try to get your friend a job with someone he hates?"

"Because I'm not entirely convinced Phoenix hates him. He was furious because Harper dated his identical twin brother Dallas for a while. Doesn't that sound like jealousy? If so, maybe it means he secretly has a crush on Harper."

"Or maybe he just hates him."

I shrugged and said, "Then he'll say no to the job offer. It won't hurt for Harper to ask."

"True. Also, why didn't I know Harper Royce is gay?"

"He's actually bi, but he tends to be more public with the women he dates." I got up and said, "Come on, let's go tell Gina and Will that Harper has arrived. Then you and I can find a ringside seat for when Gage Lang finally corners him."

"I actually feel bad for Harper. He seems like a nice guy."

"He is, but the lectures are kind of funny. I keep picturing Lang in his action star days when he played a modern-day Zeus in that superhero film, and Harper in his most famous movie role as Robin Hood. How often do you get to watch Zeus tear Robin Hood a new one?"

The morning went exactly as predicted. After Lang cornered Harper and delivered a dad-worthy 'time is money' lecture, everyone moved over to the house. Gabriel and I watched Will and Harper recite the same lines through almost two dozen takes. Then on our lunch break, we visited the taco truck that had strategically parked near the set and attracted half the crew.

The three actors playing Liam's parents and sister arrived on set at one, along with a publicist, a photographer, and a huge entourage. Everyone was buzzing with excitement because Melinda Howard, who played Liam's mom, was Hollywood royalty with a lengthy movie career and a ton of awards. I wondered how they'd convinced her to take such a small part, until I learned she and Gage Lang were friends. He'd obviously called in a favor.

Ms. Howard turned out to be kind and generous. She signed autographs and posed for photos with the crew, and it totally made Gabriel's day when she let us take a picture with her. That excitement carried us through the afternoon, as we watched the dinner scene being filmed and I divided my time between touching up Will's makeup and assisting Gina.

At the end of the day, we joined Phoenix in Will's trailer. As we sat on the couch, the cat climbed onto my lap and Gabriel leaned in and kissed me. "I'm glad I came along today," Gabriel said. "Everyone was so nice, and I loved getting to watch you work."

"It meant a lot to me that you were here." Phoenix was sitting at the table with his laptop, and when he shut it I asked him, "Did you make any progress on your job hunt?"

My friend sighed and adjusted his blue baseball cap. "Harper actually asked me to come back to work for him, but I'm not that desperate."

"He really needs your help though," I said. "The guy's barely holding it together. Wouldn't it be satisfying to get him organized and on a schedule?"

The words 'organized' and 'schedule' were like catnip to Phoenix. He chewed his lower lip for a few moments as he considered the possibilities, but then he shook his head. "Harper is a pain in the ass. He's also an overgrown child. You should see his house in L.A. He actually put a miniature golf course in the backyard, and he lives with a whole menagerie of animals. I even heard he brought his pet chicken with him while he's here in San Francisco. Who the hell does that?"

That all sounded great to me, but I said, "That's why he needs a responsible adult in his life. And do you really have to like him to work for him? It'd only be until July anyway, when you're planning to go back to work for Will."

"That's true. He offered me three times my usual salary, so he must be desperate. But I just don't know."

"Well, maybe you should take some time to think about it," I said. "He probably doesn't need an answer right away, and you still have six days left on Will's contract."

"Yeah, I'll give it some thought over the weekend." Phoenix stretched his arms over his head as he asked, "Speaking of Will, did you see him out there? I thought he'd be done by now."

"After filming wrapped, he started talking to a tall older man with white hair. I'm not sure who he is, but he'd been hanging out on set for the last couple of hours." Since the cat had settled onto my lap, I picked up her pink rhinestone harness and tried to fit it around her, while she resisted by going totally limp.

Meanwhile, Phoenix got up and moved a few things from the mini fridge to a small cooler as he asked, "If you two aren't busy, want to grab dinner?"

"We have plans, but you should join us," Gabriel said, as he scratched Madame Leota's ear and the cat leaned into it. "Two of my friends are amazing artists, and they want to teach a class for kids at an art center run by another friend of ours. They're not sure if their kinetic sculptures are actually buildable in a two-hour time-frame though, so a few of us are going to be their test subjects while they do a run-through of the class. In return, they're buying us pizza, and it's definitely a 'more the merrier' type of event."

Phoenix hesitated before asking, "Are you sure they wouldn't mind one more?"

Gabriel pulled his phone from the pocket of his cardigan and said, "I'm sure, but I'll ask anyway so you don't have to worry." He typed a message and sent it, and his phone beeped less than a minute later. After he glanced at the screen, he told Phoenix, "This is from Christian, my friend who founded and runs the community art center where we're going. He says there are twenty building kits, about ten people are coming, and he's ordering enough pizza to feed a small country. He also wrote 'so please bring your friends'. That means you, Phoenix."

"Okay, I'll come. It sounds fun," Phoenix said.

Will and Lorenzo joined us a few minutes later. Will looked a bit dazed as he dropped onto the bench seat beside the table, and I asked, "Are you okay?"

"I'm great, actually," he said. "The most amazing thing happened. I was just telling you this morning about my awful meeting with the author of *Alex and After*. Well, guess who came to the set this afternoon?"

Gabriel asked, "Is that the man who pulled you aside after you finished filming?"

"Yeah, that was him. He was here because he was concerned about the scenes the screenwriter added. Well, he ended up loving them, and me." Will shook his head in disbelief. "He told me he'd been wrong, and that I was actually perfect as Alex. I feel like I just won an Oscar."

Lorenzo sat beside him and took his fiancé's hand. "I'm glad he finally came to his senses, but everyone else has always known you're absolutely brilliant in this role."

"Thanks for saying that. It was important to me to have the author's approval though, because I think I know what Alex meant to him. I also think it's going to be a little easier to say goodbye to this character now, because I feel like I did him justice."

As we all got ready to leave, we invited Will and Lorenzo to join us at the art center. "Thanks for the offer, but we're going on a date tonight," Will said. "It's our last weekend in San Francisco. I still can't believe it's almost over."

"Well, the filming anyway," Phoenix said. "You're going to be spending all kinds of time promoting the film over the next year and a half or so, especially once it hits the theaters. In the process, Will Kandinsky is going to become a household name."

Will murmured, "That's weird to think about."

"My advice to you? Enjoy your anonymity while you can," Phoenix told him. "Pretty soon, you'll have paparazzi following you down the street and fans asking for photos and autographs, no matter what you're doing. Nice quiet evenings out are going to become a rarity."

"Do you really think I'm going to become that famous?" Will looked skeptical.

"This role is a career maker. I fully expect you to be nominated for every award there is after *Alex and After* is released, and that's going to throw the spotlight on you in a big way," Phoenix said as he picked up the cat and held the door open, then followed us outside and locked up behind us. Meanwhile, Lorenzo and Will exchanged worried looks, as if they were just beginning to grasp how completely their lives were about to change.

On our way to the SUV, we were intercepted by Harper, who said, "Hey, guys. Anybody want to grab some dinner?"

Phoenix's brow instantly creased into a frown, but I chose to ignore that as I told Harper about our plans and invited him along. It surprised me when he actually agreed to join us, but then he probably didn't know a lot of people in San Francisco. He asked, "One thing though, do they allow pets in the art center? I'm trying to stay on my new pet sitter's good side, and she's supposed to be off at six."

Phoenix said, "If you're talking about a chicken, I doubt they'll want a farm animal running around crapping all over the place and getting in the art supplies."

"Okay first of all, she's litter box trained," Harper informed him. "Second, I'll keep her in her stroller so she doesn't get into trouble."

Phoenix stared at him like he was out of his mind, but Gabriel said, "Let me ask if they're okay with pets in the art center." He sent a text, and by the time we reached the SUV he had a reply. "It's not a problem. The building is closed to the public tonight, and the art center's founder says he's looking forward to meeting the chicken."

"Okay, great." Harper took his phone from the pocket of his light blue button-down shirt and sent a text as he said, "I'll have Loco meet us there. What's the address?"

Gabriel looked it up for him as Phoenix said, "If you're trying to stay on your new pet sitter's good side, shouldn't you go get the chicken instead of making her drive it across town? Also, did you really name your pet 'crazy'?"

"The chicken's full name is El Pollo Loco," Harper explained. "And the pet sitter just needs to put Loco in an Uber. I'll do the rest."

Phoenix raised a brow and said, "So, you named your pet after a fast food chain that serves chicken. That's great. Don't even get me started on the Uber."

"Don't judge me." Harper sent his text, then turned to the rest of us and asked, "Can we all fit in here, or should I take my car?"

"We'll fit," Will assured him. "It'll be cozy at first, but Lorenzo and I are getting dropped off in just a few minutes. After that, there'll be plenty of room."

We all wedged ourselves into the SUV, and Gabriel ended up sitting on my lap with his arms around my shoulders. I loved the fact that he was happy. It radiated from him and shone in his dark eyes. When I touched his cheek, he focused that sparkling gaze on me and smiled, and it felt like my heart tripped over itself.

After Phoenix dropped off Will and Lorenzo, Harper slid over and made room for Gabriel, who climbed off my lap but kept leaning against me and holding my hand. To make conversation, I asked Harper, "Do you always travel with your pet chicken?"

"I have to if I'm going to be gone longer than a couple of days," he said. "She gets lonely without me, even though there are lots of animals at my house and plenty of people to take care of them. She even has a bunch of chicken friends, but Loco just wants her daddy."

Phoenix frowned at him in the rearview mirror and said, "Yeah, that's normal, calling yourself a chicken daddy."

Harper shot him a look in the mirror. "Don't chicken-shame me."

I asked, "What made you want a pet chicken?"

"I happened to be in a feed store that had baby chicks, and I fell in love with Loco, who was the saddest, tiniest little chick of all. I took her home and hand-raised her. After a while, I thought she might be lonely for her own kind, so I got several more chickens." He took out his phone and started showing us photos like a proud Dad. The first was a scrawny white chicken that honestly didn't look like much, and he said, "This is my Loco girl." Then he started flipping through more photos as he rattled off names. "This one's Chickira, and that's Meryl Cheep. And here's Attila the Hen. She's better than any guard dog, let me tell you. And these two are Pox and Noodle."

Phoenix muttered, "If I agree to go back to work for you, I'm writing a 'no chicken-sitting' clause into my contract."

Harper perked and asked, "So you're actually considering taking the job?"

"I said 'if'," Phoenix muttered. "There's still time for me to come to my senses."

Eventually, we pulled up in front of a huge, blocky building with a mural on the front of it, depicting kids on a playground. A sign told us it was The Zane Center for Art and Music. I stood on the sidewalk and looked up at the exceptionally well done mural as I asked Gabriel, "You said a friend of yours founded this place?"

"Yeah, my friend Christian."

"I'm still astounded by how incredibly rich some of your friends are."

"Christian happens to have a famous dad, but he's totally down to earth. He's using his money to run this place, which offers free art and music lessons to kids, adults, and seniors who couldn't afford them otherwise."

In other words, this guy was both rich and a saint. It was pretty tough not to develop an inferiority complex around Gabriel's social circle.

It was also impossible not to like Christian the moment I met him. He had a wide, friendly smile, and he was dressed in worn-out Levi's, flip flops, and a paint-stained, faded Rage Against the Machine T-shirt, not exactly what I'd expect from a silver-spoon type. He grabbed Gabriel in a hug and told him, "It's been too long!" His light brown curls were pulled back in a short, messy ponytail, and the sides of his head were shaved. I couldn't help but notice a thick scar above one ear.

He hugged me when we were introduced. Phoenix and Harper got hugs too, and Christian told the actor, "Dude, you're awesome. I loved that Robin Hood remake you were in last year, and normally I hate shit like that."

Harper chuckled and said, "Yeah, me too. I literally took the job just because I wanted to learn archery from the best in the business and get super good at it." Phoenix was standing behind him, and he rolled his eyes so hard, I thought he might tip backwards.

Christian led the way into an open and airy central workspace with high ceilings and bold artwork on the walls. When he introduced us to his tall, handsome husband Shea, I almost told him he looked exactly like the actor who played Captain America, but I was pretty sure he heard that all the time.

Three people were playing guitars on a stage at the far end of the huge room, and we were soon joined by two more men who both had dark hair and slight builds. Gabriel yelled with excitement and grabbed the younger man in a hug. Then he said, "Zachary, this is Riley. I'm so happy the two of you finally have a chance to meet!"

Zachary studied me carefully as we shook hands, and he said, "What an absolute miracle that you two found each other again." He seemed friendly but cautious, and I got the impression his big, brown eyes didn't miss much. When I was introduced to his husband TJ, he came across exactly the same way.

Suddenly, an absolutely mind-blowing electric guitar solo rang out from the stage and I turned to see who was playing. I squinted at the man with long brown hair and a beard and blurted, "Holy shit, is that Zan Tillane?" Zachary nodded, and I asked, "What's he doing here?" The man was a huge star and an absolute legend, and had been for at least three decades. He also happened to be one of my favorite singers of all time.

"My dad and his husband Gianni flew in to spend the weekend with my son," Christian said, with a lopsided smile.

Before I could ask a million more questions, Gabriel blurted, "Wait. Your son? When did that happen?"

Christian glanced over his shoulder at the trio on the stage, and I followed his gaze. In addition to Zan and a man with dark hair who must be Gianni, there was also a skinny little boy of maybe eight or nine, who was perched on a stool with a kid-sized guitar. It seemed like he was struggling to follow Zan's instructions, and after a few moments the boy jumped up and exclaimed, "I'm terrible at this! I give up!"

As Zan knelt down and patiently talked to the boy, Christian said, "Shea and I had been talking about opening our home to a foster kid for a long time, and we finally decided to take the plunge. A few weeks ago, Cooper came into our lives and stole our hearts. We knew right away that he belonged with us, so we started the adoption process. There's a long road ahead and a lot of hurdles to jump through, but we got the best lawyers we could find, and they're doing everything they can to make sure we get to be a family." There was a lot of emotion in his green eyes as he watched his dad and son.

While we were talking, Harper crossed the room and introduced himself to Zan and Gianni, then the little boy. Cooper seemed excited as he shook his hand, and we heard him exclaim, "I've seen you on TV!"

"Cooper has no idea how famous my dad is," Christian said, as we sat down at a long table and watched the group onstage. "It's pretty funny. When he told Cooper he's a singer, the kid asked if he'd ever performed with Billie Eilish. Zan asked who that was, so Cooper told him there was no way he was famous if he didn't know that. Now my dad feels like a dinosaur and is spending all his time listening to current pop music. He's actually become a big Demi Lovato fan."

Harper took a seat behind a drum kit on the stage, and Cooper joined him. The two of them worked in tandem and started banging out a decent rhythm. Zan joined in on the guitar while Gianni accompanied them with a tambourine, and soon the four of them were improvising a pretty great rock melody.

Harper kept joking with the kid while they teamed up on the drums, and Cooper howled with laughter as Phoenix muttered, "He can be so fucking charming."

I turned to him and said, "You say that like it's a bad thing."

"It is in Harper's case. All he has to do is dazzle people with his dimples and that huge personality, and he gets anything he wants."

A few minutes later, Shea came into the room carrying a big stack of pizzas, and Christian hurried over to help him. Shea called, "Is anyone expecting an Uber? There's one waiting out front."

Harper jumped up and said, "That's for me. Coop, want to come help me with my pet chicken?"

The little boy squealed with delight and raced Harper across the room. On the way by, the kid yelled, "Guess what, Christian and Shea? Harper has a pet chicken! Also, I want to be a drummer, not a guitarist."

They disappeared into the lobby, and Christian said quietly, "Maybe someday he'll want to call us Dad. But he's not there yet, and we respect that."

Gabriel asked, "Are his biological parents totally out of the picture?"

"Yeah, they are. Cooper's been in foster care since he was two," Shea told us. "It broke our hearts when we found out how many different foster homes he'd lived in over the last seven years."

"But that's all behind him now," Christian said, as he took Shea's hand. His husband nodded and kissed Christian's forehead.

A minute later, Cooper rushed into the room with a skinny white chicken in his arms and exclaimed, "Look, it's a real live chicken! Her name is Loco and she's really fluffy! Can we get a pet chicken? Please?"

The two men exchanged alarmed glances, and then Shea said, "We'll think about it. For now, let's put the chicken down and go wash your hands. We're about to eat."

The little boy, who had unruly light brown hair, big brown eyes, and a face full of freckles, wrinkled his nose and said, "I'm not hungry. I just want to play with the chicken."

"It's pizza, your favorite," Shea coaxed, "and you can play with the chicken after you eat." The kid didn't look convinced.

Harper joined us with what looked like a huge diaper bag over one shoulder, and he was pushing a weird combination stroller-birdcage. He told Cooper, "If you want, I'll let you give Loco a special treat. But only after you wash your hands and eat some dinner."

Cooper considered that for a few moments, then thrust the chicken at Harper and said, "Okay." He ran off in the direction of the restrooms while Harper kissed the chicken on the top of her head, then put her in the stroller. I tilted my head and took a closer look at the chicken. It seemed as if each eye was looking in a slightly different direction.

As we gathered around the table, I was introduced to Zan and his husband Gianni Dombruso. I was so starstruck that I stammered something like, "Oh my God, it's such an honor Mr. Tillane. I can't believe it's really you."

Zan's eyes crinkled at the corners as he shook my hand and said, with his distinctive English accent, "It's always nice to meet a fan." When he was introduced to Phoenix, he exclaimed, "I've met who I can only assume is your twin brother, Dallas Jaymes! He's a hell of a guy."

I could tell Phoenix was making a real effort not to frown as he muttered, "Yeah, he's awesome."

We all filled our plates, then took our seats around the long table. Cooper insisted on sitting next to the chicken, and after he ate half a slice of pizza, he insisted he was full and shifted impatiently from one foot to the other until his dads told him he could go and play. Harper opened the door to the birdcage stroller, and as promised he produced an oat and strawberry granola bar so Cooper could feed the chicken. Loco pecked at it for a few seconds, then half-flew, half-tumbled to the floor and took off running with Cooper right behind her.

When the kid was out of earshot, Christian turned to Shea and said, "Shit. We're going to end up buying him a pet chicken."

His husband sighed and said, "We totally are. It's impossible to resist those big brown eyes."

After we ate and cleared the table, Zachary and TJ brought out a pile of small boxes. On the top of each was a photo of a tiny metal rabbit. While I opened my box and started to fiddle with the pieces, Gabriel pulled up a video on his phone and showed me the screen as he said, "Here's the type of thing Zachary and TJ make out of recycled bits and pieces."

The video was of an incredibly intricate metal dragon that was maybe five inches long. Its motion was surprisingly lifelike as it stomped across a tabletop, slowly swinging its head from side to side like it was scanning the area. When I turned the screen toward Harper, he exclaimed, "Woah, that's super cool!"

"We obviously tried to simplify our design as much as possible so kids could do it," Zachary explained. "And we already know this'll have to be for ages twelve and up with these small parts, but even then we're worried it might be too frustrating."

They walked us through the building process for the next hour or so. At the end of that time, all of us had a tiny rabbit sculpture except for Harper. He chewed his lower lip and fumbled with the pieces, until Phoenix finally sighed and said, "Let me help you."

Harper dumped the parts into Phoenix's outstretched hand, and not three minutes later, Phoenix handed back a completed rabbit. "This is why you need to come back to work for me," Harper said, as he unleashed the full force of his perfect, dimpled smile and cranked up the charm. "You know I'm totally lost without you." Phoenix was probably the only person on the planet who was immune to Harper's appeal, and he just shot him a look that said, *oh please.*

"Okay, it looks like everybody's done," TJ said. "Now here's the test to see if they went together properly." He pushed down on one of the tiny rabbit figurines, and when he let go, it took three hops forward.

All of ours worked, including Harper's, and his face lit up in absolute delight. "That's awesome," he said. "Do you sell the stuff you make?"

Zachary told him they did and recited the name of their website. Christian got up to make some coffee while Harper and I both pulled out our phones to take a look at their work. A few moments later, Harper grabbed his wallet, dumped out a small avalanche of credit cards, receipts, and business cards, and fished through them until he found a platinum Visa.

By the time Christian and Shea served a platter of cookies and the coffee five minutes later, Harper had finished placing an order. "Thank you for that," Zachary said. "Which piece did you get?"

Harper stuffed the cards and receipts back in his wallet and flashed the couple a smile. "All of them."

TJ blinked and asked, "Um, did you look at the prices?"

"Yeah, and you guys should really think about charging more, because your art is super cool. I'm definitely going to check back when you put some more pieces online." Harper reached for the cookies and piled three on a paper plate while I did the math. The couple's original kinetic sculptures sold for three or four hundred dollars apiece, which meant Harper had just spent about four grand without batting an eye.

Cooper ran into the room, as if magically drawn by the presence of cookies. The chicken was right behind him, and she was now wearing a little rainbow-colored tutu. Shea asked, "Where'd you find the chicken skirt?"

"It's from a doll in the daycare room. Can Loco keep it? Look how perfect it fits her," Cooper said. Meanwhile, Loco ran across the room, bumped into the stage, switched direction like a Roomba, and kept going.

"Sure. She can definitely have the tutu," Christian said. A moment later, the chicken dashed into a supply room, and Cooper ran after her. "Oh yeah, we're definitely going to end up with a pet chicken," Christian muttered. "He just chose her over cookies."

We all gravitated across the room to watch when Zan picked up an acoustic guitar and started playing. His husband sat down right beside him on the edge of the stage, and Gianni rested his head on

Zan's shoulder while the rest of us sat on a mismatched collection of chairs.

A moment later, there was a small crash, and the chicken ran out of the supply room sporting a brightly colored comet trail of crepe paper streamers. Harper started to get up, but Gabriel grinned and said, "I've got it. I've been wanting some chicken time."

I couldn't help but smile as I watched Gabriel and Cooper running around and laughing as the chicken dodged them. After a minute, a voice beside me said, "You're crazy about him, aren't you?"

I turned to Zachary, who'd taken a seat beside me, and said, "He's absolutely everything to me."

"After just two weeks?"

"After about five years. That first year, he was my port in the storm, my best friend, and the only reason I could find to keep going most days. Then for the last four years, he was the person I thought about every day, longed for, and never gave up on. Two weeks ago, he became my miracle."

Zachary seemed surprised. "You really put it all out there, don't you?"

"Not with everyone. But I know you mean the world to him, so I want to be totally up front with you."

His dark eyes studied me for a few moments, and then he admitted, "I really didn't know what to expect from you. You're different than the type of man he usually dates, and I was surprised when he told me you'd gotten together. You seem like a good guy though, so I hope it works out for you."

"What's his usual type, someone like Roger?"

Zachary shrugged. "I guess so. He usually goes for older men. He's drawn to caretakers, but then…"

He stopped talking, probably because he was afraid of saying too much, so I finished for him. "But then he resents it when they actually take care of him."

"Basically."

I asked, "If you had one piece of advice for me, what would it be?"

"Never betray his trust. That's everything to Gabriel," he said. "I suppose that's true for everyone, but him especially."

"I think that's a side effect of battling addiction and coming out the other side. Trust means more to us than most people. I really believe that. Maybe it's because we've had to learn to trust ourselves, so we realize how absolutely vital it is."

"You may be right." After a pause, he said, "I don't know how much Gabriel told you about me, but my husband and I are both former addicts. That means TJ understands me in a way few people can. I think the fact that you and Gabriel have a similar history is a good thing, because you can support each other the same way we do."

"Thanks, Zachary."

"Why are you thanking me?"

"Two reasons," I said. "First, for giving me a chance, instead of immediately writing me off as some dumb kid who's not good enough for your friend. Second and most importantly, thanks for being such a wonderful friend to Gabriel. I was so worried about him the last four years, but now I know he had you in his life, and that means a lot."

Zachary tried to downplay it by saying, "I did what any friend would do."

"Yeah, you know, most people don't buy their friends cars to make sure they're not too isolated during their recovery. It takes a special person to go above and beyond like that."

He grinned a little, even though he was clearly embarrassed by my praise. Then he tilted his head in the direction Gabriel, Cooper, and the chicken had run off in and changed the subject with, "Why don't you go see what your man is doing? I have a feeling you're missing something cute right now."

He was right. I left the main part of the building and found Gabriel at the end of a long hallway. He had the sweetest smile on his face as he leaned against a doorframe and watched Cooper, who was in a cozy little reading nook in the far corner of a classroom. The little boy sat on a beanbag with one arm around Loco, reading her a children's book. It really seemed like the chicken was paying attention and looking at the pictures on the page.

Gabriel whispered, "Isn't that the cutest thing you've ever seen?" I kissed his shoulder, and when he leaned against me, I wrapped my arms around him. Then he asked, just as quietly, "Do you ever think about becoming a dad?"

"It's something I can imagine in the distant future, maybe in ten years, but I'm definitely not ready now. What about you?"

"Same. I love kids, but it's something to consider way down the road, not now."

I nuzzled his hair and said, "You know, your friends are pretty amazing."

"They are. It's astonishing how much they've accomplished. Just look at Christian and Shea with this art center. They're really making a difference in people's lives."

"I noticed Christian's scar. Is he okay?"

"He is now," Gabriel said. "He had a brain tumor that almost killed him, but after a successful operation he's been doing great. He actually founded the art center because he thought he was going to die, so this place was meant to be his legacy. Now it's his life's work, that and painting."

Christian joined us a couple of minutes later and smiled when he saw Cooper reading to the chicken. He snapped a photo on his phone and said, "Shea needs to see this," then sent his husband the picture.

"Cooper's a special little kid," Gabriel said.

"He really is." There was so much love in Christian's eyes when he said that. "He was dealt a truly shitty hand in life, but he's so strong and resilient. He just has this unshakable optimism, and he finds joy in whatever he's doing. I think I learn as much from him as he learns from me."

"Well, life certainly dealt him a great new hand when he found you and Shea. You're both amazing dads," Gabriel said.

"Thanks. I know we don't always get everything right, but we're trying our best."

Gabriel asked, "Do you think being a dad has changed you?"

"Yeah, in some ways. A tangible change is that I paint my murals on big canvases now, instead of on buildings that don't belong to me. Before, getting arrested only affected me, but now it could jeopardize the adoption and Cooper's entire future." Christian grinned and added, "I probably should have outgrown the graffiti outlaw thing by now anyway, even if Cooper hadn't come into our lives."

I asked, "What does Shea do for a living?"

Christian immediately took out his phone again and beamed with pride as he pulled up a photo. "He's a brilliant comic book artist. Check it out, this is the gay superhero series he's been publishing for the last six months. It totally sold out its first and second runs. We're thinking about going to Comic Con in San Diego next year to promote it. Cooper says if we do that we need to plan a family costume, and his top choice is to go as a trio of Ewoks. God help me."

I took a look at the photo of a professional-looking comic book cover and said, "Okay, it's official. All of Gabriel's friends are the coolest people ever."

Christian smiled at me as he returned the phone to his pocket. "Make sure you tell Cooper that. He thinks Shea and I are dorks."

I said, "He'll be right if you wear those Ewok costumes," which made him laugh.

When we turned back to Cooper, his eyelids were heavy, and he kept listing toward the book. Apparently all that chicken chasing had worn him out. Christian went into the classroom and said, "It's about time to head home, buddy."

The kid immediately got teary-eyed and exclaimed, "No! I want to stay with Loco!"

Christian gently set the book aside and picked up the boy, who was hugging the chicken. "How about asking our new friend Harper if we can visit Loco again sometime?"

"Tomorrow!"

"Okay. Let's go see."

As we followed them back to the main part of the building,

Cooper started to nod off, but before he did, he muttered, "Dad, can we get a pet chicken?" He fell asleep a moment later.

When we reached Shea, his brow creased with concern as he asked his husband, "Is everything okay?"

That was when I noticed Christian's eyes had filled with tears. "He just called me Dad," he whispered, "right before he fell asleep. I didn't realize just how much I wanted to hear that until he finally said it. I'm sure he'll revert back to my name tomorrow when he's wide awake, but that felt amazing." I barely knew these guys, but I was overjoyed for them.

Over the next few minutes, everyone packed up the leftovers and did a quick clean-up while Christian and Harper exchanged numbers and set up a playdate for the chicken. Then we headed out as a group, being careful not to wake the sleeping kid. Thank yous and goodbyes were exchanged as Shea locked the main door behind us. Then Christian and his family headed out in a black SUV, and Phoenix offered to drive Harper, the chicken, all of the chicken's belongings back to Harper's car. I thought it was a good sign that Phoenix was willing to offer that olive branch.

Meanwhile, Gabriel and I squeezed into the backseat of TJ's vintage Mini Cooper. As we pulled away from the curb, Zachary turned around in the passenger seat and asked, "Did you guys remember your rabbits?"

I'd actually forgotten about them, but Gabriel pulled two from the pocket of his cardigan. I recognized mine because the ears were wonky and leaning to the left. He asked his friends, "What do you guys think, is the class a go?"

"Definitely, with some minor modifications," TJ said. "We're going to try to source slightly bigger parts and assemble some of each kit ahead of time, to make it easier for the kids."

Gabriel said, "I think it's great that you decided to teach kids how to make your artwork."

"We're so lucky to be able to make a living doing something we both love," Zachary said, as he rested his hand on TJ's thigh. "Call it karma or whatever you want, but it just feels right to give something back after being given so much."

After we reached the apartment building, we said goodnight and pried ourselves out of that tiny backseat, then walked into the building hand-in-hand. "I love your friends," I said.

"Me too."

"Also, I met Zan Tillane tonight! I still can't believe it."

Gabriel said, "If I'd known you were such a fan, I would have introduced you sooner. He and his husband live on Catalina, and they spend a lot of time at the resort."

"Is that just a weird coincidence?"

"No. Gianni's brother Dante is an investor in Seahorse Ranch, and once or twice a year he reserves the whole property and brings a big group of friends and family from San Francisco. That's how Zan and Gianni and a couple of my friends ended up falling in love with Catalina. My friends got jobs at the resort, and then they invited me to come down and apply when some positions opened up."

"Good thing you got that job, so I could find you in the most unlikely place imaginable."

He grinned at me as we boarded the elevator, and when we reached the apartment he unlocked the door and said, "It's still early. Do you feel like a movie night?"

"Definitely. I just want a quick shower first."

"I'll make us some snacks while you do that."

After I got cleaned up, I put on a white tank top and a pair of gym shorts and followed the smell of fresh popcorn to the den at the other end of the apartment. It was a fairly small, cozy room with dark blue walls, floor-to-ceiling overstuffed bookshelves, a huge TV, and a big, comfortable couch...although by fairly small, I meant it was basically the size of my entire studio apartment.

When I reached the doorway, I whispered, "Good lord."

Gabriel had changed into a wine-colored cropped camisole and matching boy shorts, which hugged his body. His back was to me, and he was bending over to read the labels on some Blu-ray discs on a lower shelf. I immediately started to get hard, and I came up behind him and ran a hand over his hip. He responded by leaning back and pressing his ass against me, while he shot me a flirty smile over his shoulder.

If our relationship was ever going to turn sexual, now was the time. All the kissing and cuddling was great, but I knew we both wanted more. I really felt like the longer we waited, the tougher it would be to get to that next level. So, when he straightened up and turned to face me, I finally stopped overthinking and pulled him into my arms.

I claimed his mouth with a demanding kiss, and he moaned against my lips. Then I swung him around and pressed his back to the wall. He laced his fingers with mine, and I pinned his hands over his head, which drew another soft moan from him.

Being the one in charge felt backwards in a way, but it also felt good, because I could clearly see it gave him pleasure. That was what spurred me on. As soon as I began to think of taking control as a way to please Gabriel and make him feel good, it all fell into place.

The way his body responded was incredibly gratifying. I leaned back just far enough to meet his gaze and said, "Tell me what you want."

He arched against me, breathing fast as he whispered, "Please let me suck your cock."

"Get on your knees, Angel." He complied immediately, then began rubbing his cheek against the front of my shorts as he looked up at me. His hard-on strained against his underwear, showing me I was definitely on the right track.

I stepped back and took off my clothes as he held my gaze, his chest rising and falling in time to his quick, shallow breaths. Because I understood what being made to wait did to a submissive, I took my time and began stroking my cock as I watched him. I was putting on a show more than anything, and it worked perfectly to build his anticipation. A little whimper slipped from him, and he whispered, "Please."

It was empowering to realize I could give him exactly what he needed. After that epiphany, there was no more self-doubt. I could do this.

When I moved closer, he opened his mouth in eager anticipation. I said, "Not until I give you permission," and then I ran the tip of my cock over his lower lip. Another little whimper slipped from him as he held my gaze. A pink flush warmed his skin while his hard-on strained against his underwear, showing me just how much he was enjoying this.

Finally, I said, "Okay, go ahead." He grasped my hips with shaking hands and dove onto my cock, sliding his lips from the base to the tip, then sucking me as if his life depended on it.

The sensations he sent through me were so intense that I had to reach out and brace myself against the wall. Within minutes, I muttered, "I'm going to come, Angel." Next time, I'd try to make it last. Not today though, not after all those days and nights spent aching for him.

Instead of backing off, he just sucked me harder and faster. I cradled the back of his head with one hand while I lightly fucked his mouth, until his moan of pleasure pushed me over the edge. I came hard, yelling as I shot down his throat, and he kept sucking me until I was completely spent.

I was shaking and lightheaded when he finally let my cock slip from his mouth. I had to press both hands against the wall to hold myself up, and Gabriel gently nuzzled my thigh while he waited for me to catch my breath. Finally, I stepped back and grinned as I said, "Your turn."

I moved to the dark blue sofa on weak legs and sat down. Then I looked around and opened a drawer in the end table. There was a tube of hand cream in there, and I grinned and murmured, "That'll work." I patted my thigh and told him, "Take off your clothes and come sit on my lap."

He stripped himself quickly with hands that were still shaking, while I squirted some cream into my palm. Then he crawled to me and did as I asked. I cradled him as I began jerking him off, and he looked up at me with so much trust in his eyes.

I brought him right to the brink of orgasm three times, then eased him back down. That made him writhe and whimper and beg for release as his cock throbbed in my hand. When I finally said, "Okay Angel, come for me," a jagged yell tore from him and he shot all over his stomach and chest. That massive orgasm went on and on until he was left shivering, sweat-drenched, and totally exhausted.

I scooped up my tank top with my foot and used the shirt to wipe the cum from his body. Then I pulled a soft gray blanket from the back of the couch and wrapped him up in it. His soft little, "Thank you," made him seem so vulnerable, and I was overwhelmed by the urge to protect him.

I stroked his hair as he slowly came back to himself. Eventually he said, "That was totally unexpected."

"Which part?"

"All of it." He wrapped his arms around me and said, "A week ago, it seemed like you were struggling with taking charge."

"I was."

He asked, "How could you come so far in such a short time?"

"Tonight, it finally dawned on me that I can give you what you need and be true to myself at the same time. I guess it was just a question of changing my perspective." I kissed the top of his head, then shifted a bit before continuing, "I'm a pleaser, right down to my core. I'll do whatever it takes to make my partner feel good, and that makes me feel wonderful in return. Being in control doesn't come naturally, but pleasing you does. As soon as I shifted my perspective to look at it that way, taking charge become the easiest thing in the world."

"That was quite the revelation."

He snuggled closer, and after a pause I said, "There's something else I've been worried about, and I've been afraid to bring it up in case it proved to be a deal-breaker."

"What's worrying you?"

I just had to put it all out there. "Is the fact that we're both bottoms going to be an issue?"

"It really doesn't have to be." A grin spread across his face, and he said, "We just proved we can absolutely satisfy each other. Now imagine what two creative bottoms could do with a great, big pile of sex toys." I had to grin, too.

Chapter 8

Six days later, I stood on the balcony watching the sunset and thinking back over the past week. It had been perfection. Gabriel had come to work with me twice, we'd spent time with some of his friends, and we'd gone to see Emory's drag show, which was fantastic. But the best moments were when it was just the two of us, 'playing house' in this gorgeous apartment. I didn't know what else to call it. We'd been living like a married couple and had settled into a wonderful, comfortable routine, but that was about to change.

I really wished we hadn't made plans to go out, because this was our last night alone in the dream home. Tomorrow, the owners of the apartment were returning from the UK. While I was looking forward to meeting them, it was a little depressing too because I knew things wouldn't be the same with them here. We'd go from playing house to being guests in their home, and no matter how welcoming they were, I knew I'd feel like I was in the way.

One final evening alone here with Gabriel would have been heavenly. But it was Will and Lorenzo's last day in San Francisco, and they'd invited us to join them for a night on the town, along with some friends they'd made among the cast and crew. They meant a lot to us, and we didn't want to let them down.

When I got home from work, I took a shower and did the best I could to get dressed up for our night out. That meant a black button-down shirt, jeans, and my ever-present leather jacket. Everyone was meeting up at a restaurant in the Castro, then going out dancing. I knew Will would be dressed up because he always was, but I hoped everyone else kept it fairly casual.

Now I was just waiting on Gabriel, who was still getting ready. And my God, was it worth the wait. He joined me on the balcony a few minutes later dressed in his high heels, a pair of slim-fitting black pants, and a cropped black sweater, which showed off about three inches of skin and the little silver ring in his belly button. He'd also applied a perfect line of liquid eyeliner along his upper lashes and added a bit of mascara and red lipstick. I loved the fact that he was feeling confident enough to let his feminine side shine.

I murmured, "You look beautiful," as I drew him into my arms.

"Thank you. I should have let you do my makeup, though. It took me three tries to get this liner right."

"It's perfect, and so are you."

"Hardly." He kissed me, and then he grinned and ran his thumb over my lower lip to remove a smudge of lipstick. "Do you think our friends will notice if we sneak out early? I really want to enjoy our last night alone in this apartment."

"I was just thinking the same thing. They've invited a bunch of people, so we'll probably be able to slip out after dinner. Not that I wouldn't love to dance with you, but we can do that right here, in private."

"Exactly."

After a few moments, I ventured, "Have you thought about what we're going to do when we leave here? There are only three weeks left on my contract, and if they fly by as fast as the last three, we'll be heading back to Southern California before we know it."

"I want to be wherever you are," he said. "I know we could still date if you're in L.A. and I'm on Catalina, but after these last three weeks together, I'd really hate that much separation between us."

My heart started to race, but I tried to act casual as I asked, "Would you maybe want to move in with me?"

"I'd love to."

"Really? You don't want some time to think about it?"

"I've been thinking about it for days. I know I want to be wherever you are, and it's not like we just met, so living together just makes sense," he said. "There's no way we'll both fit in your studio apartment though, so we'll need to look for a one-bedroom when we get back to L.A."

"I don't know if I can afford a bigger apartment."

"I can. I have enough in savings for the deposit and the first couple of months' rent, and it should be pretty easy to find a job in a hotel now that I have some experience."

I asked, "Won't you miss Seahorse Ranch and your friends?"

"Definitely, and I want to visit them often. I'd rather be with you, though."

I met his gaze and said, "This sounds perfect, except for one thing. You need your savings for your lingerie company."

He shook his head. "That isn't going to happen."

"You don't know that." Even though Gabriel wouldn't like it, I wanted to tell him I'd met with Roger the week before, and that he'd promised to get back to me with some reliable contacts in the apparel manufacturing industry. But Roger had been evasive when I'd followed up with him, so I really didn't know where any of that stood. For now, I just left it at, "It's too soon to give up on your dreams."

"I'm not giving up. I still would absolutely love to sell my lingerie someday, but at this point in my life, it's just not realistic. I'd much rather use my money on a nice apartment for you and me, instead of throwing it away on a half-baked idea."

"But maybe there's another alternative. What if I apply for a job at the resort? If I get hired, it might come with room and board. Then you and I can live there together while we build our savings and work on getting your company off the ground."

Gabriel caressed my cheek and said, "There's no way I'm letting you trade your dream for mine. You're a brilliant makeup artist, Riley, and it's just a matter of time before you land the perfect job.

Just look at all the new followers you gained on social media after you posted the fantasy makeup photos."

That really had been a pleasant surprise. We'd done two more shoots over the last week, and my Instagram had pretty much exploded after I posted the photos. But I told him, "You're so much more important to me than any of that."

He kissed me again, then grinned and ran a fingertip over my lips. "You really are the sweetest boy in the world, and this discussion's not over. But Phoenix is going to be here any minute, so we should go downstairs."

We both went inside, and while I locked the door to the balcony, Gabriel picked up his phone from the coffee table and tapped the screen. Then he said, "Well, it looks like we won't have the apartment to ourselves after all. I got a message from Sawyer, and he and his husband will be getting home in a few hours. They spent the last two days in New York, but Alastair got a touch of food poisoning so they decided to cut their east coast visit short."

"Why would anyone choose to board a plane with food poisoning?"

"That'd be awful on a commercial flight, but they're on a private jet, so it's probably not so bad."

I muttered, "Good lord, they have their own plane?"

Gabriel shrugged and said, "Well, they travel all the time for business," as if that justified it somehow.

When he returned his phone to the table, I asked, "Aren't you bringing that?"

He flashed me a smile and said, "I must be losing my touch if you haven't noticed how tight these pants are. The phone will never fit in my pocket. In fact, it was all I could do to wedge my I.D., some cash, and the keys in there."

"Want me to carry it for you?"

"Nah. We have yours if we need to call someone."

When we got downstairs, Phoenix's dark blue Bronco was parked at the curb. As I climbed into the backseat, I grinned at my friend in the rearview mirror and told him, "You smell purdy."

He muttered, "That means I used too much cologne, right?"

"Nope, it's perfect. You look nice, too," I said. He'd exchanged his usual flannel shirt for a dark gray button-down, trimmed his beard, and made an effort to style his slightly overgrown hair. I just had to ask, because I couldn't help myself. "Are you hoping to capture the attention of your new employer?"

"Fuck no. It's bad enough that I agreed to go to work for Harper Royce. I'm sure as hell not trying to get in his pants."

"But since you said yes to being his assistant, that must mean you don't totally hate his guts."

"I said yes because he kept offering me more and more money until it became ridiculous for me to turn it down. Plus, it's just four months. I can tolerate just about anything that long, even babysitting a man-child and his goddamn chicken."

"Chickens," Gabriel corrected with a wicked grin as he settled into the passenger seat. "There are more at home."

As he pulled away from the curb, Phoenix muttered, "Fuck my life."

When we arrived at the hotel and I spotted Will and Lorenzo, I said, "Shit, I'm underdressed."

"No you're not," Phoenix insisted. "They're overdressed."

I nodded in agreement. "Okay, let's go with that."

Will and Lorenzo were both wearing perfectly tailored suits, Will's in pale gray and his partner's in charcoal. As they slid into the backseat, I said, "Well, damn. You two look like a million bucks."

"Will always looks like a million bucks," Lorenzo said. "That's why I had to up my game and get this new suit."

"Great investment," Gabriel said, as he pivoted in his seat to look at them. "You know, you could get married in a suit like that."

"Speaking of which," Lorenzo said with a big smile, "we've finally nailed down the date of our wedding, and it's in two months and two days. You'll all be receiving official invitations very soon."

"Yeah, like next week," Will said. "Is it tacky to just email every-one? We're not giving people a lot of advance notice, so we want to get on their calendars as soon as possible."

Phoenix asked, "Why'd you give yourselves such a short window?"

"We really want to get married at Seahorse Ranch, since that's where we met," Will said, as he flashed Lorenzo the sweetest smile.

"And we didn't want to do it on a weekend that's booked up with a lot of reservations, because we want our friends and family to be able to stay at the resort," Lorenzo continued.

"The weekend we chose was actually reserved by Beck and Ren's business partner Dante Dombruso and his family, but they only need half the rooms, and they were nice enough to let us book the other half," Will explained, as he took over the tag-team conversation. "Every other weekend from April to October is almost totally full, so it was a choice of pulling a wedding together in two months or waiting until the end of the year."

"And we really didn't want to wait," Lorenzo said. "We're actually planning to keep it pretty casual, so two months shouldn't be a problem."

"All we really need is our friends and family and a wedding officiant. After that, we can order pizza for all I care." Will and Lorenzo beamed at each other.

The wedding conversation continued as Phoenix drove us across town. When he turned onto Castro Street, the SUV immediately ground to a halt. As usual, San Francisco's gay neighborhood was bustling with activity. Traffic was backed up, and the sidewalks were crowded, including a long line at the Castro Theater's box office. I chuckled when I glanced at the marquee and saw they were doing a *Moana* singalong.

Phoenix muttered, "I really should've taken a side street," as we rolled forward about three feet, stopped, and then repeated the process. "I have no idea where I'm going to park, either, so I'm just going to drop y'all off in front of the restaurant and then hope for the best. Feel free to start without me, since I might be a while."

"No chance. Dinner can wait until you get there," Will said, as he squeezed Phoenix's shoulder. "Also, in case I haven't said it enough, thank you so much for driving us around the entire time we've been here. We really appreciate it."

Phoenix said, "I was happy to have something to do. I barely earned my keep as your assistant. You were just so normal and nondemanding. Not once did you phone me at two a.m. and send me on an errand because you had a craving for a gluten free cheese bagel."

I asked, "Did someone actually do that to you? If it was Harper, I'm so sorry about encouraging you to go back to work for him."

"It wasn't him, but that did happen. This was earlier in my career, before I realized I could say no to silly shit like that and set boundaries." The SUV rolled forward three feet and came to a stop again, and Phoenix swore under his breath.

A minute later, Gabriel glanced out the passenger window, then turned back toward it and exclaimed, "What the hell!"

We all followed his gaze, and when I spotted what had caught his eye, I whispered, "Oh no." A storefront's huge display window, which was probably eight feet high and six feet wide, was completely filled with a poster of Gabriel wearing lingerie.

I recognized it immediately as one of the first photos I'd taken the day of our Fallen Angel photo shoot. It was shot from the side and slightly behind him, and he was leaning on the balcony railing dressed in heels, high-cut black panties, sheer thigh-high stockings, and an equally sheer robe. The curve of his ass was on full display as the robe blew back in the breeze. Even though his face was turned away from the camera, he was perfectly recognizable to anyone familiar with the large tattoo of black lilies that ran from the side of his hip almost to his knee, since it was front and center in the photo.

Gabriel bolted from the car and ran to the shop. I caught up to him a few moments later, and he stammered, "What's this doing here? I don't understand." Then he moved closer to read the tagline across the bottom of the poster, which said: *Fallen Angel Lingerie—Coming This Summer*. He turned to me and asked, "What's going on, Riley?"

I blurted, "I didn't know he'd do this. I told him not to get carried away!"

"Told who?"

"Roger. I met with him last week to ask for some manufacturing contacts, and apparently he went totally off the deep end."

Gabriel stared at me in disbelief. "I told you not to involve him! So, you totally ignored that and went behind my back?"

"I was just trying to help."

His voice rose, catching the attention of people passing us on the sidewalk. "I was perfectly clear about not involving my ex-boyfriend! And you must have known it was wrong, since you didn't tell me about your meeting."

"I didn't know how to help you, and he did."

"That doesn't matter! I didn't sign off on any of this, including displaying that photo in the middle of Castro Street," he said. "It wasn't even one of the shots we posted on social media, because I decided that outfit was too trashy. How could you give it to Roger?"

"I didn't, I swear! I handed him my phone to show him the photo shoot, and he emailed some pictures to himself. He wanted some photos that clearly showed the outfits, so his contact in apparel manufacturing could see the types of products we wanted to produce."

He looked disgusted as he asked, "You let my ex download pictures of me in lingerie?"

"I know it sounds bad, but you and I had posted some of the photos, so I thought it was okay to show him."

"We posted *some* of them, the ones I signed off on. Not that one! Choosing to post certain images on social media and letting my ex have his pick are two very different things."

"You're right, and I'm so sorry. I made a mistake."

"It's not even about this photo, although that's really not okay," he said, much more quietly. "It's about the fact that you snuck around behind my back, did something I specifically asked you not to, and betrayed my trust. You get that, right?"

I'd expected him to be mad. It had seemed like a small price to pay for getting his business off the ground. But he wasn't just angry. He was hurt, and that was so much worse.

I'd sworn never to hurt him, and the moment I saw the pain in his eyes, I knew I'd failed. "I'm really sorry, Gabriel. I totally fucked up." Those words weren't enough. Not by a long shot.

"You were the only guy I'd ever been involved with that I

thought I could absolutely trust. The only one." He said that softly. Then he started walking away from me, heading out of the Castro.

I called, "Please wait," and started to run after him.

But he whirled on me with tears in his eyes and yelled, "No! I don't want you to follow me. Just leave me alone."

He took off running, his heels clicking against the pavement as Will came up to me and asked, "What's happening?"

"I fucked up. I hurt him, and I promised never to do that."

Will gestured toward the street with a worried expression. "Phoenix is tying up traffic. Why don't you come with me?"

I shook my head and tried to swallow the lump in my throat. "I can't. Not now. Go without me."

A horn blared in the street, and he gave me a quick hug and said, "I have to go, but I'll talk to you soon, okay? Call me if you need anything, and don't worry. I'm sure you two will work it out." A few more people started honking their horns to try to get Phoenix to move, and when I nodded, Will turned and ran back to the SUV.

It felt like my whole world had just ended.

I went back and stood in front of that huge poster, and then I pulled my phone from my jacket pocket and sent Roger a message, which said: *What the fuck did you do?*

He replied a moment later with: *You have to be more specific, mate. I do a lot of things.*

I felt like punching him in the face. *Why is there a fucking eight-foot-tall poster of Gabriel on Castro Street?*

Roger's next text said: *Blimey. You saw that already, did you? It's only been up about two hours.*

I ground my teeth and responded: *It's pretty fucking hard to miss. Gabriel saw it, too. I think he just broke up with me.*

He wrote: *Where are you now?*

I sighed and replied: *Right where he left me, in front of that goddamn poster.*

A moment later, the door to the shop opened and Roger joined me on the sidewalk. I'd never seen him in jeans and a sweatshirt before, and there was a streak of pink paint on his cheek. I said,

"Even though I know you can snap me like a twig, I really want to punch you right now."

He held his hands out to the sides and said, "Go ahead, mate. Free shot. Just not the face, yeah? I'm a bit of a bleeder, if I'm honest."

"I'm not going to hit you, but what the fuck, Roger? Remember me telling you not to go nuts? In case I was unclear," I waved my hands at the building and yelled, "this is what going nuts looks like!"

"But look at this fucking location, mate! It's prime real estate. You think shops on this block come available every day? Let me answer that for you. No, they bloody well do not."

"He didn't want this, Roger. Not the shop, the 'prime location', the fucking eight-foot poster, or any of it. He also didn't want your help, but I thought it'd be okay to go to you anyway and just get the names of a few contacts. That's it. Just some *names*. Not this!"

"Well, in for a penny, in for a pound as they say."

I asked, "What does that mean?"

"Gabriel needed my help, so I gave it to him. Did I do more than you asked? Yes. Did I get carried away? That's open to interpretation. But look at this place, Riley! We're in the very heart of gay America, and all these people? They're his target audience. It couldn't be more perfect."

I sighed and pushed back my hair with both hands. "I met with you ten days ago. Ten days! How the hell did you do this in such a short time?"

"I already had the storefront," he said. "Well, Sawyer did. He'd leased it the moment it came available, because he was thinking about putting a Sawyer MacNeil's here. But then one of the penny-pinching stiffs on his payroll convinced him this is too close to his flagship U.S. location, which is about three blocks from here. Bollocks if you ask me, not that anyone did. He'd make a bloody fortune in this location. Long story short, before Sawyer could put it back on the market I came along and offered to sublet it from him. All the paperwork became nice and final just this morning, so here we are, mate."

"Damn it, Roger, Gabriel specifically asked not to involve Sawyer and his husband!"

"And I haven't! I just told them I was investing in a business venture, that's it. I know Gabriel didn't want to feel like he was taking advantage of their friendship, so no worries there because they've not been bothered."

I muttered, "I can only imagine what it's costing you to sublet this place, and I hope you can get your money back."

"I signed a year's lease, but I'm not worried. As soon as Gabriel calms down, he'll be thanking both of us for what we've done for him."

"Don't you mean he'll be thanking you? Gabriel knows I'm broke," I said. "I couldn't afford a shop like this in a million years, so he's going to figure out pretty quickly that you're trying to buy his affection. Joke's on you though, because the last thing he wants is a sugar daddy."

Roger scowled at me and said, "This wasn't some elaborate scheme to undermine your relationship or get back in his good graces. I'm just not that cunning, mate."

"Aren't you? Because from where I'm standing, it looks a hell of a lot like you just pulled the rug out from under me."

His expression softened, and he said, "I know you're scared of losing Gabriel, so I'm not going to take offense at whatever you have to say right now. Look, take this." He grabbed my hand and pushed a set of keys into it. "When he calms down, bring him here and show him the shop. Give him a chance to fall in love with it. He's not going to stay angry forever."

"The thing is, he's not just angry. He's hurt, and there's absolutely no excuse for hurting him."

"I never meant to hurt him. You know that, right?"

"Neither did I, but it happened anyway."

He looked upset as he blurted, "But we were trying to do something good! We wanted to help him, and give him a company he could be proud of."

"But maybe he wanted to do it himself. Or maybe he didn't want to do it at all! When did he ever say he wanted a storefront in

San Francisco, or anywhere else for that matter? Let's face it, we both treated him like a child when we went behind his back and made decisions for him. He trusted me, and I betrayed that trust by meeting with you after he specifically told me not to. And I get it now. It's not just that he knew you'd totally get carried away, although," I waved my hands at the storefront.

Then I continued, "Whether we meant to or not, we just sent the message that we don't think he's a strong, capable adult who can do things for himself. What he needs more than anything—way more than a damn company—is to believe in himself and to know we believe in him, too. He's had such a long, hard road with his recovery, and the only way he can keep moving forward is by believing he's strong enough." I sighed and muttered, "Damn it, I really should have realized this sooner, and I never should have gone to you for help."

"But you meant well, mate. We both did." Roger was never going to get it. That was becoming perfectly clear. I just nodded and turned to stare at that gorgeous, totally inappropriate poster. After a few moments, he told me, "Like I said, bring him back and show him this place. I'm sure he'll forgive us both when he sees what we're trying to do here. Keep those keys, I have another set."

I murmured, "Yeah, okay," because I'd officially given up on trying to make Roger understand just how profoundly we'd fucked up.

"Alright then, I'm going to head out. Go in and take a look at the place, then be sure to lock up before you leave. I'd planned to spruce it up a bit and make it more his style before showing it to Gabriel. The previous owners were a bit stodgy." He started to leave, but then he turned back to me and said, "He'll forgive you and take you back. Don't worry, Riley."

"He broke up with you. Why wouldn't he do the same with me?"

"Because he loves you. He never once looked at me the way he looks at you, mate." It cost him something to admit that, and it made me feel sad for him.

He turned and walked away, and I watched him until he disappeared down the crowded sidewalk. Then I sighed and went into the shop.

It was open and airy with high ceilings. A few clothing racks, partially disassembled mannequins, and random items had been left behind by the former occupants. The wall to my left was mirrored, and on the opposite beige wall, Roger had painted no fewer than twenty swatches in various shades of pink. That made me feel bad for him all over again, because he was trying so hard to win over a man who'd never take him back.

I sat on the tan carpeting with my back against the mirrored wall and studied those paint swatches for a while. Gabriel didn't even particularly like the color pink. He'd probably prefer deep plum on that wall, or garnet. I found myself imagining the décor that would go with either of those colors, and then I muttered, "What the hell are you doing?"

I was as bad as Roger. I just wanted to fix everything for Gabriel, to take care of him and make him happy. That sounded okay on the surface. It was what people in love did all the time. But not like this, not by keeping secrets and going behind his back, and definitely not by making decisions for him. I should have listened when he told me not to contact Roger, instead of assuming I knew best.

Gabriel probably needed some time to himself after all of this, so instead of running back to the apartment and begging his forgiveness, I did what I thought was the mature thing. I sent him a text that said: *I'm truly sorry. I didn't realize just how wrong I was until tonight. Since you probably need some space right now, I'm going to leave you alone and come see you tomorrow, so we can talk this out. If you want to talk sooner, all you have to do is message me and I'll come running. I love you, Gabriel.*

After I hit send, I remembered he'd left his phone at the apartment. Even though I knew it would take him a while to get back there and see my message, I still refreshed my screen for the better part of an hour to see if he'd replied. I also reread my text message a bunch of times and thought of better ways to say all of that.

Damn it, why did I have to go behind his back and involve

Roger? And after I was dumb enough to do that, I should have confessed right away instead of letting him get blindsided. Not that I ever imagined he'd find out in such a completely overwhelming and in-your-face kind of way. What a shock it must have been to see himself on that poster! Not that there was a good way of finding out your boyfriend and your ex were keeping secrets and making decisions for you, but anything would have been better than that.

Right about then, it finally occurred to me that I really should take down the poster. Actually, I should have done that first thing, but I hadn't exactly been thinking clearly.

I got up and crossed the room to the huge plate glass window. The vinyl poster was fastened to a rolling bar that hung across the top of the window, and it was anchored below the sill with a black cord tied to a floor-mounted metal bracket. Nothing happened when I unfastened the cord. I wondered if it operated like a retractable shade, so I pulled down on the bottom of the poster. When I let go, it shot up so quickly that it made me jump. It worked, though. The poster was now coiled up and out of sight.

It startled me when I realized someone was standing on the other side of the window, looking in. I couldn't see much more than his outline, since it was lighter in the shop than it was outside. That meant I was mostly just seeing my own reflection in the glass.

It seemed kind of creepy that he kept standing there. He'd probably been admiring the sexy poster, but it was long gone and he hadn't budged.

I squinted to try to see him more clearly, which of course didn't help at all. All I could tell was that he was tall and broad-shouldered, and that his hair was blond because it was backlit by a streetlamp. Why did I feel like there was something familiar about him?

Curiosity made me take a step forward. He did the same thing, which put him under a light at the front of the building. His gaze locked with mine. A jolt of panic shot through me when I realized I was staring into the ice-blue eyes of Mason Simeck, the man who'd once called himself my Dom.

Chapter 9

We both made a move for the door at the same time, but before I could lock it, he pushed it open. Then he asked, "Riley? Is that you?" His voice was deep. Resonant. Familiar. I shook my head, but he answered his own question. "It is. I'd never forget those hazel eyes. The rest of you though, my God look at you. You're so different now."

He took a step toward me, and I took two stumbling steps back as the door swung shut behind him. He looked confused as he asked, "Are you afraid of me? You never were before."

That was true, actually. I probably should have been since he was a thug who carried a gun, but he'd never actually scared me back then. But in this situation, he was terrifying.

Even so, I squared my shoulders and tried to keep my voice level as I said, "Yeah, well, you never appeared out of nowhere and almost gave me a heart attack before."

"Apologies, it wasn't my intention to startle you. I saw Gabriel's poster, so I had my driver pull over. I wanted to ask the shopkeepers if they knew where to find him."

In an instant, rage replaced fear. I strode toward him and pushed him as hard as I could as I yelled, "Just stay the fuck away from him, or I swear to God I'll make you sorry you were ever born!"

Mason Simeck was six feet of solid muscle, and he barely moved when I shoved him. He held his hands up, palms facing me, as if that would calm me somehow. Then he said, "You really have changed. The old Riley never would have stood up to me like this."

"The 'old Riley' grew up, Simeck. And I meant what I said about leaving Gabriel alone."

"Yes, or you'll make me sorry I was born." He sounded amused as those piercing blue eyes held my gaze.

My hands curled into fists. "Want to find out if I'm bluffing?"

Simeck moved to the center of the shop, righted an overturned chair, and sat down on it. He was perfectly calm and contained. He wore an expensive tan overcoat and a three-piece suit, like he was a refined gentleman. I knew better.

As he rubbed his square jaw with a perfectly-manicured hand, he asked, "What exactly do you think I intended to do to him?"

"Nothing good."

"Actually, I just wanted to ask him some questions." His smile was as ice cold as his eyes. "You're certainly protective when it comes to that little whore."

I picked up something that turned out to be a mannequin's forearm and held it like a club as I hissed, "Go ahead and call him a whore again. I fucking dare you."

"Now, now, Riley, let's just calm down, shall we? I apologize for my choice of words, although the boy is actually a prostitute."

I glared at him and said, "Was, not is, and don't act like you're better than him. He might have been a sex worker, but you were the loser who had to pay boys to fuck them."

"I didn't have to pay you, did I?" His tone was teasing, which infuriated me.

"Of course you did. My payment came in the form of heroin and alcohol. I must have cost you a fucking fortune."

"I suppose that was a type of payment, and you were worth every penny, Riley." He got up so suddenly that it startled me, and I took a step back. "I've never found another boy like you in all these years. You were so fragile, so perfect, and when you finally broke, it was the most beautiful thing I've ever seen in my life. It's such a shame you're not that boy anymore."

I growled, "You sick fuck."

He started advancing slowly, and I backed up until I bumped into the mirrored wall. "That's a bit hypocritical don't you think, calling me sick? Sure, I got off on hurting you in every way imaginable, but don't pretend you didn't love it."

"Like hell I did." He tried to reach for me, but I slapped his hand away and snarled, "Don't you fucking touch me!"

When he tried to reach for me again, I held up my makeshift club like I was going to strike him with it and yelled, "What the fuck did I just say?"

"Go ahead and hit me if it'll make you feel better."

"It won't make me feel better, because I'm not a fucking sadist like you." I tried to put some bite into that.

"You're trying to say that like it's a dirty word, but it's exactly what I am. It's like calling a bear a bear and expecting it to be insulted. I'm definitely a sadist and you were my perfect, masochistic other half. Now you're acting like I'm some kind of monster, but you came to me willingly, we negotiated our arrangement, and you signed a contract. In it, you agreed to no limits and no safe words. You weren't a kid when you did that. You were over eighteen and able to give consent."

"Are you fucking kidding me?" I circled around him so my back wasn't to the wall anymore and lowered my improvised weapon as I asked, "Do you actually think a heroin addict was capable of giving consent?"

"You weren't high when you signed the contract."

"No, but I was craving my next fix. I needed it so bad that I was about to crawl out of my skin. I was also broke, so I had two choices —sell myself to you in exchange for drugs and let you torture me, or take my chances turning tricks on the street corner. I honestly have no idea why I found you less frightening than hopping in some stranger's car and potentially winding up in a shallow grave."

He said, with a total lack of irony, "Because you knew I'd never hurt you." A humorless laugh slipped from me. "I'm serious. Yes, I'd absolutely inflict pain during our sessions to get myself off, and you do raise a good point about dubious consent. But when you weren't naked in my dungeon, did I ever once raise a hand to you? Did I ever give you a reason to fear me?"

"No. But how the hell can you stand there and somehow justify keeping me so drugged that I barely knew up from down? You preyed on my addiction, Simeck."

"Yes, I probably did." I was surprised to hear him admit it. "I had little else to offer you and no other way to convince you to stay with me. But let's face it, you would have been using with or without me. Heroin was the center of your universe. That and Gabriel, which is why I kept buying him for you."

"Don't act like you were this saintly guy who kept hiring Gabriel for my benefit. I know you fucked him."

"Of course I did. He's a beautiful boy, and I enjoyed the hell out of him. But afterwards, I'd always let him go upstairs and spend the night with you, because I knew you needed him."

I rubbed my forehead to try to ward off the headache that was brewing and muttered, "I really hate how you keep trying to make yourself the good guy in every scenario."

"No, I'm definitely not trying to do that. I'm rotten through and through. I know this about myself, but I just—"

He stopped talking abruptly, so I asked, "What?"

Simeck shrugged. "I guess I want you to see me for who I really am, which, granted, is a pretty awful picture. But the picture you've painted of me seems to be a hundred times worse, so I can't help but argue my case, even if it's a giant waste of time."

A few seconds ticked by. Then I asked, "Why'd you come into this shop looking for Gabriel?"

"Because he was the only person who knew where you'd gone, and I wanted to find you. There was no other way to track you down. I didn't even know your last name, since the one you gave me was a lie. I figured whoever had made that advertisement would have a way of getting in touch with him, and that in turn would lead me to you. I obviously never expected to find you here in person. That was a shock."

I said, "I'm surprised you recognized him with his face covered."

"I knew it had to be him the moment I saw the photo, because I remember that tattoo and that tight little body vividly." His leering smile made me sick to my stomach.

"After I left, there was a night when your men tracked Gabriel down and tried to bring him to you." I held his gaze and asked, "If they'd succeeded and he refused to answer your questions, what would you have done? Would you have killed him?"

"Certainly not."

"But you definitely would have slapped him around, maybe even tortured him."

"I really wanted to know where you'd gone." That was a yes.

After a pause, I said, "Gabriel spent the last four years absolutely terrified of you. Obviously he was afraid you'd catch him and try to beat my location out of him, but I don't think that fully explains it. What did you do to make him that scared of you?"

Simeck crossed the room and sat back down in the chair while I watched him closely. He unbuttoned his suit jacket to get comfortable, then leaned back and said, "Gabriel was pretty savvy. He understood the nature of the agreement you and I had made, and he knew it was mutually beneficial. I know he asked you to leave repeatedly, but he didn't try to drag you out of my house, even though it must have broken his heart that you were letting yourself get tortured. I think he assumed, like I did, that as a masochist and a submissive you needed what I was doing to you as much as you needed the drugs." That actually wasn't what I'd needed at all, but I didn't bother to correct him.

He paused for a few moments before continuing, "Everything changed the day he came over early and saw me beating the living hell out of…let's just call this man a business associate. I was brutal and enraged and totally out of control, and Gabriel lost every bit of trust he had in me that day."

"Did you kill that man?"

"No, but I came very close."

"Why, what did he do? Did he owe you money or something?"

"He and I had a business agreement, and he double-crossed me," Simeck said. "Where I come from, if someone wrongs you, that's how you deal with it."

"But isn't that basically what I did? I signed a contract and promised I wouldn't leave without your permission, and then I ran away when you weren't looking. Why aren't you trying to make me pay for breaking our agreement?"

He just grinned, which was confusing. Was he imagining things to come? Then he got up and said, "I should go. I'm late for an appointment."

"I can't believe you're willing to just walk away, after wanting to find me for years."

He paused at the door and buttoned his suit jacket. "Careful what you wish for, I guess. Finding you again turned out to be a huge disappointment."

"Why is that?"

"Because I found out the lovely, delicate boy who once belonged to me doesn't exist anymore. As for the man who took his place, no offense, but you're really not my type."

I muttered, "No offense either, but I'm glad to hear that."

He tried to sound upbeat as he said, "This tough guy thing you've got going on is cute, though. I can only assume you and Gabriel are still together since you're in a shop with a giant picture of him on it, and I hope he appreciates the new you." Why did it feel like he was fishing for information about Gabriel and me? I decided it was best to remain silent.

He opened the door, then took one last look at me over his shoulder. There was something hard and dangerous in his eyes, which made me flinch. Then he said, "I'll be seeing you, Riley," and left the shop.

This was far from over. I knew that for a fact.

I hurried to the door and locked it behind him before tossing the mannequin arm aside. Then I shut off the lights, because the shop was as private as a fishbowl when they were on. I spent the next hour sitting in the dark while trying to process everything that had just happened. It would have been a shock to have that encounter with Simeck at the best of times, but right on the heels of what had happened with Gabriel, it was totally overwhelming.

I knew I'd be sorting through that conversation for years to come. Even though it had been unsettling, I'd still learned some things about a confusing time in my life. It gave me insight not only into who I'd been then, but who I was now. I'd always wondered how I'd react if I ever saw Simeck again, if I'd cower and revert back to being totally passive in his presence. The fact that I'd had the courage to stand up to him was a surprise.

More than anything, I desperately wanted to tell Gabriel what had happened and get his opinion on all of this. But what if he didn't want to talk to me?

As I sat there in the dark, hugging my knees to my chest, the fears I'd tried to bury deep down pushed their way to the surface. What if Gabriel didn't forgive me? What if he didn't take me back? And what if we were both in danger now that we were back on Simeck's radar?

I got up from the floor and took a deep breath. I had to keep telling myself this would be okay. I'd go see Gabriel tomorrow, and we'd have a nice, long talk. We'd get this all worked out. Then we'd figure out what to do about Simeck.

Since it clearly wasn't doing me any good to sit there and worry, I left the shop and locked the door behind me. Then for lack of a better idea, I started wandering down Castro Street. It felt different than it had before, as if a dark shadow was hanging over the neighborhood.

After a few minutes, I passed the restaurant where Will, Lorenzo, and Phoenix were having dinner with their friends. I just kept walking. I had one other friend in this neighborhood, but I didn't go to the drag venue where Emory worked directly. Some (possibly paranoid) little part of me was so rattled by my encounter with Simeck that I took a few odd turns and cut through a building, then paused and watched from the shadows to make sure I wasn't being followed. I felt kind of silly when I realized I was alone, but why take chances? I didn't know what Simeck was going to do, but it would be totally out of character to just let me go without any consequences.

Eventually, I made my way to the drag venue where Emory was a featured performer. It was fairly early, so I knew he'd still be working. I found a table at the back of the bar to wait until he was done.

When a waiter in full drag came by to take my order, I asked for a Coke. That earned me a big grin and the question, "You sure you don't want something stronger, honey?"

I actually did, and that was so depressing. I'd prided myself on how well I managed my cravings these past few years. I was never even really tempted, until that night. But I said, "I'm sure. Just the soda."

There was no way I was going to throw away four years of sobriety for a few hours of oblivion. Actually, I didn't want to dull what I was feeling anyway. Yes, it hurt like hell to be without Gabriel, and I was terrified he wouldn't forgive me. But I'd brought this pain on myself when I went behind his back, and I didn't want an easy way out. I just wanted a chance to make it right.

A few minutes after I arrived at the club, Emory took the stage in all his Polly Swallows glory. He was known for his comedy and his style was retro glam, so he lip-synced to 'Chapel of Love' by the Dixie Cups while wearing an enormous white beehive wig, a very short bell-shaped wedding dress, and platform go-go boots. While he sang, he pantomimed a disastrous wedding with a go-go boy as the groom and several drag queens as bridesmaids. When he finished, he left the stage to thunderous applause and a deluge of tips.

He worked the crowd, bantering and flirting as he made his way through the club. The transformation in him always astonished me. It wasn't just the change in his physical appearance, even though that was truly remarkable. His entire personality changed. While Emory would have been sitting in the corner hoping no one noticed him, Polly lived for attention and exuded charisma and confidence.

When Emory/Polly spotted me, he (she?) hurried over and loudly exclaimed, "Well, hey there, handsome! Fancy meeting you here!" When he drew me into a hug, he whispered in my ear, "Are you okay, Riley? You look like you want to cry."

"I've been better. It's been a rough night."

"Come backstage and tell me what's going on."

As soon as he straightened up from our hug, he was back in character. He grabbed my hand and started to tow me through the crowd as he announced, "Coming through! Look what I caught, isn't he cute? I think I'll let him ring my bell!" He swung his hips as he said that, which made his bell-shaped minidress sway.

Once we were backstage, he took off that big beehive and his clip-on chandelier earrings as I said, "I know you're busy, and I didn't mean to interrupt you while you're working. We can just talk later if you're free."

He ushered me down a long hallway to the dressing room, which was crowded with drag queens in various stages of costume changes, and he said, "I have fifteen minutes until my next number. What's going on?"

I told him a short version of what had happened with Gabriel and left out the part about Simeck, because that last bit was too much to try to explain right now. Emory chewed his lip for a few moments before saying, "Okay. But like, if someone tried to help me launch a business and sugar daddied me a shop in the heart of the Castro, I think I'd marry him, not break up with him. What am I missing here?"

"You just have to know Gabriel and what he's been through in his life. He has the hardest time trusting people, and I kept secrets and went behind his back. Also, keep in mind it wasn't me who leased that shop. I could never afford something like that. It was his ex-boyfriend, and he's probably the last person Gabriel wants to feel indebted to."

"Okay, I definitely get that part," Emory said. "I would never want to feel like I owed something to any of my exes." While we were talking, he took off his boots and wriggled out of the dress, which he tossed onto an overstuffed clothing rack. That left him in a tight bodysuit, a stuffed bra, a hell of a lot of pads to give his body a voluptuous shape, and several pairs of tights layered one over the other.

He sat down at a makeup table, wiped off his pink lipstick, and applied a deep red lip liner as a blond drag queen at the neighboring table quipped, "What exes? From what I've heard, no man has ever stuffed little Polly's pocket." Emory sighed dramatically, and the blond leaned over and asked me, "So like, could I just go ahead and get the name of that sugar daddy? Because I've got no problem with men buying me buildings or whatnot."

Emory clicked his tongue and tried to shoo the blond away with both hands as he snapped, "Mind your own business, Martin!"

"I'm just saying."

The blond went back to touching up his eye makeup while Emory told me, "You don't need this craziness right now. Let me give you the keys to my apartment. Go upstairs and make yourself a nice cup of tea. I'll be up in about an hour, and we'll figure this out. Also, you're more than welcome to spend the night on my couch if you need a place to stay."

"Oh my, maybe I spoke too soon about Polly and her pocket. Way to get 'em on the rebound, honey," the blond quipped with a huge smile, and Emory rolled his eyes.

My friend fished a set of keys from the pocket of some jeans that were crumpled on the floor and handed them over. I gave him a hug and said, "Thank you. I really appreciate this."

He tried to shrug it off by saying, "You'd do the same for me."

His apartment was on the top floor of the same building that housed the drag club. To access it, I had to go back outside and use one of the keys to unlock a security gate at the side of the building. Then I walked to the end of a narrow service alley and used another key to open a door that led to a staircase. After that, it was a four-story climb and another trip down a long hallway which led back to the front of the building.

His one-bedroom apartment was definitely on the small side, and he'd basically turned the living room into a closet for his costumes, but it was cozy. After I did as he suggested and made myself some tea, I took off my shoes and folded myself into a corner of the couch. Then I took a look at my phone. There were no messages. Gabriel would definitely have made it back to the apartment by now, so that meant he was choosing not to answer my text.

I spent the next hour or so lost in thought. The forgotten tea had gone cold by the time Emory let himself into the apartment. He was dressed in a hot pink outfit he'd referred to as 'Black Barbie' when we'd caught his act earlier in the week. I blinked and murmured, "How'd you manage that if I have your keys? I thought I'd have to let you in."

"My landlord was working behind the bar tonight, so I asked to borrow his spare set. He owns the whole building, including the club. I thought you might have fallen asleep, so I didn't want to disturb you."

"That was very considerate."

Emory mumbled, "It was just common courtesy." He was carrying a big bundle of clothes, and he shifted them in his arms as he headed into the bedroom and said, "Be right back, I'm going to take a quick shower."

When he reappeared fifteen minutes later wearing gray sweats and his thick glasses, it was a bit jarring. It was almost a Clark Kent-Superman kind of thing, except his Superman was actually a gorgeous, confident woman who commanded attention wherever she went.

My phone was still in my hand, and he pointed to it as he sat down on the other end of his red sofa and asked, "How many times have you texted Gabriel tonight?"

"Just once, because I'm trying to give him some time. I keep checking to see if he's sent me a reply, but he hasn't."

"What did your text say?"

I pulled it up and handed him the phone, and he read the message and handed it back to me. "After I sent it I thought of so many more things I could have said, but I didn't want to blast his phone so I just left it at that."

"I think you're doing the right thing by giving him some space," Emory said, as he tucked his feet under him.

"I'm definitely going to go see him tomorrow and beg him to talk to me. I won't be able to hold out any longer than that."

He studied me for a few moments before saying, "You seem to be handling this pretty well, all things considered."

"I'm really not," I admitted. "It's all I can do to stop myself from running to the apartment and throwing myself at his feet. I feel all shredded up inside, and if he doesn't take me back I don't even know what I'll do."

He said, "Well, then you're just going to have to get him to forgive you. It's as simple as that."

That wasn't simple at all, but I nodded in agreement anyway.

Chapter 10

I called in sick to work the next day, both because I was a wreck, and because I wanted to talk to Gabriel as soon as possible. I'd barely slept the night before. Instead, I spent hours staring into the darkness and rehearsing imaginary conversations, trying to work out what I wanted to say to him so I didn't mess it up. I hadn't thought of anything brilliant by the time I finally gave in to sheer exhaustion and fell sleep just after dawn.

Around nine, Emory tip-toed into his kitchen, which opened onto the living room, and tried to get some coffee going without making any noise. I sat up on the couch and murmured, "It's okay, you don't have to be quiet. I'm awake."

He turned to me with a sympathetic expression and asked, "Did you sleep at all?"

"A couple of hours, I guess."

"How are you doing?"

I tucked myself into a corner of the couch and pulled the cream-colored blanket up to my chin as I admitted, "I feel lost, and I really need to talk to Gabriel. Until I do, it'll just keep feeling like my whole life is in limbo."

"You really love him, don't you?"

"More than anything. Everything I've done over the last few years has been because of him, and for him. When we were apart, I turned all my attention to building my career, so when I found him again I'd be a man he could be proud of."

Emory murmured, "I can't even imagine loving someone that much."

"And I can't imagine feeling this way about anyone but him."

While he waited for the coffee to brew, Emory asked, "What would you have done if he'd just wanted to be friends when you found him again? Or what if you'd never found him?"

"He's all I ever wanted, so I had to keep believing we'd find each other, and that he'd want me the same way I wanted him. Then it actually happened just the way I hoped it would, and it felt like a miracle. To be able to talk to him, and hold him, and listen to the sound of his voice, to take care of him and be taken care of by him in turn, it just—it was all I'd hoped it would be, and so much more."

Emory's voice was wistful when he said, "I hope I find that someday."

"You will. I really believe that," I told him. "You're such a great guy, Emory. You're kind, and smart, and cute, and sooner or later the right guy is going to come along and realize you're what he's been looking for all his life."

My friend grinned at me. "I've never met anyone who's as much of a hopeless romantic as you are, Riley."

I grinned too and said, "I like to think of myself as a hopeful romantic, not hopeless."

"In that case, you should keep believing everything's going to work out with you and Gabriel." I nodded in agreement, and he opened the refrigerator and told me, "I'm going to make us some breakfast. You have a big day of groveling to win back your true love ahead of you, so you're going to need some energy."

When I still hadn't heard from Gabriel by mid-morning, I sent him a text. That got no reply, so I sent another. I resorted to pacing around the apartment while Emory sat on the couch, offering words of encouragement and patiently hand-beading a yellow dress he'd made for his act.

He and I also talked strategy, but we were both such novices when it came to love. We spent a solid hour weighing the pros and cons of going to talk to Gabriel versus giving him some space, and I sent three more texts. They all went unanswered.

"I don't get why he's not responding, even if it's just to tell me to fuck off," I said after a while.

"I don't like this silent treatment," Emory said. "I might not know much about relationships, but I do know they only work if you actually talk to each other."

I decided to call him, but it went to voicemail. I left a message that said, "We really need to talk, Gabriel. Please call me."

That didn't get a response either, so I reached for my jacket and said, "That's it, I'm going over there and doing whatever I can to get him to talk to me. I tried to be patient and give him some time, but we can't fix this if we don't talk it out."

Emory walked me to the door and gave me a hug as he said, "You've got this, Riley. Go get your man." I promised to keep him updated.

I took a bus across town to the high-rise apartment building, then went upstairs and knocked on the door. Gabriel had our only set of keys, but even if I'd had a set I still wouldn't have barged in. It just didn't seem like the right way to handle this situation.

It startled me when a very tall, muscular guy opened the door. He was barefoot and dressed in white shorts and a white top with spaghetti straps, which showed off his big arms and broad shoulders. The stranger flashed me a dazzling smile and asked, "Are you Riley?"

"Yeah, are you Sawyer?" I'd completely forgotten that he and his husband would be here.

"I am, and it's so nice to meet you!" He grabbed me in a hug, and when he let go of me he peered out into the hallway and asked, "Where's Gabriel?"

"He's not here?"

He shook his head, then stepped back and held the door open as he said, "Come in."

I stepped into the foyer, but then I paused and asked, "When did you get back?"

"At about two a.m. I don't know if Gabriel told you, but my husband ended up with food poisoning so we came back a little early. Alastair's taking a nap, but he's been looking forward to meeting you."

I asked, "Was Gabriel here when you got home?"

"No, so we assumed you two were spending the night at a friend's house or something. He forgot his phone, though. It's been beeping on the coffee table all day."

"That's because I sent about a million messages. If he didn't come back here, where would he go last night?"

Sawyer looked confused as he ran a hand over his short, light brown hair. "You mean you don't know where he is?"

"We had a fight yesterday evening, and he walked away and left me in the Castro around seven p.m." I pulled my phone from my pocket and said, "I just assumed he'd come back here, but maybe he went to Zachary's apartment, or one of his other friends. I don't have anyone's number, though. Do you?"

"Yeah, I do. Come on in. It's most likely he'd reach out to Zachary, so let's call him first."

We both sat down in the living room, and while he messaged Zachary, I sent a text to Roger. Not that I expected Gabriel to be there, but I could imagine him going to Roger's apartment to yell at him after discovering the shop and the poster, so maybe Roger would know where he went afterwards.

After a few minutes, Sawyer looked up from his phone and said, "I messaged three of Gabriel's friends, and no one's heard from him. Now they're worried. What exactly happened last night?"

I told him the story as concisely as possible, and then I asked, "Do you mind if I check the guest bedroom? I want to see if he came back here to change and just forgot his phone before heading out again."

"Go right ahead."

Sawyer followed me down the hall and watched me curiously. All our stuff was right where we'd left it, and Gabriel's wallet was on the dresser. I took a quick peek in the closet, then said, "I started to wonder if he'd gone back to Catalina. He wouldn't leave all his stuff though, and I really think he would have wanted to come back here and change first, since he was wearing his most uncomfortable heels. Even so, it won't hurt to check with his friends at Seahorse Ranch."

"Yeah, might as well."

I called the front desk, and when Beck answered, I asked him if he'd head from Gabriel. Then I had to spend the next couple of minutes reassuring him everything was alright. When I finally got off the phone, I told Sawyer, "They haven't heard from him. So, where else would he go? He didn't have anything with him, just his I.D., some cash, and the keys to this apartment. I can't imagine him checking into a hotel, or wandering around aimlessly all night."

Sawyer's blue eyes went wide, and he asked, "Do you think something bad happened to him?"

Mason Simeck immediately came to mind. What if he'd spotted Gabriel walking down the street all by himself, then abducted him to get back at us for daring to defy him?

"I need to go," I blurted. "Please call me if Gabriel comes back, or if you hear from him."

We quickly exchanged numbers, and then he ran with me through the apartment and asked, "Where are you going?"

"I thought of someplace he might be. I hope I'm wrong though, so please keep reaching out to anyone you can think of."

Before Sawyer could say anything else, I ran out the door. Then I rode the elevator back to the ground floor and sprinted across the lobby. Once I reached the street, I flagged down the first cab I spotted, climbed into the backseat, and recited Mason Simeck's address. I actually had no idea if he still lived there, but I had to start somewhere.

I leaned back and caught my breath as the cab driver began to make his way across town. My phone rang after a minute, and Roger's name appeared on the screen. When I answered, he said,

"I've just seen your text, mate. Why are you asking if I've spoken to Gabriel?"

"Because he didn't come back to the apartment last night, and no one's heard from him. The last time I saw him, he was heading out of the Castro. Do you happen to know if any of his friends live nearby?"

"I'm not sure, although Gabriel could have just hopped on a bus and gone anywhere in the city."

"That's true. Sawyer's messaging everyone he can think of, but would you have any names that he doesn't?"

"No. We know all the same people," Roger said. Then he asked, "Are you in a car?"

"A cab. I have a theory about where he might be, and God do I hope I'm wrong."

"Where are you headed?"

I told him about Simeck and our unexpected encounter, and then I said, "Actually, it's good that someone knows where I'm going, in case I don't come back. The address is 464 Gephardt. If you don't hear from me in a couple of hours, call the police. I don't know why Simeck walked away without incident last night, but maybe it was just too public to do anything to me. That won't be the case when I'm at his house."

Roger exclaimed, "Hang on a minute! It's not going to help Gabriel if you go bursting into a potentially dangerous situation and get yourself taken prisoner, or worse."

"But now you know where I'm going, so you can call for help if something happens to me."

"A lot of good that'll do if you've already ended up with a bullet in your noggin."

"Simeck's not going to shoot me," I said. "He'll enjoy it so much more if he makes me suffer."

Roger muttered, "Well, this bloke sounds fan-fucking-tastic."

"Yeah, he's great."

"Let's just slow down and think this through, alright? What are the chances Simeck actually abducted Gabriel? First of all, he'd have to stumble across him. The chances of that are slim, even if they were both in the same neighborhood last night. Then he'd have to get him into his vehicle. How's he going to do that without a hundred people spotting him and reporting it? Next, there's the motive. You said it yourself, he walked away last night without incident, so maybe he's not holding a grudge like you think he is."

"Or maybe he knows the way to really hurt me is through Gabriel," I said. "Simeck saw how defensive I was last night when he brought him up, so it must be obvious I'm totally in love with him. You have to think like a sadistic criminal here. A man like Simeck would absolutely make someone suffer by going after their loved ones."

"What type of criminal are we talking about here? That address you just gave me is in an extremely posh part of town. Something tells me this bloke's not just robbing liquor stores."

"Given the armed thugs guarding his house, I always assumed he was involved in organized crime, but that's just a guess. And if you're wondering why we'd have anything to do with a man like that, you have to look at that time in our lives and the choices we made through the filter of addiction. You don't know what it feels like to be so strung out and desperate that nothing else matters but your next fix."

Roger was silent for a long moment before saying, "Gabriel was quite upset last night. Do you think that might have caused him to fall off the wagon? What if we can't find him because he's using again and doesn't want us to know?"

"I doubt it. He's been doing so well with his recovery, and I can't imagine him throwing that away just because we made him angry." Although I had actually been tempted to take a drink last night…but I shook my head. "It's only been about seventeen hours since the last time I saw him. Maybe he's just with a friend he's never mentioned before, or something. I really want to give him the benefit of the doubt here."

"You're right, it's been less than a day," he said. "Given that, should you really be making a beeline for the home of a known criminal?"

"While I'm willing to give Gabriel the benefit of the doubt, the same can't be said for Mason Simeck. How can it be a coincidence, running into him right before Gabriel disappeared? They were even in the same neighborhood last night, you yourself just pointed that out."

"I see what you're saying, but we don't actually know Gabriel's disappeared or been abducted," Roger pointed out. "In fact, we don't know he's in trouble at all. He could just be avoiding us. Isn't it too soon to be jumping to all these conclusions?"

"Yeah, but I have a feeling in my gut that something's wrong."

"That's a pretty flimsy reason to put yourself in danger," Roger said. "How do you envision this going, anyway? Are you planning to knock on the door, then enquire politely if Simeck might possibly have abducted your boyfriend?"

"I don't know. I'm making this up as I go along. Also, my phone's almost out of charge, so I should go. Remember though, if you don't hear from me in two hours, send the police to that address." Roger was protesting loudly as I hung up on him.

When I glanced out the window and realized we were just minutes from Simeck's house, I started to get nervous. I knew I risked angering a dangerous man in a big way by coming to him with this accusation. Whether or not he was involved in Gabriel's disappearance, this was going to stir up a lot of trouble between us. But if there was even a chance he'd taken Gabriel and was hurting him, I couldn't sit back and do nothing.

I tried to come up with a strategy, but I had very little to work with. I knew I'd be totally outnumbered when I got there, so there was no way to threaten Simeck or pretend to be a tough guy. All I could do was plead with him and offer myself in place of Gabriel. It wasn't much, but it was all I had.

I sent a text to Sawyer, just to see if anything had changed in the last few minutes. He replied right away and told me he'd reached out to everyone he could think of, and no one had heard from Gabriel. He added: *Alastair, Zachary, TJ, and I called the local hospitals to make sure he hadn't been admitted. We also spoke to a friend who's a police offi-cer. We can't file a missing-persons report yet, but he's going to unofficially put the word out and circulate a photo. If Gabriel's out there somewhere and needs our help, we'll find him.*

It was good to know his friends were taking this seriously and leaving no stone unturned, but so far they'd all come up empty. I sighed as I returned the phone to the pocket of my leather jacket. This terrible plan with Simeck was all systems go, because I just didn't see any other alternatives. Gabriel wasn't out there just wandering through the streets for seventeen hours. The only reason he wouldn't have ended up on a friend's doorstep by now was if something had happened to him. If I was wrong about Simeck's involvement, great. But I had to find out, one way or another.

As we approached our destination, apartment buildings gave way to lavish homes. I had to wonder how anyone could afford these multi-million-dollar properties, although it wouldn't surprise me if most of that exorbitant wealth had come from sources as questionable as Simeck's.

The moment we turned onto the 400-block of Gephardt, a huge, black SUV pulled out in front of us, blocking the road. The cab driver started to back up, and when a second black SUV boxed us in, he muttered, "What the hell?"

A bunch of men in dark suits climbed out of the SUVs. After a moment, I realized they were waiting for me to get out of the cab. I could only assume these were Simeck's thugs, and that they'd been watching for me. The only reason they'd do that was if he really had abducted Gabriel and had been waiting for me to take the bait.

I climbed out of the taxi slowly, and when the cab driver rolled down his window and started to ask questions, one of the men handed him a big wad of cash. He took the money and rolled up his window, and when the SUV behind the taxi pulled to the side, the cabbie backed up, then drove off and left me there.

A tall man with dark hair, a short beard, and mirrored sunglasses came up to me and said, "Riley Palma I presume."

Something wasn't right about that, and after a moment I realized what it was. "How'd your employer figure out my last name? I made a point of never telling it to Simeck."

"We don't work for Simeck, kid. Get in the SUV and I'll explain everything."

I hesitated and told him, "You guys look like the men in black, and getting in your vehicle seems like a terrible idea. I feel like you're going to zap my memory or something."

The man shot me a look over the top of his sunglasses and said, "Jesus kid, this isn't a sci fi movie. What do you think, that E.T. is going to show up next? Now get in the SUV before Simeck and his men figure out something's up and pull out a rocket launcher."

If these guys worked for Simeck, I was sure they would have picked me up and stuffed me in a trunk by now, so I got in the backseat without further argument. The tall man climbed in after me, and as another guy slid behind the wheel, I asked, "Who are you?"

"Dante Dombruso. We have some mutual friends."

It took me a few seconds, but all of a sudden I remembered where I'd heard that name and blurted, "Oh, you're Zan Tillane's brother-in-law!"

Dante took off his sunglasses and stared at me for a long moment as the SUV pulled onto a side street. Finally, he said, "Technically, yes. That's just not what people usually say when they meet me."

"What are you doing here?"

"Roger Foster sent me a message and told me about your suicide mission. I'm here so you don't get yourself killed."

"But I just got off the phone with him a few minutes ago. How'd you get here so quickly?"

Dante gestured vaguely. "I live two blocks over."

"And you just happened to have half a dozen henchmen in suits hanging around?"

He raised a brow and said, "Lucky for you, I happened to be having a business meeting."

"What type of business are you in, exactly?"

"The type you really need on your side today, kid. Time is of the essence here, so tell me where you think Gabriel might be if he's in Simeck's house."

"My guess would be the sex dungeon in the basement. There are a lot of ways to restrain someone in there."

Dante nodded, and then he asked, "How many men does he usually have in his house, and are they armed?"

"Four or five, and they're always carrying guns in shoulder holsters. I should probably mention there's a chance I could be wrong here. Simeck might not have abducted Gabriel."

"Roger mentioned Simeck has been hounding you two for years," he said. "Even if he's innocent in this case, I plan to get him off your back once and for all."

"How are you going to accomplish that?"

A grin spread across his face, and he said, "I can be very persuasive." I totally believed it.

"Okay, so what's the plan here?"

Dante shrugged and said, "Basically, we go in there and scare Simeck shitless, and if Gabriel's in the house, we extract him."

"Are you going to shoot your way in?"

"That won't be necessary."

I asked, "Then how are you going to get through the door?"

His grin got wider, and he said, "With my considerable charm and charisma." Then he picked up a walkie talkie and spoke into it. "Let's do this, boys. We're going in calm, so no shock and awe. I'm talking to you, Vincent."

As we rolled down the block to Simeck's mansion, I asked, "Wouldn't a cellphone make more sense than a walkie talkie?"

"Now where's the fun in that?" A few seconds later, three black SUVs converged on Simeck's house. Dante's dark eyes sparkled as he said, "Show time. Just follow my lead."

"You love this shit, don't you?"

"You have no idea." He stepped out of the vehicle and put his sunglasses back on. Then he pulled up his game face and strode toward the house, with about half a dozen men behind him. Meanwhile, three of Simeck's bodyguards had gathered on the porch. Their game faces weren't nearly as good as Team Dante's, because they were clearly nervous.

One of Simeck's flunkies tried to sound tough as he barked, "What do you want?"

Dante infused his voice with steel as he said, "Tell Simeck Dante Dombruso is here to see him, and he better not keep me waiting."

Apparently that name meant something to the rent-a-thugs, because all three instantly looked like they wanted to shit themselves. One of them literally ran into the house, while the other two backed up, then turned and retreated through the open doorway of the stately Italianate mansion.

Dante and his men marched through the front door like they owned the place, and I wandered in after them. A tall man in glasses, who looked so much like Dante that they had to be brothers, grinned at me. Then he draped an arm over my shoulders and led me to the front of the pack as he whispered, "Don't worry, Riley, we've got this. Try to look pissed off, it helps sell the whole gangster vibe."

"Okay. Thanks, um…"

"Vincent Dombruso."

I whispered, "It seems like you've done this shit before, Vincent."

He shrugged and looked amused as he said, "Once or twice."

Mason Simeck rushed into the marble foyer, hastily pulling on a tan suit jacket as he blurted, "Mr. Dombruso, I wasn't expecting you! Is there a problem?" All of his attention was focused on Dante, who was unquestionably the leader of this operation.

"That's what I hear. Do you know how disappointing that is, Simeck? I allowed you to live here, in my neighborhood, and how did you repay me? By harassing a member of my family." I didn't know if it was intentional or not, but Dante was channeling *The Godfather* in a big way.

It struck me as hilarious, but it clearly didn't have the same effect on Simeck, who looked terrified as he exclaimed, "I would never do that, Mr. Dombruso! I don't even know what member of your family you're referring to."

Vincent and I reached the front of the pack at that moment, and Simeck's mouth fell open when he saw me. I glared at him as

Dante said, "I've recently been informed you've been bothering my cousin Riley and his boyfriend Gabriel."

"Your cousin? I had no idea!" He looked like he wanted to cry. I almost felt bad for Simeck. Almost.

Dante slowly walked toward our reluctant host with his hands folded behind his back. He was a huge guy, maybe six-four, and he towered over Simeck. "Gabriel is currently missing. You don't know anything about that, do you?"

Simeck's eyes bulged, and he started to sweat as he blurted, "No, I swear! I haven't seen him."

"In that case, you won't mind if my people search the house."

"No, go right ahead. I have nothing to hide." When Dante nodded, four of his men fanned out into the building. Simeck's uneasy bodyguards stayed behind. So did Dante and Vincent, who flanked me on either side, and an enormous guy on Team Dante with a crewcut, who stood near the front door. I thought it was a nice touch that my newfound 'cousin' Vinny still had his arm around my shoulders.

Simeck looked confused as he glanced at me, then looked at Dante, then glanced at me again. I couldn't resist getting in on the act, and I asked, "Don't you see the family resemblance?"

"I do, I see it. I just had no idea," he stammered. "You never said a word."

I shrugged and muttered, "Well, now you know."

"Let me make something crystal clear," Dante said. "Whether or not you had a role in Gabriel's disappearance remains to be seen. But either way, you need to understand that both he and Riley are under my protection. Not just the Dombruso family's, but mine. If you ever do anything to harm or even annoy either of those two men, I'll consider it a personal insult. You get what I'm saying?"

Simeck nodded and blurted, "Yes, Mr. Dombruso. I get it." I'd never seen him so flustered. In fact, I'd never seen him flustered at all. He really must be terrified to fall apart like that.

Dante lowered his voice and sounded so menacing that it gave me goosebumps. "You better hope Gabriel is found unharmed, and soon. Otherwise, I'm holding you personally responsible, Simeck."

"But I didn't do anything!"

Dante removed his sunglasses and stared him down. "Why don't I believe you?"

Simeck wailed, "I'm telling the truth, I swear!" I had to wonder what Dante had done to inspire such fear, especially since he seemed like a really nice guy. Well, to me anyway. Simeck clearly had a different perspective.

A few minutes later, Dante's men returned and announced they'd searched the entire house and basement, but they hadn't found Gabriel. Simeck blurted, "See? I told you he wasn't here."

"No, but now that I know you've been harassing a member of my family, I want you out of my neighborhood. Scratch that, I want you out of my city," Dante said. "You have forty-eight hours to pack up and leave. Do I make myself clear?"

"But—" Dante cut him off with a poisonous glare, and Simeck nodded and said, "Forty-eight hours. Understood, Mr. Dombruso."

Dante let him squirm for a long moment, and finally he announced, "We're done here."

His men started to head for the door, but I whirled on Simeck and growled, "If anything ever happens to Gabriel, you'd better hope Dante gets to you first. Because if I do, there won't be anything left for him to finish off." Simeck looked dazed as he stared at me with wide, panicked eyes.

Dante and Vincent fell into step with me as I left the house. Two of their men had been flanking the door, and once we passed they brought up the rear. It was all so smooth and coordinated that I wondered if the Dombrusos recruited from the Secret Service, or possibly a super buff marching band.

After we all climbed back into the SUVs and drove down the block, Dante turned to me and asked, "Okay, so how can we help find Gabriel?"

"I don't know. I really thought he'd be there."

"Simeck wouldn't be keeping him off-site, would he?"

"I don't think so," I said. "If Simeck had him, I think he'd want to use Gabriel to lure me to the house."

"How long has Gabriel been missing?"

"It's been about eighteen hours at this point. That might not sound like a lot, but I'm worried sick about him."

Dante took off his sunglasses and said, "If my husband Charlie went missing for eighteen hours, I'd fall apart." We'd pulled up in front of an attractive, modern home, which really was just about two blocks from Simeck's. As we climbed out of the SUV and stood on the sidewalk, he asked, "What are you going to do now?"

"The only thing I can think of is to rent a car and drive around San Francisco, on the off chance I happen to spot him. I know that sounds stupid, but I'm out of ideas."

"You don't have to rent a car." Dante turned to Vincent and said, "Give Riley your keys."

Vincent frowned and asked, "Why don't you give him your keys?"

"Because I need to go to Costco this afternoon," Dante informed him. I had to fight back a laugh. I literally couldn't picture a less likely thing for that super tough gangster to do.

His brother's frown deepened. "I know. I'm supposed to go with you."

"Well, then we can take my car." Dante flashed him a big smile.

Vincent shot him a look. Then he took two keys off a leather fob and handed them to me as he said, "The tank's full. Keep it as long as you need it."

I murmured, "I can't believe you're both doing so much for a stranger."

"We might have just met you, but we consider Gabriel family," Dante said, "and family means everything to us. By the way, he should have come to us sooner with that Simeck situation." He really should have. I wondered if he had any idea what his friends were capable of.

I told them, "Thank you both for everything, including the use of your car and giving me the satisfaction of turning the tables on Mason Simeck. It felt pretty great to have the last word."

Gabriel was going to be so relieved when he found out Simeck wasn't a threat anymore. Now I just had to find him and tell him.

Chapter 11

I'd been driving around San Francisco for about an hour when I finally gave in to an idea I really hadn't wanted to consider. I chewed my lower lip for a few moments, and then I pointed the big, black SUV toward one of the worst parts of the city as I whispered to myself, "I really hope I'm wrong about this."

I'd have assumed the shiny, high-end SUV would draw a lot of people to it in my old neighborhood. There was always someone looking for a handout around there, and people in expensive cars were an obvious mark. The top-of-the-line Land Rover had the opposite effect, though. Everyone gave it a wide berth when I pulled to the curb, as if they'd learned vehicles like this one spelled trouble.

The night Gabriel and I had visited this neighborhood, he'd shown me where he used to live. I took a moment to look around me and find the right building. Then I climbed out of the SUV and locked it with the push of a button.

There were a lot of people loitering on the sidewalk, and they watched me closely as I walked up to the building. Because I really didn't feel like being hassled, I took a page from Dante's playbook and kept my game face on.

My only plan was to ring everyone's buzzer in that building and ask if they knew Gabriel, in the hope of finding his ex-roommate. I never got that far though, because as soon as I reached the foot of the stairs, I spotted him curled up in the shadows beside the front door. He was barefoot and hugging his knees to his chest, and when I said his name, he looked up at me with a startled expression.

He said, "You shouldn't be here." His voice was thin and shaky.

I replied, as calmly as I could, "Come with me, Gabriel."

He looked like a frightened child when he shook his head. "Just leave me."

As much as I wanted to run up those half a dozen stairs and grab him in a hug, I felt like I'd spook him if I did that. So I said, just as calmly but with a little more insistence behind it, "Please get in the SUV. I'm not leaving without you."

He hesitated for a few moments, but then he picked up his shoes and followed me. I unlocked the Land Rover and held the door open for him, and I was relieved when he climbed into the passenger seat.

I hurried around the front of the SUV, slid behind the wheel, and locked the doors behind me. Then I glanced at him as I started the engine. His hair was tangled, and there was a smudge of dirt on his face. He put the shoes in the footwell and wrapped his arms around himself, and I asked, "Are you hurt, Gabriel? Do we need to go to a hospital?"

"No. I'm okay." It came out as a whisper.

I reminded him to fasten his seatbelt, then drove us out of that neighborhood and asked, "Do you want me to take you to Sawyer and Alastair's apartment?"

"No." His voice was so soft.

"Do you just want to drive around a little?" He nodded and turned his head to stare out the passenger window.

Something was very wrong, but I had no idea what it was. I drove aimlessly with the only plan of putting as much distance as possible between ourselves and our old neighborhood, and after a while he asked, "How did you know where to find me?"

"It was the only place left I could think of. None of your friends knew where you were, but you'd mentioned your former roommate Scottie, so I thought you might have gone to see him."

"I tried," he said, "but I found out he moved out of state over a year ago. The two women who live in our old apartment told me that."

We ended up at the coast, so I pulled into a parking space right on the edge of Ocean Beach, facing the Pacific. Unlike most other coastal cities, San Francisco sort of turned its back to the ocean, focusing instead on the bay. Maybe that was because it was always cold and windy here, a beach much better suited to long walks in a sweater than sunbathing.

On this particular Friday in March, the beach was almost empty with the exception of two surfers heading into the water and a woman walking her dog. When I opened the door, the crisp, briny smell of the ocean rushed in. The cool air felt good, so I left the door open while I went around to see what was in the back of the SUV.

I knew at a glance that Vincent was a family man. In addition to a case of water, there was a snack tote, a blanket, and several toys. I searched the bag and selected a couple of things, then went around and opened the passenger door. Gabriel looked so lost as he turned to face me.

I unfastened the seatbelt and put the blanket over him, then handed him a bottle of water and said softly, "Drink this, Angel." He took a few sips while I removed a wet wipe from its pack. As I gently cleaned the dirt from his face, I asked if he was hungry. When he nodded, I unwrapped a soft granola bar and fed it to him piece-by-piece.

After he finished, I took the empty water bottle from him and set it aside, and then I smoothed his hair as I asked, "Can you tell me what happened, Gabriel?"

His left hand slipped out from under the blanket. He was making a fist, and he held it up to show me. Then he uncurled his fingers and revealed a little baggie. I didn't have to ask what it contained. I'd seen enough heroin in my life to recognize it at a glance.

I felt like I'd been punched in the chest, and I asked, "Did you use any of it?" He shook his head, and I took it from him and shoved it in the pocket of my jeans. Then I went back around and climbed in the driver's seat.

We both just sat there for a while with the doors open, as the wind stirred our hair and we stared out at the ocean. It finally occurred to me that a lot of people were worried about Gabriel, so I sent a quick text to Sawyer and Roger letting them know he was alright. I knew they'd spread the word from there.

As I tossed my nearly-dead phone onto the dashboard, Gabriel asked, "Who did you message?" I told him, and he asked, "Did you tell them about the drugs?"

"No, I only told them you're safe. A lot of people were worried about you when you didn't come home last night."

"I didn't mean to worry anyone."

"I know."

He burst into tears a moment later, so I climbed over the console and joined him in his seat. He crawled onto my lap and buried his face in my shoulder, and I held him and just let him cry. It took a while, but eventually the tears lessened, then stopped. I reclined the seat partway and rubbed his back as he took a few shaky breaths.

When I thought he was calm enough to answer, I asked, "Can you tell me what happened last night?"

"I fucked up." I kept rubbing his back as I waited for him to continue. Finally, he said, "I was mad and hurt when I walked away from you on Castro Street. I know you were just trying to help, but you did things behind my back, and I just never expected that from you. I always thought you and I would tell each other everything, not keep secrets."

"I'm so sorry, Gabriel. I know I was wrong to make decisions for you and do things you specifically told me not to. For what it's worth, I learned my lesson and I'll never do that again."

He was quiet for a while before saying, "Even though that was upsetting, it's not really what made me spiral. As I walked down Market Street, I started thinking about how much that shop must have cost, and how much trouble you and Roger had gone through.

It started to feel like this huge obligation, like I had to do this no matter what, because so much money had already been poured into it.

"That pressure started freaking me out, because I don't know how to run a business. I also worried about what it would mean for you and me if I had to stay in San Francisco to run the shop while you went back to L.A. for your career. I got scared I'd lose you, and the shop would go under because I didn't know what I was doing, and Roger would lose all his money and end up hating me, and I'd fold under the stress of it all and start using again."

He paused for a few moments and exhaled slowly before continuing, "I ended up sitting down on the curb and having a full-blown panic attack. I don't think I've ever had one of those before. Not like that, anyway. I couldn't breathe, and my heart started racing, and I got so light-headed that I was pretty sure I'd pass out. It seemed to go on for a really long time, and when it finally ended I was so angry at myself. I'd melted down over a bunch of what-ifs. I thought, how could someone who'd freak out over things they'd only imagined have any chance whatsoever of maintaining their recovery?"

After another pause, he said, in a detached sort of way, "So, as I'm sitting there, literally in the gutter, this guy comes up to me and asks me if I want to score some H. It felt like a cruel joke, a drug dealer showing up and offering me my drug of choice, just as I was questioning whether remaining clean and sober was even something I was capable of. And in that moment, I gave up on myself. I took all the money I had on me and held it out to him, and in exchange, he gave me that baggie of heroin."

I said, "But you didn't use it."

He sat up a bit and met my gaze as the tears started to well up again. "But don't you see, Riley? The fact that I bought it shows I can't be trusted. Once I realized I couldn't be around you anymore, I just lost it."

"Why do you think you can't be around me?"

"Because I refuse to drag you down with me. I just won't do it. I love you way too much to put your recovery and your life at risk."

I caressed his cheek and said, "That's not how this works, Angel. You're not going to drag me down. Instead, I'm going to hold you up, until you're strong enough to stand without my help."

His dark eyes searched my face as he whispered, "You are?" I nodded, and after a few moments, he said, "I scared myself last night, Riley. I thought I lost everything when I bought those drugs, including you and the life I'd been trying to build for myself. All that was left for me was a short slide back into addiction. I ended up walking to my old neighborhood and looking for my former room-mate, because I figured that was where I'd probably end up. Once I found out he'd moved away, I just ran out of steam. I sat down on the front stoop and stayed there all night. I didn't know what else to do or where to go."

"I'm so glad I found you."

"Me too. I really needed your help." He was quiet for a minute or two before saying, "I don't know why I have to be such a contradiction. On one hand, I really want to be taken care of. But then, whenever anyone tries to do that, I resent it."

"There's nothing easy about accepting help. For one thing, there's pride involved. But more than that, I think you and I both learned early on not to rely on other people, because they can let you down. I used to think the only person I could trust was myself. Everyone else would just end up hurting me, so it was best not to depend on anyone. But then my trust in myself was shaken when I became an addict, and it's taken me a long time to rebuild it."

"That's it exactly."

When he yawned, I said, "We need to get you to bed."

"I'm embarrassed to face Alastair and Sawyer after all of this. What must they think of me?"

"That you're their friend and they love you. They're going to be so happy to see you."

I returned to the driver's seat, and after we got ourselves situated I headed back across town. After a while, Gabriel murmured, "It must have been so expensive to rent this nice SUV."

"Actually, it belongs to a new friend of mine. His name's Vincent Dombruso, or as I like to call him, my cousin Vinny."

"How do you know Vincent?"

"It's a long story. I promise to tell you all about it later, after you've gotten some sleep."

He asked, "Does everyone know I disappeared last night?"

"Yeah. All your local friends were calling around and trying to find you. I even spoke to Beck, in case you'd gone back to Catalina. Sawyer and Roger are going to let everyone know you've been found." I glanced at him and added, "By the way, all anyone knows is that you didn't go back to the apartment last night. It's totally up to you how much you want to keep private. For all they know, you had a credit card with you and used it to spend the night in a hotel."

"I definitely want my closest friends to know the truth, like Zachary and TJ, and Sawyer and Alastair. They've been a part of my recovery from the start, and they'll understand that I'm still struggling." He thought about that, and then he said, "Actually, I'm fine with everyone knowing. There's no reason to treat this like a dirty little secret. I made a mistake. My friends will understand that."

"You're right, they will. Your friends are all pretty amazing." I glanced at him and asked, "Are you sure you want to leave San Francisco when I finish my job here? I know you had your reasons for leaving, but you also have an absolutely fantastic support network in this city."

"I've been thinking about that over the last few weeks. I'd love to stay, but your job is going to keep you in Southern California, and I want to be wherever you are."

"I could try to find a job here. There are special effects makeup studios in most major cities, including San Francisco. There are a lot more of them in L.A., since it's the hub of the entertainment industry, but that doesn't mean it's impossible to find work in my field somewhere else." After a moment, I added, "Although you did have some concerns about coming back here."

"You're right. I was worried spending time in this city might trigger a relapse, but what happened last night wasn't because I was in San Francisco, it was because of me. I have a lot of work to do, not just with my recovery but in terms of learning to manage my stress and anxiety. That stuff goes with me no matter where I am, and being here hasn't actually made it worse." Then he said, "So really, there's only one reason why we shouldn't stay in San Francisco."

"If you mean Mason Simeck, he's not a threat anymore. You know that long story about the Dombrusos that I promised to tell you later? It actually involves him."

He blurted, "Did Simeck find you?"

"Yeah, last night, after he spotted that giant poster of you on Castro Street. Don't worry, he didn't hurt me. We just had a conversation, and then he left. I spent the night on Emory's couch, and around noon today, I found out you never made it back to the apartment. I was terrified Simeck had abducted you, so I went to his house to confront him."

Gabriel asked, "By yourself?"

"I planned to go alone, but I was intercepted by some of your friends." I asked with a grin, "Did you know the Dombrusos are big-time gangsters?"

"I'd heard they had roots in organized crime going back generations, but I thought this generation had gone legit."

I shrugged and said, "Maybe they have, but either way, their reputation certainly precedes them. Dante and Vincent and some of their...support staff went with me to see Simeck, and he almost pissed himself. Dante told him you and I are under his protection and ordered him to leave town, and Simeck swore he'd leave us alone. He was terrified of the Dombrusos, Dante in particular, so I know he won't do anything to cross them."

Gabriel muttered, "I can't believe all of that happened in the last twenty-four hours. I also can't believe you were waiting to tell me about it!"

"We had more pressing things to deal with. By the way, Dante said you should have come to him sooner to get Simeck off your back."

"It never even occurred to me. First of all, who knew Simeck was terrified of Dante? But also, I wouldn't have expected the Dombrusos to stick their necks out for us."

"Dante considers you family." I grinned and added, "Speaking of which, he told Simeck I'm his cousin. You should have seen Simeck's face."

Gabriel pushed his hair back and exhaled slowly. After a minute, he said, "This is a lot to process."

"I know. That's why I was waiting to tell you."

"I want every detail of your conversation with Simeck," he said, "but you're right that it should probably wait until I've gotten some sleep. I'm pretty overwhelmed right now."

"I'll definitely tell you everything. I also plan to grovel and apologize a million times for going behind your back and asking Roger for help when you told me not to. In case you're wondering, I met with him about a week and a half ago to ask for some contacts in the manufacturing industry, and that somehow turned into him leasing a storefront."

Gabriel said, "I feel bad complaining because I know he was only trying to help, but this is what he does. He makes decisions for me and goes totally overboard."

"He really cares about you, though. He's actually the one who called the Dombrusos and sent them to help me with Simeck."

"He's a good person with a heart of gold, and I hope he finds someone who absolutely loves and appreciates him."

"He will. Somewhere out there is a man who's looking for a take-charge kind of guy," I said. "It's just a matter of time before he and Roger find each other."

When we reached Sawyer and Alastair's building, we parked in the underground garage. Gabriel winced as he put his shoes on, and he was limping a little as we walked to the elevator hand-in-hand.

We knocked when we got to the apartment. A few seconds later, a slender, blue-eyed blond in a white polo shirt and khaki shorts threw the door open. Then he tackled Gabriel in a hug and exclaimed, with a posh English accent, "I'm so glad you're alright!" He kissed Gabriel's cheek before letting go of him, and then he stuck his hand out and flashed me a dazzling smile. "You must be Riley. I'm Alastair."

I shook his hand and said, "It's great to finally meet you."

Alastair led us into the apartment as he asked, "Why'd you knock, did you lose your keys?"

"No, but now that you're back, we didn't just want to barge in," Gabriel explained.

"Our home is your home," Alastair told him. "You know that."

We reached the living room the same moment Sawyer did. He whooped with delight and grabbed Gabriel in a hug, lifting him off his feet as he exclaimed, "I'm so glad you're back! We were worried about you."

"I'm really sorry," Gabriel said, as Sawyer put him down again. "I really didn't mean to worry anyone."

Sawyer draped his arm around his friend's shoulders and gave him a squeeze as he said, "We know."

Gabriel turned to Alastair and asked, "How are you feeling? Sawyer left a message saying you had food poisoning."

"I'm much better, although I'm sticking with tea and toast for the time being. The thought of anything else makes my stomach wobbly."

They chatted for another minute, and then Gabriel told them, "I really need a shower and a nap, but after that I want to hear all about your trip and everything that's going on with both of you."

"Yes, we'll catch up soon. In the meantime, a nap sounds like a brilliant idea," Alastair said, as his husband put an arm around him. "I think we should do the same."

While Gabriel was in the shower, I changed into a clean T-shirt and sweats. Then I plugged in my phone and sent messages to Emory and Beck, letting them know all was well. Emory actually had no idea about Gabriel's brief disappearance, but I'd promised to check in and wanted to let him know we'd worked it out. I figured Sawyer and Roger had contacted everyone else by now, but those two guys wouldn't have been on their call list.

Beck sent back a message asking where he'd been. I thought about how to answer that, and then I replied: *He went to visit an old friend.* That was technically true, even if his former roommate hadn't been there when he'd gone looking for him. Even though Gabriel had said he was going to be open about what had happened, that really wasn't my tale to tell.

My next text was to Roger, which said: *Thanks for calling the cavalry. I really appreciate it.*

He responded with: *No worries, mate. I spoke with Dante and heard it all went splendidly. Thanks for your earlier message letting me know Gabriel had been found. Is he really okay?*

I wrote: *Yeah, he is. He's about to take a nap, but I'm sure he'll talk to you soon. I need to ask one last favor. Could you please tell Vincent his SUV is in the parking garage of Sawyer and Alastair's building? I don't actually know how to get in touch with him.*

His next text said: *Consider it done, mate. Happy to help. If there's anything else you think of, just let me know.*

Gabriel emerged from the bathroom a few minutes later wearing his most comfortable pajamas, which were midnight blue flannel and a bit oversized. He was holding a box of bandages, and he muttered, "I'm never wearing those shoes again. They ripped my feet to shreds."

I took the box from him and said, "Let me help."

He sat on the edge of the bed, and I knelt at his feet and carefully covered his blisters. When I looked up at him, he was watching me with the sweetest expression. "I really love you, Riley," he said. "Not just as a friend. I really, truly love you."

"I love you, too. More than anything." I picked up his hand and kissed his knuckle. Then I tucked him into bed and told him, "I'm going to brush my teeth. I'll be right back."

I scooped up my dirty clothes and brought them with me to the bathroom, shutting the door behind me. Before putting them in the hamper, I removed a small packet from the pocket of my jeans. Then I tore open the baggie and flushed its contents down the toilet, rinsed it out, and wrapped it in toilet paper before throwing it in the trash can. It was a relief when it was gone, not because it was tempting, but because I couldn't stand the sight of it.

After I washed up a bit, I returned to the bedroom and slipped under the fluffy white blanket. Gabriel was almost asleep, but he slid close and wrapped himself around me. As I stroked his hair, he murmured, "Did you get rid of it?"

"Yeah. It's gone."

"Good. I felt horrible about bringing that stuff into Sawyer and Alastair's home."

He fell asleep a few moments later, and I continued to stroke his hair. There was so much I needed to do. First and foremost, I had to help Gabriel find a local counselor, and I wanted to find a support group for both of us, because I'd been reminded that recovery was an ongoing process. Then I'd have to work on finding my next job, possibly in San Francisco, and figure out where we were going to live.

But right now, this was exactly what I needed to be doing. I closed my eyes and let myself relax as I held my boyfriend in my arms.

Gabriel woke up around seven that night. I was sitting beside him with my laptop, and I set it aside when he stirred and mumbled, "What're you doing?"

"Researching companies in and around San Francisco. I found four special effects makeup studios that all sound great. I also updated my resume and online portfolio. I haven't applied for any jobs yet though, because we'd just begun talking about staying here, and I wanted to confirm it was what you really wanted before I did anything else."

"I would love to stay here."

"Okay. Then I'll send out my resume."

He tucked himself under my arm and said, "You're amazing, you know that?"

"In what way?"

"Instead of sitting back and hoping, you make things happen. Meanwhile, I've been just sort of daydreaming about a lingerie company for years."

"It's so much easier to try to find a job than launch a company," I said. "Look how far I got when I wanted to open my own studio. Although I know now that it would have been premature. I'd rather spend the next three to five years working at an established company and building my skills before branching out on my own."

"That sounds like a good idea."

After a few moments, I said, "I'm sorry again about going behind your back with Roger. I feel like my apology kind of got lost among all the things that happened over the last day."

"It's okay, you don't have to beat yourself up about it. I know you feel bad, and I also know you meant well."

"I feel terrible about losing your trust," I said. "I know how important that is to you, and I promise to do everything I can to earn it back."

"You didn't lose it. When I first found out you'd been planning things with Roger, I got upset and might have said some things, but I still trust you with my life. You made a mistake, that's all. I shouldn't have freaked out and overreacted."

"You don't have to let me off the hook so easily. I know I fucked up."

"I fucked up too, by walking away instead of talking to you when you did something I didn't like. All we can do is learn from our mistakes and try to do better next time." His stomach rumbled, so he sat up and grinned. "I'm really hungry. We should probably get up."

"Vincent dropped off a huge, cheese-stuffed casserole a couple of hours ago, when he came by to pick up his keys and the SUV. We can warm that up if you want to. He said the food was both because he knew we'd had a rough couple of days, and because he and Dante bought way too much stuff at Costco and it wouldn't all fit in their refrigerators."

We both climbed out of bed, and he said, "I love the Dombrusos. Do you think they'd adopt me if I asked nicely?"

"I think they already did."

He changed from his pajamas to jeans and an oversized black sweater, which reminded me we'd officially shifted to 'guest' status in this apartment. Then he took a big gift bag out of the closet, and I asked, "What's that?"

"A thank you gift for our hosts."

We found the couple in the living room. Sawyer was sitting on the couch, and Alastair was stretched out with his head on his husband's thigh. Alastair sat up when we joined them, and as Gabriel handed over the bag, he explained, "On the surface, it may look like this is just for Sawyer, but it's actually for both of you. Sawyer can wear it, and Alastair can enjoy the view."

Sawyer pulled a black silk corset from the bag, and a huge smile spread across his face as he said, "Oh yeah, we'll definitely both enjoy this. Thanks, Gabriel."

"There are four complete outfits in there. I think I got your size right, but I can make some alterations if the fit's a bit off."

"Everything you've ever made for me has fit perfectly," Sawyer said, as he pulled a black silk and lace camisole from the bag. "Wow, this is beautiful. You went to a lot of trouble to make this stuff, so how can we repay you?"

Gabriel told him, "This is meant to be a thank you gift for letting us stay here. We want you to know we really appreciate it."

"It's not a big deal," Alastair said. "The apartment would have just been sitting empty, which always feels like a waste. We're both glad you got some use out of it."

There was a knock at the door, and Sawyer got up and said, "I'll get it."

As he left the living room, Alastair peered into the bag and smiled. Then he said, "You're right, this definitely is a gift for both of us. Thank you. It means a lot to Sawyer, too. You know how much he loves lingerie, and it's almost impossible to find things that fit properly. Even stuff that's supposedly made for men tends to be cut for a slim, androgynous body type, which doesn't work for him."

A few moments later, Sawyer and Roger came into the room. Roger was dressed in a dark blue suit and white shirt, but he'd left off the tie, which passed for dressing casually with him. He was carrying a pink bakery box and a small carton of cookies, and there was a large, padded mailer under his arm. After he put everything on the coffee table, he and Alastair grabbed each other in a back-slapping embrace and exchanged greetings.

Then Roger handed Alastair the carton of cookies, which had a picture of a baby on it, and said, "I heard you were puking your guts out mate, so I brought you your favorite digestive biscuits. They used to be the only thing you asked for when you were a kid and felt ill."

"I love these," Alastair said, with an embarrassed grin. "In fact, I was wishing I'd brought some back from the UK, so thank you."

Roger turned to Gabriel and said, "I'm really sorry about going overboard and leasing that shop without even asking if it was something you wanted. I've brought you a dozen chocolate croissants, which I hope will distract you from being angry with me."

Gabriel crossed the room and gave him a hug. "I'm not angry. It overwhelmed me at first, but I know you were trying to help. I'm worried about you though, because I know that must have cost a fortune, and I doubt you can get your money back if you signed a lease."

Sawyer and Alastair had both returned to the couch, and Sawyer said, "I feel like we missed something. What are you two talking about?"

Roger sat in one of the gray armchairs around the coffee table, and Gabriel and I settled into the other as he explained, "That storefront I subleased on Castro Street, after you decided not to put another coffee house in that neighborhood. I got it for Gabriel when I heard he wanted to start a men's lingerie company, but I didn't bother checking with him first. That led to a bit of a fallout."

Sawyer looked confused. "I didn't know you were planning to start a company, Gabriel. Why didn't you tell me, so I could help you?"

Roger's brows shot up, and he blurted, "Shite! I've fucked up again, haven't I? Gabriel didn't want your help, so I probably shouldn't have been talking about this."

Gabriel quickly jumped in and said, "I just didn't want to bother you and Alastair with this. You've both already done so much for me by letting me stay in this apartment, and I would have felt like I was trying to take advantage of our friendship."

"We know you'd never try to take advantage of us," Sawyer said, "and I'd love the opportunity to invest in your company."

Gabriel said, "I decided to hold off on this idea, because I don't know how to run a business, and I can't afford the start-up costs."

"But that's exactly where I'd come in," Sawyer said. "I know it's been a rough couple of days, so I don't want to push. But can we sit down together on Monday and talk about this? It's something I'm really interested in, and if you think you might still want to move forward with it, I have all the resources you need to make it happen."

"Are you sure? I'd feel awful if the business failed and you lost money because of me."

Sawyer shrugged and told him, "That doesn't worry me in the slightest."

"Okay. I guess we'll talk Monday, then." Gabriel seemed a bit dazed.

"You know, my family owns several manufacturing facilities in the UK, including some that make apparel," Alastair said. "We should team up."

"Speaking of which." Roger picked up the large, padded envelope and told Gabriel, "I almost chucked this in the bin after the shop fiasco, but then I thought there was no harm in showing you. I spoke to a pal of mine who works at one of those facilities last week, and he got back to me with some samples to give you an idea of the quality of their work. This just arrived today." To Alastair he said, "I gave old Dobbie up in Manchester a jingle, and he expedited these for me as a personal favor."

Gabriel took the mailer from him and tore open one end. He glanced inside, then dumped several items into his lap. In addition to four silk camisoles in a rainbow of colors, there was also a price list and a bunch of fabric swatches gathered on a large metal ring. He picked up a red top with lace trim at the neckline and ran it between his fingers as he murmured, "This is beautiful."

I was worried all of this was a little too much on the heels of the night he'd had, so I got up and said, "I'm going to heat up Vincent's casserole. Gabriel, maybe you could give me a hand." Then I asked Sawyer and Alastair, "Have you guys eaten?"

They said they hadn't, and Roger got up and murmured, "I should get out of your way. Enjoy your weekend, all."

He started to head for the door, but Gabriel called, "Why don't you join us for dinner?"

I could tell that meant a lot to Roger, but he tried to act casual as he said, "Sure, I could do that, as long as it isn't any trouble."

"No trouble at all." Roger returned to the armchair, and Gabriel told him, "Thanks for requesting those samples. You're a good friend."

Roger looked surprised as he muttered, "My pleasure."

When we reached the kitchen, I pulled a huge pan out of the fridge, and Gabriel peeled back the foil and asked, "What do you suppose is under those twenty pounds of mozzarella, a lasagna?"

"I took a core sample with a spoon after Vincent left, and I'm pretty sure it's stuffed manicotti." I turned on the oven, and then I pulled Gabriel into my arms and whispered. "It seemed like the whole business thing was starting to snowball, so I asked you to join me in case you were starting to feel overwhelmed."

"That really was a lot at once. I'm glad Sawyer realized that and suggested meeting on Monday."

"Is that actually something you want to do?"

"Yeah, it is. He really reassured me that I wouldn't be taking advantage of him, and I want to get better about asking for help when I need it."

"That's great. I was afraid you wouldn't want to do anything with the company after the shop fiasco."

"It means too much to me to let it go that easily," he said. "I know I have a lot to learn, but that's not as intimidating if Sawyer's willing to team up with me." After a moment, he asked, "You don't think he was just being nice though, do you?"

"Nope," Sawyer said with a grin as he came into the kitchen. "I really want to invest in your company, and not just for your sake. It's something that means a lot to me. Remember when you and I met?

It was at a party, and I was wearing a corset under street clothes while you were openly being your true, authentic self. I somehow found the courage to lift up the hem of my shirt and show you we were the same, and that was huge for me."

Gabriel smiled at his friend and said, "I do remember. The night we met was the same night you met Alastair."

"Yeah, it was, and our conversation gave me the courage to show him the real me later that night." Sawyer's smile lit up his whole face as he said, "The rest is history."

Gabriel said, "You don't know how happy I am that it worked out for you."

"Same. I can't even imagine my life without Alastair. And I'm proud of myself too, because I've come really far since the night of the party. I dress how I want to now, and if it makes people uncomfortable to see a big, muscular guy in what they consider 'women's clothes', good. Maybe it'll make them examine what they've been taught to believe about gender, and about this ridiculous idea that we're all supposed to be the same.

"I mean, what's the big deal about a guy who wants to express his feminine side? Why are people so threatened by that? I'm so tired of our society's rigid gender roles that tell us we have to look and dress and act a certain way, that we have to blend in, conform, 'be a man', and all that other bullshit. Why not just let people be themselves and be happy? It doesn't cost anything to accept others instead of judging them."

Gabriel exclaimed, "Exactly!"

Sawyer chuckled, and then he moved to the huge commercial espresso maker and flipped a few switches as he said, "Okay, I totally got on my soap box there, but what I'm trying to say is that I really believe in you and your idea for a company, Gabriel. It's not just about making pretty things, although yay for that. There's a bigger picture here, one that has to do with personal expression and smashing gender stereotypes, and I'm totally here for this. Let's start a fucking revolution, one silk panty at a time!"

Gabriel started laughing and burst into tears at exactly the same moment. He crossed the kitchen and grabbed Sawyer in an embrace as he said, "I really love you. I hope you know that."

"Right back at you, my friend." When they let go of each other, Sawyer joked, "I'm going to put that bit about a panty revolution on a T-shirt. We'll include one free with every purchase."

"You're not only making me believe I can do this," Gabriel said, "but that I need to." That made both Sawyer and me smile.

The stove beeped, and I placed the huge casserole in the oven while Sawyer pulled some milk from the fridge and said, "So, we'll talk Monday and make this happen. For now though, we decided we're going to have dessert first, since that fifty-pound saucy, cheesy pasta thing is going to take a long time to heat through."

"Good idea. We can share the croissants Roger brought," Gabriel said, "and Alastair can have his teething biscuits."

Sawyer chuckled, then started pulling mugs from the cupboard as he said, "I'm making cappuccinos. Who wants one?"

"Everyone," Gabriel replied.

"This is amazing," I said with a smile, as Gabriel came over to me and I wrapped my arms around him. "I can't even believe the man himself, Sawyer MacNeil, is making me coffee. It's as if Mr. Peanut showed up and offered me a bag of nuts."

Sawyer laughed at that and said, "You should probably say no if someone called Mr. Peanut offers you his nuts. Also, I am so fucking sorry I named my coffee houses after myself. In my defense, I never actually expected them to take off the way they did, but suddenly I'm a brand name."

"It's awesome. Just own it," Gabriel told him.

"Besides mate, Riley's wrong to compare you to Mr. Peanut," Roger said, as he and Alastair joined us in the kitchen. "You're not a company mascot, you're the head honcho. You're basically Chef Boyardee, Little Debbie, or Granny Smith. In fact, you're a bit of all three! I'm going to start calling you Chef Little Granny."

While the friends laughed and bickered, I held Gabriel a little more securely and let myself enjoy the moment. We'd gone through a lot in the last twenty-four hours. To wind up like this at the end of it felt like the most amazing gift.

Chapter 12

The next three weeks passed in a blur. Before I knew it, filming on *Alex and After* was completed, and the cast and crew gathered for a lavish wrap party. The best part about that was seeing Gabriel so excited. He got all dressed up in a black on black outfit that included a sheer long-sleeved shirt over one of his lace and silk camisoles, slim-fitting pants, and ankle boots with a three-inch heel. He even let me do his makeup, and the red lipstick and smoky eye accentuated his natural beauty. I loved seeing him so confident and comfortable in his own skin.

Will and Lorenzo flew in from L.A. for the party. They were both excited, because they'd just had an offer accepted and were buying their first home. They sat at our table in the swanky Japanese restaurant, along with Phoenix, who seemed frazzled. While we ate, I asked him, "So, how's it going with Harper?"

That resulted in a ten-minute rant which prominently featured the words man-child, aggravating, irresponsible, and chickens. It concluded with, "He almost brought the chicken to the party tonight. He wanted to put her in a little tuxedo. It was all I could do to talk him out of it."

Will slid his chair closer and put his arm around Phoenix's

shoulders as he said, "Hang in there, buddy. I plan to steal you away from him as soon as my next film gets going."

Phoenix muttered, "Thank God."

Will looked great. He'd cut his hair short and shaved once the role of Alex had wrapped, and he was dressed in a sharp, deep blue suit and a white shirt, which was open at the collar. His fiancé's suit was in a complementary shade of blue, which made me think they secretly coordinated their outfits, even though they denied it. He told us, "I feel like I haven't seen you guys in a year! How has it only been three weeks?" Then he turned to me and asked, "What's new with you, Riley? Do you have your next job lined up?"

"As a matter of fact, I do. I just got hired by a special effects makeup company here in San Francisco, and I start Monday. It's a job doing exactly what I'm interested in, and it's even a step up from entry-level." That was definitely because of the fantasy makeup photoshoots Gabriel and I had done together, which had really impressed them.

"So, you're staying in San Francisco," Phoenix said.

Gabriel nodded. "We decided this was the best place for us, since we have a lot of support here."

"Plus, this is going to be the headquarters for Gabriel's lingerie company," I said with a smile. "He's partnered with his friend Sawyer MacNeil, and they're going to be launching an online retail site this summer."

Phoenix asked, "*The* Sawyer MacNeil, as in the name on those awesome coffee houses?" When Gabriel nodded, he said, "I didn't realize you had friends in such high places."

Gabriel grinned and told him, "I've known him since we were both in low places."

Lorenzo asked, "Isn't that a country song? Something about friends in low places?"

"It is," Will said, "and that reminds me. We were promised karaoke, and I want to get my Salt 'n Pepa circa 1987 on."

I said, "You're kidding."

"Nope. In fact, Lorenzo and I have a whole choreographed dance routine that goes with it."

Will looked really proud of that, but Lorenzo colored slightly and muttered, "That's like, something we do in private."

I grinned and said, "Kinky," which made Will chuckle.

The karaoke started a few minutes later. Everyone headed to the lounge, and Harper was the first to take the stage. He really did seem to crave the spotlight.

Gabriel whispered, "I need some fresh air for a minute," and led me away from the crowd. The restaurant was built around a serene, meticulously landscaped courtyard, and we took a seat on an ornate red bench beside a small fountain. He put his head on my shoulder and said, "It's been such a busy week. I feel like we've barely had a chance to catch our breath."

In addition to working on getting his business off the ground with Sawyer, Gabriel and I had been attending a long-term recovery support group every Wednesday night, and he'd been meeting with a drug and alcohol counselor every Monday and Thursday. The counselor was one of Zachary and TJ's friends, and Gabriel had nothing but good things to say about him.

At the same time, I'd just completed my last week of work on the movie. It was bittersweet. On one hand, I was totally ready for my next challenge. But after all those weeks together, the cast and crew had started to feel like a family, and it was always tough for me to say goodbye to people.

On top of that, Gabriel and I had been apartment hunting in the city, but that was pretty discouraging. He could use his savings now that he had an investor and wouldn't need every penny for his start-up, but San Francisco was stunningly expensive.

Sawyer and Alastair had told us we were welcome to stay with them as long as we wanted to. We were grateful for that, but it wasn't a long-term solution. I wanted enough space to keep working on my own makeup projects, even though I'd landed that job, and Gabriel needed a home office, as well as room to display his sketches and sew his samples. Most of all, we wanted a place we could call home, and we'd always feel like visitors in our friends' apartment.

I'd given notice on my apartment in L.A., and that weekend we were going to pack up all my stuff and bring it and my car back to

San Francisco. We were going to get Gabriel's things from Seahorse Ranch at the same time, but almost all our stuff would have to go into a storage unit for now, since we didn't have anyplace to put it.

Gabriel caressed my cheek and said, "You look like you have a lot on your mind."

"I was just thinking about our housing situation. What are we going to do if all we can afford is someplace as small as my apartment in L.A., but at three times the price?"

He smiled at me and said, "We're both creative people, so I'm sure we can figure out how to make a small space work for the two of us."

I slid closer and took his hand in mine. "I love your optimism."

"I think you've been rubbing off on me."

I asked, "You think I'm optimistic?"

"You kept believing for four years that we'd find each other again, against all odds. I'd say that makes you one of the most optimistic people I've ever known."

"I had to believe that," I said. "I wanted you too much to accept the fact that we might never see each other again."

He ran a fingertip across my lower lip as he asked, "Why me, Riley? Why'd you decide I was the only one for you?"

"You're the kindest, gentlest, most loving person I've ever known. In fact, you literally taught me what love was. That year I spent in Simeck's home, I was full of so much self-hate. I felt worthless and unlovable. But then one day, you appeared. You didn't know who I was or anything about me, but you saw I was hurting and you comforted me. Then you came back a few nights later, and you did it again. And again. Nobody had ever cared for me or about me before. But you did."

I continued, "You were, and are, so beautiful inside and out. I can see why I called you Angel. That beauty just radiates from you. And you let yourself be vulnerable, which just astounded me. You probably think I don't remember, and granted there are plenty of holes in my memory. But I remember some things, like when you'd whisper to me late at night and tell me your worst fears."

He asked, "What did I say?"

"You were scared you'd always be alone and no one would ever truly love you. You said even if someone tried to get close to you, you'd probably just end up pushing them away. You also said you were afraid to trust people, because trusting someone gave them the ability to hurt you."

Gabriel nodded and said, very quietly, "All of that's true."

"I should have told you I loved you, and that you could trust me. That's what I wanted to say, more than anything. But I was scared too, because I knew you didn't feel the same way about me."

"I don't know what I would have said, but I really did love you. And I felt horribly guilty that I kept leaving you there, given what Simeck was doing to you."

His voice broke, so I said, "Please let go of that guilt once and for all, Gabriel. I stayed by choice, just remember that."

"Did you stay for the drugs?"

"No, I could have gotten them somewhere else. I stayed because I think I needed the pain. Not that I got off on it, but I needed it anyway."

"In what way?"

"Being high all the time dulled everything. That was part of the appeal, but at the same time it frightened me. I felt like I was losing myself," I said. "The pain Simeck dished out cut through the haze, and it brought my mind into sharp focus the way nothing else did. I needed it, as odd as that might sound. It woke me up, while the drugs and alcohol made me feel like I was sleepwalking a lot of the time."

He asked, "Did you feel like you were sleepwalking with me?"

"No. The pain might have cleared my head, but you made me feel alive. That probably seems like a cliché, but I don't know any other way to say it. I felt numb a lot of the time, but when we were together I was able to feel safe, and loved, and cared for, even through that layer of fog I spent most of my time in."

"I actually know exactly what you mean. That's what it felt like for me, too," he said. "I don't know if you realize it, but I got as much from our time together as you did. You loved and accepted me unconditionally, and I needed that desperately."

"I'd always thought it was one-sided."

"No, not at all." He ran his hand over my cheek and told me, "That's why it was so easy to decide to be with you when you came back into my life. The sexual attraction was new, but all the other pieces were already in place—the love, the trust, the friendship, the mutual understanding. From there, it was just a short tumble to falling in love with you."

He grinned at me when I said, "I'm so damn glad you tumbled."

"So am I." When he kissed me, it was sweet and hot at the same time. Then he stood up and held his hand out to me as he said, "Let's get back to the party. It's the last chance to see our friends for a while. After that, you're mine for the rest of the weekend."

The party finally broke up around one a.m. We caught a ride with Phoenix, who was also driving Will, Lorenzo, and Harper back to their hotels. Gabriel sat on my lap, and Will leaned against us and said, "This is probably the last time I'll see you guys before the wedding. You're definitely coming, right?"

I assured him, "We wouldn't miss it."

We said our goodbyes when Phoenix pulled up in front of our building. There were lots of hugs and promises to keep in touch, and then Gabriel and I went up to the apartment hand-in-hand.

Alastair and Sawyer had taken off for a weekend getaway up the coast, and they'd left a note on the table beside the front door, letting us know where they'd be in case we needed to reach them. At the bottom of the note was a P.S. which said: *There's a surprise for both of you on the kitchen counter.*

I said, "I wonder what Alastair baked this time." He'd really been getting into it over the last week, and they kept giving us cakes and cookies and weird English puddings, probably so they didn't eat it all themselves.

"Whatever it is, it can wait," Gabriel said, as he slung my hand over his shoulder and used it to pull me down the hall. "Right now, all I want is you and me, naked in bed." I really wasn't going to argue with that.

When we reached the bedroom, I slipped off my shoes and said, "So, I did a little shopping after work today."

"Did you get some more new clothes?"

"Not exactly." I pulled a large, white shopping bag out of the closet and placed it on the bed. There was a sticker on the front of it that read 'Little Shop of Sex Toys', and I said, "Next time, I want you to come with me so we can pick out stuff together. But this time, I wanted to surprise you."

He sat down on the bed and grinned as he said, "I like surprises." Then he peered into the bag, and a burst of laughter slipped from him. "Well, damn. That really is a surprise." He pulled a two-foot-long, hot pink, double-ended dildo out of the bag. It was bent into a U-shape, and he shot me a curious look.

"So, here's the thing. You're a bottom, and so am I. That's just our reality. But all that really means is that we have to get a bit more creative when it comes to sex, as you yourself pointed out at one point."

He looked amused as he pulled three more dildos in various sizes and shapes out of the bag and said, "I think we can get *very* creative with this stuff."

Over the last few weeks, we'd been relying on oral sex and hand jobs to make each other feel good, but we were ready for more. I joined him on the bed and said, "Thanks for being patient with me while I've been building my confidence and figuring stuff out."

"I'm glad we've been taking our time, and I'm really looking forward to seeing where we go from here."

"Me too. I know we'll keep trying different things and figuring out what works best for us." I grinned and added, "Just imagine all that fun experimentation in our future."

He grinned too and said, "I think it's pretty great, actually. I feel like what we're going to end up with will be uniquely us, completely different from what other couples do, but perfect for you and me."

"It might be awkward at first though, so please bear with me. This is all so new."

"It's new for both of us," he said. "It may take us a while to figure out how to make it work, but eventually it'll become second nature."

"You're right."

He smiled at me as he got up and said, "Let's go get cleaned up, and then we can take these toys for a spin."

I dove out of bed and ran ahead of him into the bathroom, which made him laugh. As we stripped, I said, "Just so you know, all those toys have been washed and loaded with batteries, and I made sure I knew what all of them did. There are good surprises, and then there's 'oh dear lord what the hell is happening right now'. I wanted to be prepared."

When we stepped into the shower, he drew me into a passionate kiss. I soaped up my hands and ran them over his smooth, wet skin, and he cupped my ass and rocked his hips, rubbing his cock against mine. I whispered in his ear, "Turn around, Angel. Hands on the wall."

He complied immediately. I leaned against him as I reached for more soap, then caressed his cock and balls before sliding my fingers between his ass cheeks. I grazed his opening, then circled it before slipping my fingertip into him. He was tight, but I felt his body relax after a moment, allowing me to slide in deeper.

Gabriel pushed back onto my hand, trying to take me deeper still. It was incredibly gratifying to watch him respond to what I was doing. His breath caught when I grazed his prostate, and he began to moan when I started massaging it. I eased off, then increased the intensity again while I began stroking his cock. As he braced his hands on the wall and rocked his hips, fucking himself with my finger, I rubbed my hard-on against his ass.

A few minutes later, I slid my finger from him, which made him whimper. We rinsed off, then dried ourselves quickly. I grabbed two more towels and led him back to the bedroom, and after I spread out a towel on the bed, I told him, "Get on your back for me, Angel, and spread your legs."

He did as he was told, getting into position while his hard-on pressed against his stomach. I squirted some lube onto my hand, stretched out beside him, and went right back to fingering his ass while I claimed his mouth in a rough kiss.

Then I sat up a bit and watched him as I worked him open. He was beautiful, wild, and uninhibited, and I loved seeing him lost to the pleasure I was causing. His skin was flushed, his full lips parted as he gasped for breath. And to think, this was only the appetizer.

After a while, I picked up a medium-sized dildo and lubed it thoroughly before working it into him. He cried out and grasped the sheets when I flipped the little switch on its base to make it vibrate. He jerked me off while I fucked him, and after a while I picked up another dildo and started to ask, "Would you—"

I didn't even get the question out before Gabriel grabbed the toy from me. He wasted no time lubing it, and then we shifted positions and shifted again until he could reach my ass and I could still reach his. He pushed the toy against my hole, and after a moment it slid inside me, which made me moan.

We soon found the perfect rhythm. He fucked my hole while I fucked his, and with the way I was angled above him, he was able to reach my cock with his other hand and jerk me off at the same time. I came in just a few minutes with that toy buried in my ass and his hand gripping my cock. It rolled through me in waves, and I yelled as I bucked my hips, thrusting into his hand and driving myself onto the dildo in turn. It went on and on, and by the time that intense orgasm ebbed, I was covered in sweat and struggling to catch my breath.

Gabriel eased the toy from my ass and looked pleased with himself. I could barely think straight, but I wasn't done yet.

I slid down between his legs and began sucking him while I turned the toy's vibration up a notch and fucked his ass harder and faster. In a matter of minutes, he cried out and shot down my throat while a tremor rolled through him. I looped my arm around his waist and kept sucking while he arched off the bed.

Finally, he collapsed onto the mattress, as sweaty and gasping for breath as I'd been, and I eased the toy from his ass. I used the second towel to clean us both up a bit. Then I wrapped the used toys in it and dropped the bundle onto the floor before stretching out beside him.

Gabriel rolled over so we were facing each other and draped his leg over my hip. He looked groggy and happy as he murmured, "That was new."

"Yes, it was." I was sure my grin was just as goofy as his.

He reached behind him and grabbed the double-ended dildo. "Okay, so what the hell do we do with this? All I can picture is a seesaw type of thing."

I chuckled and admitted, "I have no idea. All I can think of is using it while we're both on our hands and knees, ass-to-ass and facing away from each other, but that's kind of impersonal. I wouldn't even be able to see or touch you."

"You know what I immediately thought of when you said that? Did you ever read *Doctor Dolittle* when you were a kid?"

I burst out laughing and exclaimed, "No! Do *not* make a pushmi-pullyu reference! That'll ruin this sex toy for all time."

He started laughing too, and then he said, "Okay, so what other ideas do you have?"

"That's it for now, but I'm sure we'll come up with something. There are all kinds of possibilities and it's super flexible, look."

I took it from him and twisted it, bent it, then twisted it again, and Gabriel laughed and said, "You just spelled out S.O.S."

"So, it'll be useful if we're ever lost at sea." I straightened it out, then grasped it at one end and waved it around as I said, "Or we could get a second one and have sword fights. That's good, too."

I tossed it aside, and he smiled at me and said, "I'm glad you went on that little shopping spree. It was a great surprise."

We shifted around and pulled the blanket over both of us, and he curled up in my arms. After a while, he murmured, "Have I told you how much I love you?"

"Yes, but I don't mind if you repeat yourself."

He grinned and tucked his head under my chin as he said, "I love you more than anything, Riley, and I'm so glad I'm yours." That was, without a doubt, the best thing I'd ever heard.

~

We were all tangled up together when we woke up the next morning. It was warm and cozy and I would have loved to stay in bed all day, but we actually had a rental truck waiting and a long, busy day of traveling and packing ahead of us.

After we took turns in the shower, we both got dressed in jeans and T-shirts, except that Gabriel's were black and form-fitting and looked sexier than mine. He tied his hair back in a ponytail and put on his canvas flats, and after he picked up his phone, its charger, and a jacket he said, "It feels weird to be traveling this light."

"It does, but we'll have everything we need in L.A., and we're just spending one night before coming right back here."

We went into the kitchen to make some coffee. I still wasn't brave enough to attempt the giant commercial machine, even though Sawyer had shown me how to use it more than once. Instead, I turned to the same automatic coffee maker we'd been using since we arrived (one of five different methods for making coffee that Sawyer kept in his kitchen). While I filled the carafe with water, I asked, "What do you suppose that is?"

There was a small white box on the counter, which was tied with a red ribbon and sitting on top of a business-sized envelope. Gabriel shrugged and said, "I assumed it was from Alastair to Sawyer, or vice versa."

"Didn't Sawyer's note last night say something about a gift for us in the kitchen?"

"Oh yeah. I'd assumed it meant they'd left some baked goods for us." Gabriel picked up the box, then showed me the envelope, which was addressed to both of us. He pulled out a note and read it as I finished getting the coffee brewing, and then he muttered, "Well, I'll be damned."

"What is it?"

"So, you know Sawyer was looking for a small warehouse we could use for our lingerie company, both for storing our inventory and doing the packing and shipping. Well, he found a building and went ahead and bought it yesterday. He said several people were interested in it, so he had to act fast."

"Are you okay with him making that decision without you?"

"Oh, totally," he said. "We'd talked about this ahead of time, and I asked him to handle it. Real estate is his area of expertise. Plus, it's his money, so I didn't want to tell him how to spend it. Although in the note, he says if I hate it, he can just turn around and flip it."

He untied the red ribbon and lifted the lid on the small box, then dumped the contents into his hand as he said, "There's a reason your name was on the envelope too, Riley." I glanced at the set of keys in his hand, then met his gaze as he said, "There's an apartment on the second floor of the warehouse, and Sawyer thinks it'd be perfect for us."

"You're kidding."

"He made a point of saying we're under no obligation to say yes, and we're also welcome to keep living here in this apartment as long as we want to." Gabriel grinned and added, "I think he's worried it'll come across as a scheme to kick us out of their home."

"Can I see the note?" He handed it over, and I read half of it before saying, "He's offering it to us rent-free. Why wouldn't he charge us?"

"Keep reading. He says he has no interest in being our landlord, and he really doesn't need the money. He also says it wouldn't make sense to rent it to anyone else, since we wouldn't want a stranger to have access to our offices and the warehouse."

I leaned against the counter and said, "I'm absolutely stunned. How do you feel about this?"

Gabriel smoothed back a stray lock of hair and said, "A few weeks ago, I wouldn't have been able to accept an offer like this. In fact, I was too worried about taking advantage of our friendship to even ask him for business advice. But now, I'm actually considering it. He's trying to do this out of the goodness of his heart, and there's no real reason to turn it down."

He gestured at the note and continued, "He really wants us to go see the building, whether or not we choose to take the apartment.

It's still in escrow, but he says the real estate agent is fine with us accessing it, since it's totally vacant. Why don't we stop by and take a look after we pick up the rental truck?"

I nodded and said, "That's a good idea."

∼

Less than two hours later, we pulled up in front of a fairly plain, rectangular, cream-colored building near Fort Mason, and Gabriel whispered, "Can you believe it? My company has its own warehouse."

The two-story structure sat off by itself and looked like it probably dated from the 1920s. It had a fresh coat of paint, a small parking lot to its right, and a large cypress tree to its left. There was a wide rolling door at the front of it, and we went around to the side and let ourselves in through a smaller door.

Almost the entire ground floor was wide open, except for a small office and a restroom. When we went upstairs, I said, "Your company doesn't just have a warehouse, it has a headquarters." The right side of the second floor consisted of three good-size offices, which were fronted by a glass wall. Opposite them was a solid wall with a single door in the center of it.

There was a note tacked to the door in Sawyer's handwriting, which said: *Welcome home, Gabriel and Riley!* He'd drawn two stick figures holding hands, one of which had shoulder-length hair.

Gabriel turned the key in the lock, and as we stepped into the apartment, we both murmured, "Oh wow."

It was a huge, sunny, wide-open space, and two walls were lined with tall windows. A basic kitchen was tucked into one corner, and a bathroom took up the opposite corner. The floor was worn wood, and there was exposed ductwork in the high ceiling which gave it an industrial feel, but it also felt inviting and comfortable. Gabriel whispered, "It feels like home."

It really did. I turned to him and said, "Are you sure you're not going to feel guilty saying yes to this place? I don't want anything to get in the way of your friendship with Sawyer, so if you think it's going to make things weird between you, we can go back to apart-ment-hunting."

"I think this is where you and I both belong, Riley. As soon as I walked in, I pictured you with your makeup tables beside the window, and me sitting over here in what's going to be our living room, sketching some new designs for my lingerie."

I said, "I can see it, too."

"I know I've had such a hard time letting people help me in the past, but this feels different. I get that it's not Sawyer saying 'I didn't think you could manage to afford an apartment yourself, so I went ahead and got you one'. It's also nothing like Roger leasing a shop without consulting me first and trying to spring it on me." We'd both been relieved when Roger had been able to find a tenant for that shop within a matter of days, and he was actually going to end up making a profit in his new role as a landlord. But that was defi-nitely an experience neither of us ever wanted to see repeated.

I said, "You're right, it's not even sort of the same situation."

He turned to me and asked, "What about you, though? Would it feel weird living here? I don't want you to feel like you're indebted to Sawyer forever if we move into his building."

"I really like him and trust him. Alastair, too. I don't think this would make things awkward between us. He's buying the building regardless of whether we move in here, and he won't be renting the apartment to anyone else if we say no, so it'd probably just end up as a storage room or something." I chewed my lower lip for a few moments before saying, "I'm really not used to things just getting handed to me. I barely know how to react."

"Same here. But let's say yes to this, Riley. Later on when we're more established, we'll get a place that's ours alone. But this makes sense at this point in our lives, when you're just about to start a new job and my business isn't off the ground yet."

"Okay," I said, "let's do it."

Gabriel smiled at me and kissed my cheek. Then he pulled his phone from his pocket and said, "I'm going to call Sawyer and thank him."

While he placed the call, I opened a door at the back of the apartment. It led to a landing that was maybe eight feet by ten and an exterior stairwell, which meant we could come and go from our apartment without cutting through the warehouse. *Our apartment.* I whispered, "Holy shit."

When Gabriel joined me on the landing a few minutes later, he said, "Sawyer is thrilled. He was really worried we'd say no, and it seems like it meant a lot to be able to do this for us." He looked around and added, "Check out this great deck! Let's put a porch swing out here."

"Definitely. Hey, come look at what I discovered." I climbed up on the railing around the landing, then leaned way over to the right and said, "We have a view of the Golden Gate Bridge."

I hopped down, and Gabriel climbed up and repeated what I'd done. Then he stepped off the railing and smiled at me as he said, "This place just gets better and better."

I pulled him into my arms and said, "We have a home, Gabriel. A real, honest-to-goodness home."

"It's amazing, isn't it? How did I get so lucky?"

"By being a kind, wonderful person with friends who adore you, that's how."

He kissed me before saying, "Let's take a few photos so we can show people our fantastic new apartment, and then we should get on the road." I started by climbing back on the railing, leaning way over, and snapping a picture of our view.

Once we'd finished taking some pictures of the apartment and warehouse, we locked up behind us, then climbed back in the moving van. Gabriel rolled down his window and snapped another picture of the front of the building, and then I asked, "All set?"

"Yup. Let's take the 101 instead of highway five to Southern California, okay?"

I put on my seatbelt and started the engine as I asked, "Are you sure? It'll add a little time."

"I know, but this way I can introduce you to my mom."

When I turned to look at him, he grinned at me, and I stammered, "Oh wow. Really?"

"It's high time, don't you think? I mean, we're shacking up together, so this is the next logical step."

"Sure. Absolutely. Um…how do you think this'll go, exactly?"

"It'll probably be awkward," he said. "She's met plenty of my friends, but never a boyfriend. I think it's going to throw her for a loop. She knows I'm gay, but it's one thing to think of that as an abstract concept, and another thing entirely to meet the man I'm in love with."

"Does she know we're coming?"

"Yeah, I called her yesterday. She's making us lunch, so we should try to get there by noon. It's just east of Monterey, so it should only take us about two hours."

I asked, "Why didn't you tell me sooner?"

"Because you look terrified right now, and I didn't want you to have to worry about it for twenty-four hours."

"That was a good call, actually." I started driving, and when his phone beeped a couple of minutes later, I asked, "Is that her?"

"No, she hates texting. This message is from Tracy. He's decided to move back to San Francisco and is asking if I know anyone who needs a roommate." Gabriel sat up straighter and exclaimed, "I just had the best idea!"

As he sent a text, I said, "Nothing against Tracy, but you didn't tell him he could live with us in our new apartment without bedroom walls, did you?"

"No, I had a much better idea." When his phone beeped, he grinned and said, "My plan is coming together." He sent a few more messages before turning to me and saying, "I just convinced Roger to rent his spare bedroom to Tracy. This is so perfect! Roger needs a project, and what could be better than bringing a sulky, ex-military hottie out of his shell? I can see them falling in love and getting married."

"Or they could end up killing each other, since they both seem like alpha males with strong personalities who are used to being in charge."

He thought about that before saying, "Okay, so the odds are pretty much fifty-fifty. But if it goes the way I hope it will, two people who mean a lot to me will both be happy." I appreciated his optimism.

～

Shortly before noon, we pulled up in front of an apartment building in the small farming community of Martinsville. It was a plain, two-story structure with eight units on the bottom and eight on the second floor, along a narrow balcony. It was off by itself at the end of a cracked asphalt road, surrounded by fields that had once grown crops but now grew weeds.

I asked, "Is this the same apartment you grew up in?"

"Yeah. She's lived here more than thirty years. That's our unit up there," he pointed to the second floor, "and Miss Eleanor lived in this first unit down here on the ground floor."

We came bearing gifts. Gabriel had asked me to stop at a grocery store along the way, and he'd bought a big bouquet of flowers and crammed four grocery bags with cookies, chocolates, muffins, and other goodies. "She never treats herself," he explained, "and she has a raging sweet tooth. She's going to try to say I shouldn't have spent all this money, but we'll just tell her it was your idea. Then she can't argue."

When Guadalupe Morales opened the door for us, she grabbed her son in a hug and spoke to him in Spanish before turning to me with narrowed eyes and shaking my hand. She was a tiny woman whose dark hair was pulled back in a bun and shot through with gray, and she was wearing a flowered dress and low-heeled pumps. Gabriel asked, "Are we keeping you from something, Mama? You're all dressed up."

She surprised both of us by saying, "You never brought a boyfriend home before. I wanted to look nice, since it sounds like I'm meeting my future son-in-law."

I followed Gabriel into the apartment. We cut through the tidy living room, which had a huge cross above the TV, and went into the kitchen, where we placed all the grocery bags on the counter.

Then he turned to his mother and said, "I am planning to marry Riley someday. Are you okay with that?"

She pulled a pitcher of iced tea from the refrigerator and said, "I'll admit, I had a hard time with the fact that you're gay at first, because I'd always been taught homosexuality was wrong. But I finally realized this is the way God made you, and I know you're a good boy, Gabey. You're not doing anything wrong. I already had to stand up to my whole family when I got pregnant out of wedlock, and I can stand up to them again when you decide to marry the man you love. If they don't like it, well, so what?"

Gabriel looked like he was fighting back tears, and I blurted, "Thank you Ms. Morales, that really means a lot to us."

"I just said I accepted Gabey for being gay. I didn't say I accept you yet. First, I need to find out if you're good enough for my son." She handed me the pitcher and said, "Take this to the table and sit down. You and me, we got a lot to discuss."

"Yes ma'am." I was grinning ear-to-ear as I did as I was told.

That night, we lingered over dinner with Gabriel's friends at Seahorse Ranch. They were sad about the fact that he wasn't coming back to stay, but we promised to make frequent visits to Catalina, and they promised to visit us in turn. Eventually, we went to pack Gabriel's things, and when we finished we both collapsed onto his bed. "Just think," I said, "we get to do that again tomorrow with my stuff."

"We can handle it. We're tough." He smiled at me, and I kissed his forehead. After a pause, he murmured, "Today was full of miracles, between that amazing warehouse and apartment, and my mom not only accepting our relationship but totally falling in love with you."

I grinned and said, "I don't know if she fell in love with me, exactly."

"She told you to call her mom when we were leaving. Face it, she loves you."

"That was a nice surprise."

"For both of us."

I looked around and asked, "Are you sad to be leaving?" The room had been restored to its former, fairly generic décor, and the glass doors were open, framing that beautiful view of the lights of Avalon far below us.

"I'll miss my friends, but I know it's time to move on. This place was exactly what I needed at a certain point in my life. It was a safe haven, apart from the rest of the world. In a lot of ways, Seahorse Ranch helped me heal, and I'm not the same person I was when I first came here. Actually, I'm not the same person I was six weeks ago."

I said, "I'm not, either."

"It's wild, isn't it, how much we've both grown in such a short time?"

"It makes me feel so optimistic," I said. "I think for any relationship to last, it's all about learning, evolving, and growing together, and that's exactly what we've been doing."

"You're right, and I think there's both strength and beauty in that. There's you, there's me, and then there's us, and together, we're so much more than the sum of our parts." We wrapped our arms around each other, and after a while he admitted, "I used to be afraid of the future, because it was so full of uncertainty. But now I feel like I can face anything that comes my way, because you'll be right there by my side to help me through it."

"That's exactly where I'll be," I said, as I held him securely. "Forever."

The End

The His Chance Series will continue with Second Thoughts. This upbeat story features movie star and party boy Harper Royce, his long-suffering personal assistant Phoenix Jaymes, who knows he made a huge mistake by going to work for that man-child, and a whole bunch of chickens.